Avrum

A
Renewed
Testament

R.A. GIUGGIO

Copyright © 2018 R.A. Giuggio

All rights reserved.

ISBN-13:978-1-7323818-0-3

DEDICATION

"To all who have searched for the Light
because they forgot the switch was on the wall."

ACKNOWLEDGMENTS

*Thanks to everyone who helped me so much.
Special pragmatic thanks to Mike, the brother who
wouldn't allow this story to sit hiding on my computer,
and an extended historical appreciation to the writer
Mark, the author of Chapter 14, verses 51 & 52.*

~~ 1 ~~

My Name is Avrum, and I am an old man.

I don't feel all that old. True, new aches and pains seem to appear almost daily, and I'm more likely to remember what happened five years ago than five days ago, but I am in strong health and have most of my wits about me (what wits I have ever had, I suppose). But everyone in my village treats me as an elder. Since much of what we think of ourselves is a reflection of how others respond to us, I must, therefore, be old.

Quite humorous in a way. When I was a younger man, I always looked at the elders as having achieved certain tranquility within themselves, a certain understanding of the ways of things. Most importantly, I saw them as knowing the secrets of the God of All Things and being in harmony with his plan. That understanding is crucial for us; we are Jews, the Chosen People, selected by the Almighty himself to be keepers of the sacred covenant. It is both our birthright and obligation to maintain that covenant.

However, I have achieved precious little tranquility

and even less understanding of the Almighty's purpose. If anything, as each day passes, I become more restless and more confused. Rather than being answered, the questions begin to multiply; what was once simple is now exceeding complex. As a young child, I was certain of so many things; as an elder, I am certain of virtually nothing. I find most confusing the fact that I am still here. I eat few of the foods our physicians recommend and drink far too much wine. Most of the people who were more careful about those things, including the physicians, have died. I've sat Shiva with sons of the fathers who have passed and then did the same for their sons. I have outlived generations. Most of the people I have liked or loved, or those I have disliked and loathed, have passed. Almost all of my business associates, and those with whom I shared wine and worship are gone.

The most important people in my life have died, most of them years ago. And yet Avrum continues to wake every morning. I am by Roman calculations (and all of Israel must now compute things as the Romans do) in my sixties. My mother never saw forty, my father fifty-five. My closest childhood friend died before he reached thirty-five; my closest adult friend before he was fifty-five. If the Greeks are right, and one's life is a play, I am the only actor left on the stage.

I often wonder if the God of All Things has forgotten Avrum is here. I could forgive him for that; with all that's going on in the world, I'm sure he has little time for an insignificant Jew. I imagine many of the other elders, no matter where in the world they may be, feel the same way. Or maybe the Almighty is just waiting, patiently, for me to surrender to the fates, and to get out of the way.

That being said, I have little to complain about. I am well fed, well clothed, and warm. Most importantly, I am so not because of the kindness and generosity of others, but through my own efforts. My one remaining childhood friend, Ephraim, survives only because of the charity of his son and grandchildren. Ephraim lives with them, which gives him great pleasure, and with his daughter in law, which decidedly does not. It's scarcely her fault; Ephraim is just another mouth to feed, another body to clothe, and he is not in the best of health. She tolerates Ephraim out of a sense of duty; there is no willingness, there is no love.

Conversely, I am able to provide for myself quite well. My good health and productivity assure me of that, at least for the present. Unlike many of my fellow villagers, I have earned my living not by the sweat of my brow, but by a particular skill the Almighty has blessed me with. He must have given it to me; only He knows how easily it has come to me.

Like most in Palestine, my village is composed of illiterates, those unable to read or write. I am the village scribe, the person everyone must come to for the latest news of the world, or to draw up a contract, or to hear of the most recent writings. The farmer who wishes to buy land, and the one who wishes to sell it to him; the tradesman who wants to contract his labor to a client, the merchant who needs to hear of the latest edicts from Rome (and there is never a shortage of those), all must come to Avrum. The Roman soldiers, who patrol our village, and are also mostly illiterate, must come to me. They pay me handsomely for my services; more importantly, they leave me alone.

My abilities as a scribe include a talent for languages. I am fluent in Aramaic, my native tongue, but also in Greek, Roman and Coptic, the language of the Egyptians. I can generate and reproduce just about any manuscript in the world.

These gifts have provided for me comfortably throughout my life, and they provide for me now.

Ephraim must spend his time at the town well, gossiping and complaining with the other elders; he has nothing else to do. It's also how he avoids contact with his daughter-in-law. Meanwhile, I start each day with a full slate of planned activities. There is the day to day business to be done, a very special project on which I have been working, and now this manuscript. Unlike for Ephraim, the days do not pass slowly; I often wonder where the hours have gone.

Nonetheless, I am not unaware my productivity will wane as the weeks and months pass (I no longer conceptualize time in terms of years.). To that end, I am training an assistant, Ephraim's grandson Yonni, to be my successor. The training is long and arduous, owing no doubt more to the lack of the ability of the teacher that the pupil. But Yonni is both bright and energetic; he will make a fine scribe.

I wonder sometimes if I am not unconsciously holding him back and retarding his progress. A part of me realizes that once he is fully trained, Nazareth will have no further need of Avrum; of that I am petrified. Like a farmer protecting his fields from an intruder, I protect my area of skill from those who would capture it. I hold onto my place in the community as a drowning man clings to a vine.

But this manuscript is mine; it belongs to me. Only I can write it; only I can accurately describe its details.

Perhaps it is the arrogance of old age, but I believe incredible events have happened in my lifetime, and I was blessed to see many of them, indeed to participate in some of them. Those events bear retelling, not by some far-off writer in a faraway land, but by a son of Palestine. The world is changing daily; the Occupation has become more brutal and violent, and a madman has become Caesar. Manuscripts have begun to appear about a boy from Nazareth, a boy I knew well and loved.

Nazareth knows little of these things; in fact, all they know is what I choose to tell them, and I haven't told them everything. They should be told, before my passing, and so I write this memoir.

A force within me compels me to this writing. Is the force from the God of All Things? From the Evil One? Is it the spirit of a man I loved as a boy, or perhaps one that I loved as an adult? Or is it merely my own arrogance that my insignificant existence has had some meaning in terms of what I saw and who I knew. I am somewhat sure I will never have the answer to that question.

I will die soon; I accept it. Soon Nazareth will forget Avrum bar, Jacob. I have no heirs, no immediate family, and few friends. In the blink of an eye, all those beautiful days and horrific nights of my life will be forgotten. You may have heirs, family and friends who will keep your memory alive. But they too will die, taking your memory with them; your life will be as forgotten as mine. It will only take a little longer.

My religious tradition demands of a man that he has a son, plant a tree, and write a book. Though forbidden by my nature to do the first, I have done the second, and now attempt the third.

~~ 2 ~~

As each of us defines our births, we tend to be short-sighted. The factors which led to my own beginnings, during the fifth year of the reign of Augustus, are as innumerable as the stars in the sky. One can begin with Adam and Eve and then work their way down from there. Indeed, if there were no Abraham, no Moses, no David nor Solomon, there would have been no Avrum bar Jacob. True as that may be, I begin with the place of my birth and only a generation before.

Nazareth is what is known in Palestine as a one-spring village, meaning it is a small town destined by geographical fate ever to remain a small town. The mountains onto which the first inhabitants carved their homes yield but one bubbling spring. Mankind, as we know, follows the water. There are simply not enough natural resources in Nazareth for it to be anything but a small town.

Only about sixty families live in the town, and as a result, there is a great sense of community. Family members meet at the well fed by that spring, usually plotting their visits to chat about this one or that one.

Friends arrive at the same time to catch up on whatever local news they have missed, although that news is often no more remarkable than the birth of a calf. Most days in Nazareth are like the days before; most in the future will be pretty much the same. There is little stratification in the town; whether a peasant farmer, feverishly working an arid landscape for food and crops, or a peasant tradesman, endlessly searching for opportunities, one is still a peasant. There a few specialized occupations in Nazareth; being a scribe is thankfully one of them. There is also the town councilor, who oversees town business such as it is, and a select group of residents who advise him on a part-time basis. They actually have very little importance; since the Occupation, Rome controls most things, so that many of the matters the council decides are frivolous.

The one position that is anything but frivolous is our rabbi, the resident and the guardian of the village's most magnificent structure, the synagogue. It is the rabbi who represents the real moral authority in our lives. By interpreting the Torah and other great writings, he is the one who settles disputes, performs the various rituals demanded by our faith, and guides us in our daily lives. As it can be said everywhere, Nazareth has been blessed by some wonderful and saintly rabbis but has also been cursed by some complete fools. But whether saint or fool, the rabbi is the rabbi; he is to be respected and obeyed.

One such rabbi, one of the righteous ones, was Elisha bar Abraham, whose pride in life was his only daughter Rachel. Defying the custom of the day, a tradition sadly still with us, Elisha taught his daughter to read and write, calculating that by doing so he would make her a highly desirable catch for any young man in Nazareth. Rachel took to her learning, becoming well versed in the Scripture. Unfortunately, it was an unrewarded achievement. No other woman in town could converse with her on her level, and the men simply ignored her. Rachel vowed that her abilities would not lie dormant; if she were fortunate enough to bear children, she would educate them into literacy and love of the written word.

By the age of fourteen, she had begun to notice the young men in the town, in the way young girls notice them. She especially was drawn to the hale and healthy only son of a man who owned a small olive and fig grove located on the outskirts of town. Jacob bar Judah would make an excellent husband, Rachel thought, and she was not shy about making her intentions known. That forwardness would be scandalous if not for the fact that Jacob felt equally attracted to Rachel. Their respective families agreed it was the perfect match; with Jacob's wealth and Rachel's literacy, surely the children of their union would be blessed. In a rather quick fashion, Jacob and Rachel became man and wife.

The groom's father made a generous gift for the wedding; the newlyweds would share their marital bed in their own home. It was, (and still is), a small stone edifice adjacent to the groves that would someday be Jacob's. Like most homes in Nazareth, the land centered on a small courtyard, complete with wood stove, which would serve as both a cooking area and an area of recreation. Outside of the courtyard was the entrance to the house itself; which opened into the anteroom, complete with wash basin, and the main room, which could be partitioned off by curtains depending on the size of the family. If the union was especially fruitful with many children, Jacob and Rachel could move. If not, it would be the perfect home for a small family.

Years later I would ask my mother about the early days of the marriage, and she always spoke of them with twinkles in her eye. Despite his own illiteracy, Jacob encouraged his bride's talents and took no offense. Similarly, Rachel would not shirk her domestic duties because of those talents; she did what every other housewife in Nazareth did and did so with no regrets. By all accounts, with which my father would concur, it was a blissful beginning for a new couple.

Only one thing about the marriage was disappointing. Try as they might, (and Jacob would chortle that they tried often), they remained childless. Rachel would visit apothecaries both in town and in the neighboring city of Sephoria, speaking to physicians and midwives from both. Jacob had begun to fear he had married a barren woman. The situation was made more pressing by the passing of Jacob's father. Jacob had inherited the groves, but himself had no heirs to guarantee they would remain in his family.

He too sought advice. He conferred with the rabbi, but obviously that was difficult; Rachel was the rabbi's daughter after all. So Jacob turned to the other married men in town, including his closest friend, Yusuf bar Malachi. Yusuf and his wife Agatha had produced three strong and healthy boys, all of whom still survived, and all of whom had followed in their father's footsteps as town tradesmen. Yusuf was indeed Nazareth's most respected tradesman, and with his sons became the busiest. It was his family that had built an extension onto the synagogue, with stone shelving for a variety of manuscripts, shelving that would provide me with much substance in the later years. Their work was of such quality that Romans took notice. Yusuf and his sons would build a new home for the praetor charged with responsibility for Nazareth. They would even be allowed to work in Sephoria; the city Augustus had ordered transformed from a rural village into the capital of Judea.

Jacob held Yusuf in the highest esteem, as did most of Nazareth. Both that esteem and Jacob's chagrin would grow with the news that Agatha was again with child.

From the beginning, however, it was a difficult pregnancy. The previously spirited Agatha seemed listless and drained. Many in the village feared that this birth would not have the success of the previous ones.

Those fears would be realized. The birth itself was accomplished, yielding a healthy baby boy Yusuf and Agatha named James. But Agatha had suffered the loss of a lot of blood during the delivery. For three days and nights she seemed to be holding onto her life by the thinnest of threads. On the fourth day, she lost her battle; Agatha would die holding Yusuf's hand and her newborn child close to her breast.

I was told the burial procession was among the most dramatic and emotional Nazareth had ever seen. The entire town marched the grief-stricken Yusuf and his sons to the grave-site. In what would be a scene not soon forgotten, Yusuf held James in his hands above his head as they lowered Agatha into her final resting place.

It would be the end of Agatha, but the beginning of an extraordinary chain of events that would affect legions of other histories, and not just in Nazareth. Included in those legions would be Jacob and Rachel, and their yet to be born son Avrum.

~~ 3 ~~

Everyone has darkness in their lives, and the weeks that followed Agatha's death were certainly Yusuf's darkest. Not only had he lost his beloved soul-mate, but he also had a new son with no one to take care of him. And a household to be managed with no one to manage it. And yet, many of our darkest hours are brightened by faith and friendship, and so it would be for Yusuf. Through faith, he found a way to deal with Agatha's death; through friendship, including that of Jacob's and Rachael's, he was able to deal with the practical matters of her passing. Yusuf would not suffer financially through his grief; Jacob made sure of that. And Rachel arrived at the house first thing in the morning, not to leave until dusk fell.

She would admit in later years that she had an ulterior motive. If she could prove to the God of All Things her ability as a mother, perhaps He would bless her with a child of her own. The care of James, however, was a daunting and challenging task. The infant seemed to always be ill and cried incessantly. There were times that Yusuf thought he would lose his last-born son. But with each struggle came success and James eventually began to thrive. It had been a harrowing experience for Rachel, but she would later describe it as glorious. Surely, she reasoned, she would be rewarded for her kindness. And within two years she would. But not before the life of Yusuf took an eerie and dramatic turn.

About three months after Agatha's passing, a new family arrived in Nazareth. Eliza and Anne had left the bustling city of Sephoria for the quiet life of Nazareth. Neither was young, and the constant activity in Sephoria had tried them. They were an agreeable couple and had little trouble fitting into the milieu of the village.

They brought with them their last child, a quiet and shy adolescent girl named Miriam. A pious family, a day didn't go by that the family wasn't seen at the synagogue. They became quite friendly with my soon-to-be grandfather, the rabbi, who was suitably impressed by the family's devotion and knowledge of our traditions. Though illiterate, they were able to speak freely and intelligently about our sacred scrolls.

Eliza confided to the rabbi that one of his reasons for locating from Sephoria was Miriam. He felt the men of Sephoria, with their "modern" ideas, were unsuitable for his maiden daughter. He also feared the heavy concentration of Roman men, in the city for its reconstruction; everyone knew Romans only wanted one thing from a Jewish girl. Eliza said he would die a happy man if he found a husband for his daughter; a good man, a pious man, one who would respect and care for her.

Grandfather had the perfect man in mind. Yusuf was quite a bit older than Miriam but was everything Eliza had dreamed of for his daughter. The rabbi introduced Yusuf to Miriam, and soon a relationship developed. It caused a raised eyebrow or two in the village; even Jacob, a man not given to idle gossip, remarked to his wife:

"It's always the quiet ones, isn't it Rachel. Agatha's barely cold, and the saintly Yusuf is out chasing after the young virgin."

"Hush," his wife replied. "You're imagining things; She's younger than Judah," referring to Yusuf's eldest."He must be interested in her for one of his sons."

Jacob laughed. "No man looks at a woman the way he looks at her to make of her a daughter in law. There more there than you think."

If Miriam's and Yusuf's relationship were a minor scandal, what happened next would feed the gossip mill for weeks. Rachel arrived at Yusuf's house one morning, and Judah informed her that his father would be away for a while; he did not know for how long. It quickly became apparent that Miriam had joined Yusuf on his journey. They had left Nazareth in the middle of the night; Judah could not (or would not) offer an explanation, and neither would Miriam's parents. Yusuf had left instructions with his sons about pending work to be done, and asked Judah to confer with Rachel about James. Beyond that, little was know.

"Perhaps he took her to Jerusalem, to visit the Temple," Rachel suggested.

"The Temple!" Jacob guffawed. "I doubt he took her there to do what he wants to do."

"Well, it's certainly a mystery," Rachel replied.

"An older man, a younger maiden; where's the mystery" Jacob replied.

But as is often the case in these matters, the saga of Yusuf and Miriam gave way to the daily struggles of life in Nazareth. Within weeks, the entire affair was almost forgotten.

The interest in Yusuf and Miriam would be rekindled however when, as quickly as they disappeared, they returned, again in the middle of the night. One day they weren't there; the next they were. The first one to see them was actually Rachel. Arriving at the house to care for James she was shocked to see Yusuf in his anteroom, conversing with his sons. Seeing her astonished face, Yusuf approached her.

"Blessed Rachel! How wonderful to see you; Still caring for my son and my house. How can I ever repay you?"

Dumbstruck as she was, Rachel was able to say: "Yusuf, you've returned! You've returned!"

"Yes I have, and I've returned a married man. Miriam has agreed to be my wife, and the Lord has blessed our union with a child, a beautiful baby boy." As he spoke, Rachel heard the unmistakable sound of an infant crying. Confused, she peaked into the main room, to see Miriam nursing a young baby. Miriam beckoned her to enter.

"Yusuf had told me of your kindness, dear Rachel; please accept my gratitude. You will be welcomed in my home always."

Still dazed, Rachel walked to the mother and child.

"And this is our new son; his name is Yeshu. Would you like to hold him?"

Rachel held the newborn in her arms. She would later say that the first thing she noticed was the baby's eyes; she would claim they were the kind of eyes that penetrated the soul, and saw the mystery of things. Rachel glanced at Miriam and saw those exact eyes. She began to sob, as she rocked the baby in her arms.

"He's so beautiful!"

Of course it would be no time before all of Nazareth heard the story. Their whereabouts during the exile would remain forever a mystery, but the story of the older tradesman and the young virgin would be spoken of often. All the woman in the village would claim they knew exactly how many months had passed during their exile; nine months definitely had not elapsed. The men only chuckled, of course not when Yusuf was around. Jacob led the teasing while at all times admiring his friend's élan.

"He had no choice", he would say. "They would have stoned her otherwise."

"Stop it!" his wife rebuked. "The God of All Things has blessed them as only He can."

"Quite an Almighty we have then," was Jacob's reply. "Gives us the Torah, and then promptly ignores what it says."

Ultimately, the story would once again give way to other town gossip. Yusuf, now accompanied by his new wife and two sons, would spend many evenings at the Synagogue. Jacob longed to ask Yusuf's older sons what they thought, but he was too discreet. The older boys seemed none the worst for their father's adventure; Judah married, as did Phillip, the next in line. Yusuf would soon have grandchildren not much younger than his own son. Within a year, all three of Yusuf's older sons would have married and moved onto Sephoria to take advantage of that city's' reconstruction. As such, only James and Yeshu remained at home with Yusuf and Miriam. James continued with his struggles, fighting bouts of melancholy, it seemed, routinely.

"It's only natural," Rachel said "He had a difficult birth, lost his mother, and quickly had an almost new family. Such things leave scars."

She proved accurate in her assessment (she usually was); it would take years and a series of cataclysmic events to heal those scars.

Rachel continued to help Miriam, now with both James and Yeshu. But her time with Yusuf's family was soon to be drastically reduced.

~~ 4 ~~

Within a year of Yusuf's return, Rachel began feeling those sensations a woman with child feels. A visit to the town's midwife confirmed her hopes. After years of dreaming and praying, Jacob and Rachel would be parents. Jacob could barely contain his excitement; there was now at least a possibility he would have an heir. Like all expectant fathers he claimed he cared not if the child was a boy or a girl, but Nazareth knew better.

Jacob's fondest desires were fulfilled. Rachel gave birth to a hearty and healthy baby boy. A man given to neither tears nor religiosity, Jacob openly wept, and consecrated his son to the God of All Things. In honor of his grandfather, he named the boy Avrum.

From all accounts, I was a pampered and spoiled child. Father would carry me on his back, showing me off to everybody in town; mother fussed over my every move. Each morning she would bundle me up and take me to the synagogue, where my grandfather would similarly fawn over me. I was his first grandson, the first child of his only daughter and he had big plans for my future.

After the morning meal and the entire attention grandfather would pay, mother would take me to the well. There she would converse with other new mothers, such as Miriam, and some of the older woman. In typical Jewish fashion, she would listen attentively to whatever advice the older woman gave, and then promptly ignore all of it. Her Avrum wasn't like other children; he was special. He was hers.

The early years passed and I began to walk. That meant I could now play with other children my age in the village. For me, that meant Ephraim, the son of the town smithy and of course James and Yeshu. The four of us formed an inner circle, as children will do, and played and invented games as we went along. We wrapped pebbles into some old cloths our mother gave us and stood in a circle tossing them to each other. Or we would take a branch from a dead tree and try to hit the bundles as far as we could. I got along very well with the other boys; I was proud of the day they nicknamed me "Avi."

By the age of six, every young Jewish boy has his free time curtailed by two things. First, by that age, a boy was expected to begin learning his father's occupation. Every morning at sunrise and often before, father would wake me, and we would go to the groves. I helped with the planting, the harvesting and the bundling of olives and figs. Ephraim worked with his father, farriering the village animals, while James and Yeshu could be seen carrying Yusuf's tool chest, trailing their father everywhere. My three companions seemed to enjoy their apprenticeship immensely; I was a bit less enthused by the tedious labor required of an olive grower. It was ironic in a way. As the son of a landowner, I was preparing for a life of relative prosperity, unlike my three friends who would likely remain as poor as their fathers. Most people would think I would be engrossed by the groves, while my friends would be resentful. It was quite the opposite.

Secondly, every Hebrew male of that age began his religious instruction. Two afternoons a week we would be taken to the synagogue to be instructed in the beliefs and rituals of our faith. I believe Yeshu enjoyed these times more than James and Ephraim; James was reserved by nature and sat quietly through our lesson, while Ephraim seemed totally bored. Yeshu and I were the vocal ones, responding at every opportunity as grandfather reveled us with the tales of Abraham, Moses, David, and Solomon. I soaked up all of the stories as they ignited a wealth of imagination within me. Yeshu's reaction was only slightly different; he was always asking "why." He did this so many times we nicknamed him "But why, Rabbi," and teased him constantly. If one of us had to urinate, Ephraim would chortle "But why, Rabbi?"

I was usually accepting of everything the Rabbi said. But for Yeshu, it was always a matter for discussion. The other three of us sat for a month as he barraged my grandfather with questions about the story of Abraham, who had been ordered by the God of All Things to sacrifice his son Isaac. Yeshu insisted on needing to know and understand just how a father could possibly do that. The fact that Abraham was never required to carry out the sacrifice didn't seem to mean much to Yeshu; it was again a question of "Why?"

After our lessons my three friends went home. They thought I was staying with my grandfather to enjoy the evening meal. Instead, he and my mother had devised a plan. I wasn't going to be like other boys, or like most of Nazareth. I was going to learn to read and write. So for an hour at the synagogue and later at home by candlelight, I learned to read letters, and then words, and then sentences. At the same time, I was learning to write. These abilities came so naturally to me that it hardly seemed like work. In fact, I utterly enjoyed them. There's no question that part of it was due to my desire to please my mother and grandfather; I've never doubted that. But I also knew that I would not spend my teen years seeking to discover my vocation; I already had. By the age of ten, I was reading and writing fluently, not only in our native Aramaic, but in Hebrew, the language of our ancestors. Indeed, I was also beginning to learn both Greek and Roman. It was just so easy, and mother and grandfather never missed an opportunity to encourage me.

Father was another story.

"Bah, reading and writing. I can do neither. Why bother? Can you eat books? Will they keep you warm in the harsh winter? One day you will have children, Avi, and when they are crying for food, what will you do, read to them?"

I felt rebuked, but mother always intervened. She would bear no objection to her son becoming literate; that was that. Father would never warm to the idea until many years later. For as long as I lived under his roof, he never really acknowledged my accomplishments. To him, any time spent away from the groves was time wasted. So it became a balancing act, keeping him happy by reporting to the groves each morning, and leaving the afternoons free for my passion. I tried to involve my friends in that passion, but none were interested. James had no desire, and frankly I always thought he lacked the requisite skills; besides, he was too fidgety and skittish to sit at a desk, stylus in hand, learning to write. With his interest in the Scriptures, I thought at least Yeshu would want to join me on my literary adventure, but he just smiled wryly. He was too busy, he claimed, and I had to agree with him; he was becoming as skilled a craftsman as his father. He seemed to truly enjoy his labors, even the mundane ones like breaking apart stones and boulders. Between his apprenticeship and twice-weekly battles with my grandfather, I imagined he'd find reading and writing to be boring, perhaps as boring as I found the groves.

Ephraim had developed his own passion. He seemed to know more about the female anatomy than grandfather knew about the Exodus. He once spent an entire day explaining to the rest of us what the Eighth Commandment really meant. Ephraim knew all about coveting, and what it meant in terms of your neighbor's wife. Yeshu would smile at Ephraim's descriptions of that and other carnal acts. I was embarrassed; not only was talk of such things forbidden for boys our age, but I also found most of it disgusting. It surprised none of us when Ephraim began to withdraw from our little circle in order to spend more time with the young girls of Nazareth; hopefully, it wasn't spent discussing coveting.

James was too shy to even talk to girls, and while Yeshu seemed very comfortable around them, they didn't seem to affect him one way or the other. Our time together was becoming more limited as we grew into adolescence, and we rarely spoke of our social lives.

I could easily discuss my social life; I didn't have one. It wasn't that I felt uncomfortable around girls it was that I didn't feel anything around them. I longed to talk to someone about that, but a strange feeling of shame kept me from doing so. I didn't even know why I felt ashamed. I entered my teen years with a joy for the literacy I had achieved, and a general contentment with the rest of my life.

Still, I was troubled.

~~ 5 ~~

The first summer of those years was marked by a joyous event in Yeshu's life. It was his bar-mitzvah, the most wondrous yet solemn event for any Jewish boy. Bah-mitzvah meant ascension into manhood, and all the responsibilities it entails.

But most boys realized the solemnity of the occasion was more for his parents. For him, it means a nice party, presents, and a lessening of parental authority. Once bar mitzvahed, for instance, a boy could spend time with a girl without a chaperone. Ephraim had lined up several months of these meetings before he was actually bar mitzvahed.

But for Yeshu it was all about the seriousness of it all. He confided to me that he felt unworthy to ascend into manhood.

"You're crazy," I told him. "You above all deserve the honor. There isn't a boy in Palestine more deserving."

I'm not sure it assuaged any of his doubts, but nonetheless, he went through with the ceremony. The party afterward was undoubtedly very nice, appropriate for a tradesman- to be taking his vows before the God of All Things. My parents donated generously from the grove, as did Hiram the butcher. Yeshu received many fine and practical gifts, including his first hammer, which James had forged by hand. Miriam weaved him a new tunic, which was the custom, and Yusuf built his son his own toolbox. Yeshu's eyes watered as each gift was presented. My gift to him would not be significant, I knew. During the past years, I had heard from my grandfather of Yeshu's fondness for the Book of Daniel, that book in Scripture filled with imagery and symbolism, sometimes terrifying images and symbolism. I copied the Book of Daniel on fresh parchment, and bound it securely; Yeshu would be able to keep it for decades. I had spent the better part of that year preparing the manuscript and nervously presented it to him.

Yeshu's eye sparkled.

"Avi, I cannot give you enough thanks. Always it will be in my possession, and always I will treasure it."

I couldn't resist the temptation to chide my friend about his illiteracy. "And how will you read it then," I asked kiddingly.

"Those beautiful and sacred words will have to be read me," he admitted. "You and I will have to spend much time together."

With that, he embraced me tightly, so tightly I could feel the very life force rushing through him. So Yeshu wanted to continue our friendship even though he was an adult. I was genuinely beginning to appreciate the advantage of being a scribe.

The party ended, with all the adults making predictions about Yeshu's future, his career, his marital life, and the like. Ephraim's father could be seen sizing up the newly minted adult as a possible mate for Ephraim's sister. The common consensus; Yeshu would continue his father's business, marry, and have several fine sons, who would all do likewise. And he would spend his life in Nazareth.

As the guests prepared to leave, I asked him how many of those predictions seemed right to him.

"Probably none," he responded with a smile. "But if they are what the God of All Things wills, I will be comfortable with them."

We embraced again, and I returned home, filled with the glory of the day. But the joy of that summer's day would for me be darkened that autumn. Grandfather grew gravely ill and seemed to suffer the weight of his years all at once. I had never experienced the death of anyone close to me, and I was very frightened. Through her own grief, mother tried to comfort me, but even to her, I could not explain what grandfather meant to me. From him, I had experienced a warmth and a quenching of a thirst I had for my craft. Father would dismiss those interests, occasionally even mock them. Mother, while always encouraging, nonetheless, wished I spent more time the groves. It was grandfather who was always there to protect and yet challenge me at the same time. And now he would be gone.

On what turned out to be the last night of his life, he called me near. In both a somber and frightened mood, I went to him. My main memory remains today the odor in his room, an odor I now know as what people call the smell of death. Barely able to speak, grandfather whispered to me:

"Love your father, Avrum, and honor his wishes. But never forget the learning you have been exposed to."

"I won't, grandfather, I promise," I said, trembling as I spoke.

But then with a smile that belied his condition, he said:

"And take care of your friend Yeshu. He has a great love of scripture, even if he has some strange and discomforting ideas. Keep him loyal to the word; promise me that also."

I made him that vow and kissed his forehead. During the night, he passed. Yeshu, Miriam, Yusuf, and James were the first to come to our house. I told my friend about grandfather's dying request.

"He was a wonderful man; I....I loved him, Avi."

"And he loved you, Yeshu."

"I know he did. Even though we disagreed, he always treated me with respect. I will never forget him," he said, as tears were cascading down his cheeks.

As he was speaking, other members of the congregation filled the room. The woman began to anoint and wrap the body. Many tears flowed as those responsible for what my father called the "practicalities" of death carried them out. I held my mother tightly, attempting to lessen her grief; she was so much the center of my attention that I did not cry. Her comfort was paramount to me.

Once the body was anointed and wrapped, grandfather was carried to his final resting place, in the backyard of the synagogue. There he would rest for eternity with rabbis from past generations.

Somewhat shockingly, Yeshu stepped to the edge of the grave. In a manner (and voice!) I had never heard him use, he spread his arms out wide and looked toward the sky.

"Heavenly Father, we thank you for the life of this good man, so full of love for You and Your creation. Like the greatest of men, he did not keep this love to himself; rather, it flowed to every corner of Nazareth and beyond. Watch over him, Father, and keep him from the Evil One. We will miss this man, but are secure in the knowledge that he is in your care."

Everyone at the gravesite was stunned. Orations over dead bodies were something Greeks and Romans did, not Jews. And certainly not a recently bar mitvahed young Jew. More than that, however, were the words my friend had used. Jews had had many names for the God of All Things, all acceptable as long as the name He had called Himself to Moses was not used. But to refer to him as "Father"? As a pleading child might address a parent? This was undoubtedly unorthodox, if not downright heretical.

Moreover, the majority of Jews accepted their fate as mortal beings. True, we had heard of some radicals who spoke of an existence beyond our earthly times, but they had few followers, especially among people in Nazareth. Grandfather was dead, his existence over; The God of All Things had no need to keep further watch over him. Did He?

On the way back from the grave, I could hear some of the other villagers echo many of those same sentiments and others. Yeshu had certainly spoken out of turn; as Ephraim's father remarked:

"Who is he, the son of a tradesman, to say those things? Yusuf needs to teach that boy a lesson, the kind that comes with a stick."

Others apparently felt the same way. They were confused by Yeshu's words; indeed, many were offended. For Yusuf's and Miriam's part, they remained silent.

I would not ask Yeshu about his soliloquy until many years later. Frankly, I was concerned that by doing so I would jeopardize our friendship. But Ephraim, ever the bold one, did. When Ephraim asked Yeshu how he could be so forward, Yeshu just smiled at him.

"The rabbi would have wanted me to say those things."

I did not know all of what had been discussed between grandfather and my friend during those countless sessions they had shared; perhaps Yeshu was right. But I feared he was wrong.

Either way, I wasn't going to confront him; there was just too much danger in that.

~~ 6 ~~

Especially since my grandfather's death would allow me, differently, to become even closer to Yeshu and his family. Many Nazarenes would make an annual trip eighty miles away to the sacred city of Jerusalem during Passover week. Our tradition demanded it. Actually, our tradition required four yearly trips to Jerusalem, but in a poor town like Nazareth, that was impossible. Nazarenes celebrated Moses' leading the children of Israel out of Egypt by sojourning to the city of the Holy Temple. While Passover was a solemn and serious enough observance, it was also a joyous one, commemorating the happiest time of Israel's troubled existence.

Grandfather had always led our family's trek to Jerusalem, and from the age of five, I had joined him. My parents did not participate in the journey; father would say "spring is for planting," and claim that he had too much responsibility to travel. Mother would stay with him to make the Passover seder. As such, it had fallen to grandfather to show me Jerusalem, an obligation he accepted with joy. When the time came, we loaded our provisions onto our donkeys and set off on foot to celebrate the historical acts of our ancestors.

After Grandfather had passed, I wondered if I would ever see Jerusalem again. My uncle Zebedee had replaced grandfather at the synagogue as the rabbi, but we were not particularly close; actually, we weren't close at all. Though I continued my studies and had even begun to copy some of the great works of the Greek culture, it generated a much hollower feeling than it previously had. Mother also feared that I might abandon my craft; even she did not appreciate that, hollow or not, that would never happen.

It was Yusuf who spoke to father about Passover, suggesting that I accompany his family to Jerusalem.

"It would be a shame for Avi to miss it, and he gets along with so well with Yeshu and James."

"The shame is that he'll miss the preparations of the orchards again this spring. There is so much to be done, and he has yet to learn any of it," father retorted.

As usual, mother arbitrated the dispute. I could celebrate the holiday with Yusuf and his family, but then I would dedicate the next month to the groves.

We set off on a perfect Palestine spring morning; the trip was magnificent. This was easily my favorite time of the year. As we walked along in our caravan, we moved through a variety of small villages, avoiding large cities like Sephoria; there would too much to distract us in those places. Along the way, residents of other towns would join us. Friendships were renewed, acquaintance resurrected, and news of the past year digested. I was appreciative of the many condolences I received about my grandfather; it was heartening to hear how many lives he had touched, even those of whom he had only seen once a year.

The entire trip was enthralling. Above all, this was the God of All Things' Chosen People, gathering to celebrate His goodness. Whatever bad had happened in the past year between families and villages was forgotten in honor of our ancestral tapestry.

The seven-day sojourn passed quickly, each day filled with merriment and of course prayer. This year would be the best; I would be spending most of the time with Yeshu. I wanted the journey to continue forever.

But finally, we did arrive at the glorious city. Jerusalem had always enticed me; just the sheer size was breathtaking. The number of people, residents, and visitors; the amazing variety of it all, all of it enthralled me. Imagine, there were even stalls in the main square where people purchased manuscripts, the labors of scribes like me. I could even dream of a day when my documents would be in those stalls.

Yusuf located our caravan along the southernmost wall of the city. As nomads, by Roman law, we were forbidden to set up our tents in the city proper.

Passover is a significant Jewish holiday, but as a people, we were still oppressed. The price of disobedience was swift and often brutal. It had only been two years ago that four fishermen from Galilee, who had been drinking all night, entered the city after dark. Being in the town past dusk was a crime unless you were a resident, and Romans kept a close watch. None of the fishermen ever returned, their families left to wonder if they had been imprisoned, sold into slavery, or even crucified. The Romans kept no records about Jews.

Nonetheless, we were able to camp close to the city. At daybreak, our party, now thirty strong, passed through the walls of the city, accompanied by multitudes of others. My impression of Jerusalem itself was, as I've said, its sheer size: I'd been told that thirty towns of Nazareths would fit inside those walls. The second impression was always the people. In Nazareth I saw Jews, mostly only Jews.; visitors to our hamlet were few and far between. Here, we walked through the various sections of the city and saw not only Jews and Romans, but Greeks, Syrians, and other types of gentiles I couldn't even identify. There were Cypriots, their skin as dark and shiny as the blackest olives in my father groves. All manner of dress and custom was present; you could spend weeks identifying the various cultures in the city that day.

One routine was the same every year. We'd forage around the city, seeing a world as different from Nazareth as the sea was from the land. Here the different culture mixed easily, and children seemed to run amok with little parental supervision. The only similarity between Jerusalem and Nazareth, it seemed, was the permanent presence of the Romans; they seemed to be lurking everywhere.

The afternoon was reserved for the Temple. Its majesty and magnificence awed each of us; it was a city unto itself. The enormity on the courtyard, where women could purchase linens unavailable in their villages, seemed to me to be the busiest place on earth.

The courtyard gave way to the edifice of the Temple itself. Ascending its steps, I was breathless as I looked at the large rooms where scholars would debate the subtler points of the Torah. I knew that beneath these rooms were still other rooms, where scribes and copyists were busy producing editions not only the Torah but of other books, from our culture and others.

And of course deep within the Temple walls was the Holy of Holies, where the God of All Things resided. There also would be a copy of the sacred covenant between Him and His people. It was such a holy place that only the High Priest was allowed to enter it, and he could only do so once a year.

None of these things, of course, were for the proletariat. Our primary focus was the Mick Bah, the ritual cleaning of our bodies in the springs that fed the

Temple. With our bodies purified, Yusuf led us to the front of the Temple, where we purchased animals to be given in the sacrifice to the God of All Things. Since we were peasants, that meant we brought doves to the sacrificial pyres. There we held hands and prayed to our Creator; we stood as God's Chosen Ones, united. We prayed for ourselves, our families and above all for the nation of Israel, that she someday would be free.

Yeshu had been eerily silent through most of our activities. It was as if he were a sponge fish, soaking in the sights and sounds of the city and its Temple, with hardly any conversation at all. During the Mick bah, I couldn't help but notice what a man he had become. He stood six feet tall, with a hale and hearty build, supplemented by rich ebony hair and distinctive Palestinian features. His eyes continued to sparkle, sometimes mischievously, sometimes probingly, and often even with a sense of melancholy. Those eyes continued to portray kindness, curiosity, and compassion all at the same time.

I didn't understand why Yeshu had been so silent. And I never would have been able to anticipate what happened next.

~~ 7 ~~

Solemn as he had been during our holiday rituals, Yeshu was the first to explain these rituals to the younger children in the group. Indeed, he explained things so thoroughly that even the adults were impressed. Any questions anyone had were answered in a soft yet authoritative voice: I recognized that voice pattern as my grandfather's, combined with the vocal ability Yeshu had shown at his funeral. The two in unison made a powerful impact, if not an almost mesmerizing combination. Now I realized that Yeshu had indeed been grandfather's best pupil, adopting his style as well as his substance.

And it was this sturdy, masculine adolescent who was the first to aid the old and infirmed at the Mick bah. All the while he paid particular attention to James, who remained shy and awkward, especially among the throngs of visitors. Yeshu may have been quiet, yet his every word and action spoke volumes.

At the end of the sunlit hours, we returned, physically and emotionally drained, to our campsites. I thought the evening hours would allow Yeshu and I to talk; the day had been so filled we had hardly spoken. I looked forward to spending those hours reviewing the day with my friend.

I searched throughout the campsite for him. At his family's tent, neither his parents nor James knew where he was; actually, Miriam thought he was with me. Partly to alleviate her fears, and partially to alleviate mine, I took James with me to look for him. Yeshu had reached the age of maturity; he was longer required to rejoin his family for the evening meal. Still, his absence was strange, and very unlike him.

He was nowhere to be found. Worse, no one remembered seeing him leave Jerusalem proper. Yusuf joined us after a while, his concern evident. We searched every tent in the caravan, with no results. With hope, we returned to Yusuf's tent; perhaps Yeshu had finally arrived there.

But he had not, and thus begun the eeriest vigil of my life so far. Yusuf, Miriam, James, and I each paced nervously about the tent and outside; at various times we were joined by other members of Yusuf's extended family and friends of the tradesman. Men volunteered to keep searching; woman comforted Miriam as she wept openly. Memories of the missing Galileans were all too fresh in our minds; and they were adult men, not a recently bar mitzvahed boy. Yusuf seemed to age years in that single evening.

Few of us slept. I can only remember brief periods when I rested. Evening had turned to the dead of night, and Yeshu was still missing. Our minds filled with horrible images.

The moment we saw the sun peak over the horizon, Yusuf, James and I raced to the Temple. Through his emotional turmoil, James had reasoned that his brother was most likely to be there. The God of All things was with James that day; as soon as the Temple came into our view, we saw Yeshu sitting on its steps with an elderly man who appeared to be a Pharisee. Collectively we sped to the scene; Yusuf especially was breathless as we arrived at the Temple steps. I began to berate my friend (Yusuf could barely speak) for what he had done when Yeshu spoke up.

"This wonderful rabbi and I were discussing the Book of Daniel, Avi; I thought it was more important than returning to the campsite."

I was shocked, not only by his words but by their tone; it was both almost arrogant and condescending. I feared Yusuf would take a stick to his son.

Perhaps sensing this, the Pharisee responded by firmly embracing Yusuf.

"So this is Yusuf, of whom you have spoken so highly. I am honored to meet you, sir. Do not trouble yourself over your son's actions. It was my fault more than his. Your son's understanding of Daniel is unique, especially given his youth. But anyway, it is I who owe you the apology, not he." Yusuf was about to respond when the Pharisee turned away from us and began to ascend the steps of the Temple. As he walked up, he stopped at certain intervals to look back at the teen boy with whom he had his late-night conversation, a look of puzzlement seemingly locked onto his face.

I had stood mute during the entire event, but I did speak as the three of us, now accompanied by Yeshu, made our way back to the caravan.

"You are one fortunate boy, Yeshu bar Yusuf. If I had acted and spoken like that to my father, I'd have no skin left on my backside."

"You must always honor your father's wishes, Avi," he replied. "I was merely honoring mine."

I was completely bewildered. Had Yusuf told his son to engage this Pharisee in a debate? I wanted to ask, but by the time we had reached the outer wall, we saw family and friends waiting for us, hoping for any news about my friend; it seemed the whole caravan had heard of his disappearance. A collective sense of relief seemed to permeate the entire crowd as we came into view. For the first time (it would not be the last) I began to see the powerful effect Yeshu could have on people. I believe that troubled me.

The Passover celebration ended, and we began our return trip to Nazareth. I continued to seek Yeshu out for clarification of what had happened. Yet each time I approached him, he seemed to divert the conversation to just about any other topic. By the time we reached home, I was resigned to the fact that I may never know what had occurred that evening in Jerusalem. It bothered me immensely; why would my friend not confide in me? But very quickly, other events would intervene, and I would forget the entire episode until years later.

~~ 8 ~~

I was beginning to see less of Yeshu. Not only was my time becoming more and more occupied by the olive groves, as I fulfilled my promised to my mother, but Yeshu had also seen a change in his life.

The Romans were continually in need of laborers for Sephoria's reconstruction. There were multiple opportunities for men like Yusuf and Yeshu to profit from that labor. Therefore, at the beginning of each week, the family would set off for the new capital of Judea, not returning until the following Sabbath. Weeks would go by without the opportunity for me to set my eyes on my friend at all.

But then came the feast of Jupiter, a week-long celebration of the Romans' most powerful god. There would be no work in Sephoria that week, as the Romans feted that god with food and drink and merriment. I anxiously awaited the day after Sabbath when I would spend the entire evening with Yeshu. I went to sleep the night before in eager anticipation of reuniting with my old friend. We would unite, but in a way I could never have imaged.

The death of a parent is traumatic for anyone at any time, but especially for a boy just entering his adolescence. And the situations surrounding my mother's passing would haunt me throughout my life, as they haunt me to this day. I can still feel the autumn chill in the air, smell the aromas, and see the landscape on the day my mother was taken from me. If our spirits should unite in some afterlife (like the kind Yeshu spoke of), I will embrace my mother and admit my shame. For I was at least partly responsible for her death.

The day began like most others. I agreed, with my usual reluctance to spend the morning in the groves. In the afternoons of these days, I would go to the synagogue. That peaceful compromise, devised by mother, was working well, as it halved the days between my filial responsibilities and my other pursuits. Mother had asked me in the morning to stop at the house on my way to the synagogue and retrieve water from the well. It would barely be a fifteen-minute interruption of my day.

With a child's lack of responsibility, I did not go to the well but headed directly to the synagogue, all the way dreaming of what the evening with Yeshu would bring. Mother would have been dismayed to discover that she had no water for the evening meal, and would have to get it for herself. I will always wonder if thoughts of her disobedient son filled her mind as she began walking back.

If they did, they would be her last. Carrying the bucket of water over the cobblestoned path, she tripped and fell, her head smashing into a protruding boulder. Those who witnessed the fall would say later that her head hit the stone with the most terrifying sound imaginable. They ran to see her and what they saw horrified them. The blood spurting from mother's head had turned the gravel into a sickening sea of red.

My uncle came to me at the synagogue. I could tell instantly that he was distressed. With tears flowing from his eyes, he told me to rush home, that there had been a terrible accident.

Terrified, I asked: "Is it, Father?"

My uncle shook his head.

"No. No. No!" I screamed as I ran to my house. I stood directly in front of my home, too horrified to enter. As I stood there trembling, I felt a hand gently placed on my shoulder.

"Avi," Yeshu said.

I turned to see my friend standing right behind me. Every emotion in my soul sprang to the surface. I began to wail hysterically as Yeshu guided me into the house. In the anteroom sat father, his head buried in his hands, as Yusuf stood at his side. Yeshu led me into the main room where my mother's body lay prostrated on a straw mattress, her head wrapped in linen that someone had used in a failed attempt to stop the bleeding.

"Momma!" I screamed as I fell to the floor.

Father came to me, kneeling next to me in tears. He held me as we trembled in front of mother's lifeless body. Whatever distance there was between father and son dissipated in the grief of the moment. We didn't speak, we only cried.

Yusuf knelt next to father, while Yeshu and James knelt next to me. Miriam stood behind me, holding my shoulders. All of us were shedding tears. Miriam kept repeating. "Dear Lord, she helped me so much….."

We must have stayed that way for an hour. Eventually, however, the business of the dead overtook the morning of the living; perhaps it is best that way. Yusuf and Miriam began to help father with the burial arrangements. Father had decided long ago that their final resting place, as well as mine, would be in a small area alongside the groves, a short distance from the trees that had provided for us. As the men made preparations for digging the grave, Miriam and the other woman anointed mother's body and wrapped her for burial. It was not required that I help with either task. I doubt I would have been able to.

I could not even watch the anointing. Silently I walked into our front yard, sitting at the small table Yeshu had built for us years earlier. I stared at the sky, and the tears returned. My mother had spent her last thirteen years caring for me. Even when I had grown to the age when I could look after myself, she was always there, encouraging me. Now she was gone, and I was partially responsible for her death. How could I have been so disrespectful, so uncaring, as to leave her the task of retrieving the water? I felt lower than the serpent that had tempted Eve in the Garden of Eden. Surely the God of All Things held me in the same regard.

Yeshu joined me in the yard. He said nothing as he sat next to me. The tears returned for both of us as we began to speak of mother, of what she had meant to me and what she had meant to him. Yeshu put his arm around my shoulder.

"It's all right, Avi; it's all right. Things happen for a reason, a reason only our Heavenly Father knows."

"Oh Yeshu" I wailed. "I was supposed to get the water today at the well. It's my fault mother …...."

He interrupted me. "Look at me, Avi. Is it your fault the boulder was there? In the exact spot where your mother's head fell? If it had rained today, your mother would not have gone to the well. Is the sunshine your fault?"

"You disobeyed your mother, that is true. But you are no more responsible for her death than for the boulder or the sunshine. Seldom are the times we are wholly at fault; fewer still the times we produce our own accomplishments. We can only deal with the fate the

God of All Things give us and do the best we can to obey his will."

Shaking my head in disbelief and confusion, I asked: "So it is His will that my mother died?"

Yeshu looked pensive.

"Everything that happens, everything that has happened, and everything that will happen is His will. We cannot escape that will; we may ignore it, but it is always there. I cannot say why she died, but I know of her goodness and that He will take care of her. Of that I am certain."

"Your words confuse me, Yeshu, but if you say the Almighty will take care of her, I believe you. At least, I want to believe you...." I was being motioned inside. We were to begin the funeral procession; the last time I would walk with the woman who bore me. Yeshu's words, while they were comforting, did little to lessen my grief. I frequently stumbled along the path to the grave, helped up each time by his strong arms. The men were still digging the grave that would be mother's final resting place. Job had once said we were dust, and that we would return to dust. For the first time, I understood the wisdom of that sage of the Scriptures.

But did mother's spirit live on? I prayed to the God of All Things that it did, that she was now in the same place as the father whom she had adored. As the men finished their digging, I spoke to her, hoping she heard my words. As I said my final good-byes, I kissed the shroud that covered her body.

And then it was over. A few short hours before, mother had sent me off to the groves with a hug; now there would be no more hugs, no more embraces. I would no longer hear her voice or see her smile. A mere few hours had shattered and ripped apart my world.

Yusuf's family stayed with us through the night, Yusuf and Miriam talking to my father, Yeshu to James to me. At some point, I must have dozed off. I could hear my mother's voice calling to me. I awoke trembling, with Yeshu holding me tightly. Many years later, I would remember that embrace and his words whenever I think of that terrible day.

~~ 9 ~~

I remember little of the rest of the year, and with a couple of exceptions, less about the next. Torah sages claim that time heals all wounds; father would say: "Sure it does. When you die, all your troubles are over." Yet not one day passed that I didn't think of mother. Sometimes the memory brought a smile to my face, sometimes tears. But the memory was always there.

I was bar mitzvahed during that period, but it was far from the joyous occasion it was supposed to be. Slightly delusionary, I think, I kept waiting for mother to appear and celebrate my ascension to manhood. The only thing I remember from that day was the gift I received from Yeshu. An inkwell, fashioned out of beautiful wood, it was sound and sturdy, bordering on the ornate. With three fonts and a place to keep my stylus, it was both decorative and practical. How long did I keep it? It holds my inks to this day.

Mother's death had brought father and me closer. The chasm that had always existed might not have been closed, but it indeed had narrowed. We would talk to each other every evening, sometimes father to son, but other times as man to man. I realized for perhaps the first time how much he had loved mother, and how much he missed her.

But I was somewhat taken aback when, to deal with the domestic side of his responsibilities, he hired the daughter of one of his customers. Sophia was slightly younger than father and was certainly pleasant enough, but I resented her intrusion into our lives. That feeling would grow as the weeks and months passed; Sophia was spending more and more time at our house. I felt father was paying her far too much attention. After dinner many evenings, they would leave me alone as they went to walk in the groves. Their relationship troubled me; Sophia troubled me.

In Nazareth, as in many villages my people inhabit, a boy of my age was considered to be grist for the matchmaker's mill. Sophia had begun to insinuate that father might engage one for his son. For my part, I saw it as an attempt to remove me from the family portrait.

"Sophia thinks we should have a matchmaker for you, Avi."

"No!" I emphatically replied.

"I understand your objections, son. You're educated, you will have an inheritance, and you can have any woman you want. And if I do say, you are a fine looking young man. If you do not like any of the girls in Nazareth, there are other villages."

I was relieved father had come to those conclusions. He was right; I wasn't attracted to any of the girls in Nazareth. I had begun to realize that it was unlikely I would be tempted to any girls in any other town, either. I was aware, painfully aware, of the proscriptions of the Torah; I was also aware of how I felt.

"That's it, isn't it, Avi? None of the girls in the village has caught your eye?"

"Yes, father." It wasn't a lie, but it couldn't be called

the truth.

Father looked at me inquisitively and rose to pour some wine. I knew he had sensed something; I also knew it would not be the last I heard of it.

I continued to see little of Yeshu during that time, except for three glorious days that we spent together as we had when we were children. Yeshu surprised me by suggesting that I accompany him and James on one of their trips to Sephoria. He had regaled me with so many tales of the new capital, and he thought I would enjoy seeing it for myself.

I only had to ask father once. Whether he felt I could use the time away from the groves, and the constant reminder of mother; or, as I suspected, wanted more time alone with Sophia, I didn't know. But he quickly gave his permission, and I set off with Yusuf and his sons that very week.

I had been to Jerusalem several times, and Sephoria was nowhere near the size of the Holy City. But while many of the sections of Jerusalem had been aged by time, Sephoria had been transformed into an almost new city. The stones and bricks of which most of the town was constructed still had their original luster; there were even edifices entirely built of wood. One of them earned my immediate attention. A building housing manuscripts, only manuscripts, and manuscripts of all types stood in the center of the city. It held copies of so many forms of writings, from "Oedipus Rex" to Plato's "Republic" to the latest edition of the Roman codex of law. There was even a "modern" translation of the Torah. Yeshu had been right; this was, for a scribe, paradise. I estimated I could spend the remainder of my earthly days here. I also dreamt of contributing my works.

But that was only one aspect of the emerging city. Gymnasiums and theaters had been built, allowing for a variety of enjoyments. Since Yusuf's family was still actively involved in the building of these structures, we were allowed to see how Romans enjoyed their leisure time. It was ironic of course; once completed few Jews would not be able to attend events in these places. Jews might labor in them, but we would never be welcomed as guests. But for now, we could wander them at will. Included in our wanderings would be the soon to be Roman baths.

I was fairly astonished by those baths. Not by the cleansing process itself; after all, the public baths were just like the Mick bah. But when I went to the Temple, I could glance up and see carvings and sculptures of Moses, Abraham, and those representing the God of All Things. Those icons were carved on almost every wall within the Mick bah. They were a reminder of the purpose of our cleansing, to be pure as we entered the presence of the Almighty.

The depictions on the walls of the Roman baths were anything but pure. The first image I saw was of a man and a woman, in not only the lewdest position I had ever seen, but it was also more depraved than anything I had ever imagined. And that was perhaps the most respectful one I saw, as I wandered deeper into the baths. Carvings of couples in every possible position (and some I would have thought impossible) lined the walls and ceilings. The amazement in my eyes must have been evident; Yeshu and James chuckled as we walked.

"Not quite the Temple, is it, Avi?" Yeshu teased me.

I just shook my head. This was a trip for Ephraim, not for me. He would know what the couples were doing. I was shocked Yeshu was not offended by these depictions, and I quickly told him so.

"Of course I'm offended" he replied. "It all disgusts me. They have taken the most beautiful gift the God of All Things has given us and turned it into something filthy. But He works in mysterious ways; somehow He will use this filth to bring even these people to Him."

I was unsure the Almighty would want these people brought to him. I was less sure that the act Yeshu had described as a gift. I was far from Ephraim in my knowledge of such things, but I was aware of how babies were born. For me, it seemed a necessary evil, no "gift" at all.

I would certainly not discuss with Yeshu some of the other carvings I saw. For in some, lewd acts were being consummated not by a man and a woman, but by a man and a man. I looked at them with a fascination that I could never express to my friend; I could hardly express it to myself. I walked quickly passed them, but the images had been imprinted into my mind.

Fortunately for my purity, there were more sights in Sephoria to be seen, sights that appealed to the higher qualities of a man, not the basest. We took them all in; some instructed, some entertained, many did both. The entire city was a feast for the senses.

I began to realize there was a whole new world outside of Nazareth, a world where many of the things I took for granted were no longer true. I had seen mere glimpses of this world during my treks to Jerusalem, but Sephoria had been a different experience altogether. The meshing of cultures, to which I had only paid scant attention to in Jerusalem, was exhilarating; it was also terrifying. Surely a boy raised in such an environment would be a much different boy than I, or even Yeshu, was.

I wondered as we returned to the cocoon of my native village, what those boys would be like.

~~ 10 ~~

Perhaps it was my trip to Sephoria; perhaps the subtle pressures, external and internal, that I was feeling about my social life. Maybe it was a delayed reaction to mother's death and father's involvement with Sophia. Whatever the reason, I began to believe that my destiny lay somewhere outside of Nazareth. I would leave my birthplace, my family, my friends and my synagogue. I would make whatever financial arrangements necessary with my father. With my talent for copying combined with those arrangements, I would live well, perhaps very well. The joy of my life in Nazareth would be over, but so would its pain. As for Yeshu, I would likely never see him again, never be blessed by his presence nor cursed by my developing feelings for him.

But it would be several years before I left. Things would happen in those years which would propel me to move, yet others that compelled me to stay.

It was the night of my birthday, a night that should have been dedicated to me. As was our custom, father made a small party to celebrate the anniversary of my birth. Or at least I thought that was the purpose. Quickly it became apparent that he had another agenda. With no discussion with me beforehand, he announced to family and friends that he and Sophia would marry. I was hardly surprised and had anticipated it. But I was taken aback by its timing.

But it would hardly be the most significant revelation of the night. After the guests had left, father motioned to me to walk with him.

"I hope I didn't spoil your party, Avi, but its time I took a wife."

"I understand, father" I replied dutifully.

"I need a wife, son. Our house needs a caretaker, and you need a mother."

I almost spat out my reply. "She will never be my mother."

Father paused. "Perhaps I was wrong to say that: actually, I know I was wrong to say that. I don't have your talent for words, son" he said apologetically.

I had made him feel uncomfortable; that was not my intent.

"That's fine, father; I didn't mean it that way."

"Good, Avi. You do like Sophia, don't you?"

I didn't know how to answer him. I certainly didn't dislike Sophia, and I had to admit she was right for father. Still, the speed of the courtship bothered me.

"You don't even know her well," I said.

"I know her well enough to know that she will make a fine wife. Besides, I've known her longer than Yusuf knew Miriam, and their relationship worked out well, don't you think?"

Then, with a chuckle, he added, "And Sophia and I don't have to get married."

I didn't understand what he meant. "Why do you say that, father?"

"Listen, Avi, you weren't even born yet, but Yusuf and Miriam married very quickly. And Yeshu was born quicker still. And there was the whole business of them leaving Nazareth....."

I stood wide-eyed at father's words. I had never heard anything of this; could my friend's birth have been tainted?

Under further prodding (I think father would have instead talked about Yusuf anyway), he explained the circumstances of Yeshu's birth. When he was finished, I was ashamed to admit to myself that I found those circumstances much more interesting than my father's forthcoming wedding.

I told him I wanted to walk alone and to digest all that had been said. As for his marriage, I could easily come to terms with it. I would be leaving Nazareth anyway; that would be discussed at another time. And father seemed to be happy.

But Yeshu? Was Miriam with child when Yusuf married her? Was my friend conceived out of wedlock? Was Yusuf even his father? Was that what Yeshu was trying to tell me that day at the Temple? I resolved to have all those questions answered, and answered quickly. I went to sleep that night, but rest would elude me.

Yet fate was going to play tricks in the lives of Yeshu and Avrum. Before I could have my dramatic conversation with my friend, his world would collapse around him.

Yusuf was dying. It happened slowly at first but seemed to pick up momentum almost daily. Yeshu finally admitted his father's condition. Yusuf had taken to his bed, unable to perform essential functions for himself. Tears flowed from my friend's eyes as he told me of these things, as tears also formed in my own. Whatever their relationship was before the law, few sons shared the bond Yeshu shared with Yusuf, and the reverse was equally true.

I mourned what seemed to be the inevitable. Yusuf had been a lamp in my life, a source of love and comfort, with his constant good nature, his dedication to his family and his God. Simply said, he was the type of man that any man, especially a Jewish man, would strive to be. I would have a range of emotions about various men in my life; very few would I admire. Yusuf would be one of those.

Within weeks, Yusuf would pass. All of Nazareth stopped. Fields went unplowed, and labor was suspended, as the village mourned this most wonderful man. My father, who had cried only at his wife's passing, wept openly and unashamedly, as did many of the men in the village.

I accompanied father to Yusuf's burial, as I would to the following Shiva. Father was so distraught that I had concern for his welfare. As they had laid the tradesman into his final resting place, Yeshu again surprised the gathering by speaking at the edge of the grave:

"Our Father in Heaven, blessed is Your name.

Blessed is the life You breathed into this good man,

Blessed too, the woman You gave to him as a companion.

Look after her, my Father, and her children.

Protect Yusuf from the Evil One,

And grant him eternal rest."

It was a stunning oratory. But Nazareth was becoming accustomed to Yeshu's peculiar behavior at funerals; certainly, at this one, no one would begrudge him. At the house afterward, I felt Yusuf's entire family was acting oddly. Yes, they were sorrowful, yet they seemed possessed of an eerily calm solemnity. Between tears, there was the constant talk of the God of All Things, and the wonder of His ways. Everyone knew this was a pious family, but this was beyond piety.

I said as much to Yeshu when I was finally able to

speak to him privately.

"I will miss Yusuf, Avi. His caring, his love, the way he celebrated the Lord with his every act. But he is not gone from us, because his spirit will always be with us. You yourself know of such things, my friend, because of your mother. You hear her voice even today as you did when she was with us. The God of All Things does not take away what we need. The physical presence of your mother and Yusuf may not be here, but their essence remains."

I marveled at his words, but they certainly confused me. Why did he refer to 'my mother', but to his father as 'Yusuf'? My training as a scribe had taught me to pay attention to words, and I wondered why was his so strange.

It would have of course been wrong for me to question him that night. But I vowed I would not leave Nazareth without a better understanding of my friend, who he was and exactly where he had come from.

I had no illusions; I knew my interest in Yeshu was beyond intellectual curiosity, beyond the simple caring of friendship. I loved him, I loved all of him, in all the ways a person could love another.

But I knew he was not like me. I didn't know how I knew, but I knew. My love for him would be unrequited. I accepted that, even fearing what would happen if it wasn't.

What would I do then?

~~ 11 ~~

Both Yeshu's role in his family and mine in my own, would change that year. Despite being younger than James, there was little question that Yeshu was more suitable to become the head of his household.

As for me, father did indeed marry Sophia. I would like to say that I had some profound, heartfelt reaction that day, either positive or negative. The truth was I was numb to their relationship; as long as Sophia kept her distance, it would be fine. My father's demeanor certainly improved, and he and I were getting along as well as we ever had. He no longer resented the hours I spent away from his groves; in fact, he had begun to realize perhaps that his heir would never be an olive grower. He may not have liked it, but he certainly respected it.

And my talent was genuinely beginning to bloom. I became known as the "Young Scribe of Nazareth" and was commissioned to do some minor works. But there was nothing minor about the commission I would receive one summer. Valerius Gaetus, the current Roman Emperor, had decided that he wanted a written history of all the villages in Palestine. It would be too cumbersome to put a Roman scribe in charge of the project, and so I was offered the job for Nazareth. I spent many hours with the village elders (interesting that I refer to them as elders, since many of them were younger than I am now). I began the history of my village and attacked the assignment with zeal. The amount of silver I would receive motivated me; learning the history behind Yeshu inspired me even more.

My approach was to trace each of Nazareth's families through the generations. I discovered some fascinating things; my great-grandfather had obtained the groves through marriage with an older woman. He seemed more to be an opportunistic drifter than the noble farmer.

On my mother's side, grandfather was yet another in the long lines of rabbis in his family; my uncle, of course, had replaced him, continuing the chain. I was able to go back four generations on that side of my family.

My favorite interview (for that was how I had begun to think of the process) was with the elderly Zenandra, a woman who had survived four husbands and had lived her whole life in Nazareth. Rumor was she had attained the age of eighty, but no one knew for sure. Despite her years, Zenandra's memory was acute; she was a reservoir of town history and gossip. She also seemed able to consume copious amounts of wine. I couldn't wait to ask her about Yeshu's family.

"Ah yes, Yusuf bar Malachi, the very skilled tradesman from a long line of skilled tradesmen. His grandfather built this house, Avrum. Yusuf was an excellent man, yet without the pretensions of many such men." With a chuckle, Zenandra added, "As you well know, young scribe, many of Nazareth's holiest men are only holy in the sunshine." She continued to laugh as she poured more wine.

"But Yusuf, he was a good man. A special family, wonderful people. You, of course, don't remember Agatha, his first wife, and a fine woman herself." She detailed Agatha's death, then peered at me and said, "Then Miriam came along."

I deliberately feigned a lack of concern, but my interest was at its peak. I looked up from my writing,

"Where did Miriam come from," I asked.

"From heaven, according to your grandfather," Zenandra chuckled. "Actually she was from Sephoria, the village the Romans are now turning into a brothel. From the beginning, all recognized her beauty and her remarkable eyes. She captivated all of Nazareth with those eyes, even this old lady. I believe they still captivate everyone. Her son has those eyes."

Zenandra certainly knew of what she spoke.

"And of course she was with child."

"Already with child?" I asked.

"Come now, Avrum, you're old enough to understand these things. And I know of your friendship with Yeshu; no doubt you've discussed it."

Of course, we never had.

"The men were unaware," she continued, "but men are often obtuse, too busy with their fields and animals to see what is right in front of their eyes. Only a woman can see the obvious."

Once again she laughed; once again, she poured wine.

"So she was in sin?" I said.

"Oh, Avrum, sin, sin, sin; that's your grandfather in you. Many things are allowed by our laws that are sinful. The Torah lets men beat their wives and their children; some think it encourages these things. Are they not sins? The Almighty allows the Romans to rule us as if we were dogs; is that not sinful?"

"A young woman with child and no husband; I call that a lapse in judgment," she concluded.

"Many in Nazareth would disagree," I replied.

"When they get to Zenandra's age, they will see things differently. They will take a dim view of those who call others sinners."

Zenanadra then peered directly into my eyes.

"Like with you, Avrum. I've noticed you for a long time. You remind me of my departed cousin Samuel, may he rest in peace. Samuel was like you in many ways. Like you, he was forced to hide in the shadows of his village. If many people knew the real Avrum, they'd be pointing their fingers. That is what is sinful."

I began to object, but she was smiling and sipping her wine. I didn't know how; I couldn't fathom how. But Zenanadra knew my deepest and darkest secret.

I met her gaze. I could tell the remark was meant with no malice; if anything, it had been made with compassion. All I could do was smile, and let the matter drop. For Zenandra, she had made her point.

I would spend many other afternoons with her, but the topic was never again breached.

I wrote the history of Nazareth with a speed that surprised me. The manuscript was completed within a year, and I translated it into Roman midway through the next. I presented it to the praetor.

"Caesar himself and the governor will be happy with you, Avrum. The governor is preparing for his retirement and wishes to make this history a gift to his successor, a man named Pilate. You have done a great service and paid tribute to Rome."

The service and tribute to Rome meat nothing to me; in fact, it made me uneasy. But the reward for my labor was crucial for me. It was a generous payment of silver, which I could save for my departure from Nazareth. The irony of having Rome funding that departure gratified

me.
    My exodus was approaching.

~~ 12 ~~

Three things had to be determined before I left. First, the obvious question was: where would I go? Second, financial arrangements needed to be made; wherever I went, I would be a stranger in a strange land, and I preferred not to be a hungry one. Lastly was the matter of Yeshu.

In my mind, I flirted with the idea of Sephoria. It would be close to home, and indeed the freshly remodeled city would provide a variety of opportunities, both personal and professional. But I had to admit I was less the adventurer that I might have liked to be. Everything about Sephoria was new, and I preferred a considerable collection of the old. I enjoyed tradition, even if I found it uncomfortable. The bottom line was that Sephoria was too much of Rome, too much of Greece, and not enough of Israel.

Ultimately the awe and splendor of Jerusalem continued to have its hold on me. Every time I had visited the Holy City, my love for it had grown. In Jerusalem, I could easily find work; scribes were certainly needed, especially multi-lingual ones. Most importantly, there must be other men like me there, perhaps many others. And I would not be encumbered by the possibility of running across someone I knew, as would likely be the case in Sephoria. I could never truly explore my nature in Nazareth's next-door neighbor. So Jerusalem it would be.

I had been maneuvering my father for two years about finances. The first year I would say, "If I ever leave Nazareth"; by the second, it was, "When I leave Nazareth." I convinced him that my desire to leave had nothing to do with him, or with Sophia since I thought that really concerned him. Instead, it was all about Avrum. And it was.

So a document was composed; actually, I was the one who composed it. If the union between father and Sophia remained childless, as apparently it was going to, Sophia would keep the house and whatever funds father had provided for her. All the monies from the groves would be mine. I could maintain control of them or sell them. Father found this disconcerting, however. He had always dreamt that, in the end, I would leave my world of letters to carry on the family business. But he accepted my decision, with some of what could be expected hesitation. The document was signed, and as is our custom, placed with the rabbi for safe keeping.

Those were the easy steps. Now there was Yeshu. I wanted him to know I was leaving, and within the confines of our relationship, to understand why I was moving. Yeshu was not Ephraim; a simple "goodbye, I'm off to Jerusalem" would hardly suffice.

I invited him to a private dinner at my house one winter's evening. The logs burned crisply, warming our little home. Father and Sophia were out visiting friends, so the house would be mine for several hours. Yeshu walked in and actively embraced me.

"Avi, it's been too many days….."

Over dinner and wine (I knew it would be an evening for wine), we made small talk about our families and friends, about Nazareth, and of course about the Romans. But we both sensed that this would not be the night for casual chatter. As we sat after dinner, I decided to be direct.

"I'm leaving Nazareth, Yeshu," I began. That might be the most comfortable thing I had to say all evening. He looked anything but surprised.

"I've been anticipating that, Avi, and understand that the anticipation was with no joy. I would have arranged for this evening myself if you had not done so. I've known for a while that your father's groves held no interest for you and that the books in our synagogue are too few for someone like you. Sadly, I realized that you would someday leave."

"I've been planning it for quite a while. Already I have decided where I am going, and have settled up finances with my father."

Yeshu rose and walked toward the burning logs. Peering into the fire, he said, "So things are further along than I thought. It's Jerusalem, then?"

I was somewhat taken aback. "Yes.... Jerusalem...", I stammered.

"It's a city built for you, Avi. All of those people, all of those books; and imagine, living within walking distance of the Holy of Holies! It's certainly a city made for Avrum bar Jacob."

Turning to me, my friend added "But you have to promise me something, Avi. Promise me you'll be careful."

Earnestly, I replied: "Careful is something I have always been, Yeshu; you more than most should realize that. But I will promise you."

Yeshu nodded his head, then added," In Nazareth, when evil is done, all know of it. In a city like

Jerusalem, people hide in their rooms alone, and if they see evil, they shut their curtains, less it visits them."

I nodded. "I understand, but, as you said, there is much that is good and holy there also."

"That there is my friend, that there is. But the Evil One has an ample opportunity where there are so many disconnected people, especially among the poor and hungry and lonely. Such places are his stronghold, his feeding ground. His ability to tempt in these places is strong."

"You've been discussing Daniel again" I teased, wanting to lighten the mood.

"Yes I have," he admitted with a grin. "Your uncle and I were discussing it this very day."

"Oh Yeshu," I chided him again. "Why don't you let me teach you how to read? For that, I would stay in Nazareth for as long as it took. You could actually read the Word."

"Man cannot live by just the Word alone, my friend. He must ponder the Word, and make it his own. Words are like bread; by itself, it is bread. When we eat it, it becomes the sustenance and fuel for life. Like bread, the Word must be digested and allowed to circulate the soul. As man cannot live by bread alone, neither can he live by the Word alone."

"And by the way, Avi, that's exactly what the rabbi and I were discussing that night in Jerusalem."

"I was afraid to ask you about that, Yeshu, and by the time I had worked up enough courage…..."

"I know; the entire caravan was upon me. They filled my spirit with their kindness."

"I can't believe the Pharisee agreed with you."

Yeshu smiled that unique smile of his. "I wouldn't exactly say he agreed. But he did admit our leaders in the Sanhedrin debate all day about what Moses meant when he wrote this word or that one or used this image or that. That is not the truth of the Scripture, Avi, the truth of the Scripture is that it is true."

"As usual, Yeshu, you confuse me. You seem to accept the wildest of things while questioning the simplest."

"It is confusing Avi, but trust me, it's the simplest things that are the wildest. Fortunately, Our Father in heaven is there to lead us and tame that which is wild."

I did not want this last night with Yeshu to turn into a theological discussion. But I had to understand why he kept referring to the God of All Things in such a personal manner.

"Because He is personal, my friend. He's not some abstract being that floats above, waiting to pounce on any small transgression by his people. He is there to help. He knows He has created a confusing world, where men will struggle. The idea is for us to use that struggle as a path to Him. And He is always there."

The wine was beginning to have its effect on me.

"You discovered all these things while being a tradesman? Did you ask the God of All Things for wisdom as you are breaking the boulders?"

Yeshu laughed; the wine was having its effect on him also.

"You cannot learn of the world by hiding from it, my friend. The Almighty is in the boulder I break as He is the peaceful contemplation of the mystic. Yes, I find the revelation of His kingdom in that boulder. It is not the only way; it is the way I have been given."

Teasingly, he added: 'Some have even found that revelation by transcribing manuscripts, painful as that may be to believe," he chuckled.

"Perhaps someday, through my books, I will find what you have discovered in your rocks," I laughed.

We saluted each other with our glasses.

~~ 13 ~~

"But enough of these things," Yeshu continued. "Avi is leaving Nazareth; what will I do without him?"

"I should be asking what I will do without Yeshu" I answered. "You have been with me every step of the way. The day mother died....; leaving you will be the hardest part about leaving the village."

"You're not leaving me, Avi; my spirit will always be with you. And you underestimate yourself, my friend; you always have. I may have been there for you, but you were there for me also. Always when I felt there was no earthly being who could understand me, there was Avi."

I was moved to tears to think that Yeshu held me in that regard. I rose and went to pass some of the wine out of my system. As I did so, I looked at the trees, I looked at the sky. Dare I reveal my innermost secret to him? How would he react? What would he say? What would he do?

But I would never say it.

"There I something you should know……" I stammered as I returned.

Yeshu interrupted. "There is nothing I should know

that I don't already know, Avi; nothing, nothing at all. All I need to know is that Our Father made you and specially made you, as He has made us all."

I sat, entirely uncertain how to continue. Did he know?

"But you need to promise me one thing, Avi. Promise me you will not be lonely in Jerusalem. There are many, many types there, many like you, who search for love and companionship, as you do. Love and companionship are two ways to Our Father; use them as your guide."

I stared at him. "I will try, Yeshu, I will try."

His brow furrowed.

"I have always ached that I could never be all that you needed from me. I cannot change my nature any more than you can change yours. But our friendship and love for each other are special, and always will be important to me."

"And Avi……" Yeshu paused.

"Yes?" I asked nervously.

"There is someone in Jerusalem. It is his spirit you hear calling you."

Again tears welled in my eyes, and soon a torrent followed. Yeshu too cried. But the tears were those of relief, relief that a vast chasm that perhaps we both felt had hindered our friendship had been closed. He was not like me, as he said. But he could still love me.

There are moments in all our lives like that moment; doubtless, the reader has had them. If the God of All Things had taken me at that very moment, I believe I would have died a contented man.

But He did not take me. Yeshu and I continued talking. And it was time to speak about him, with the same honesty and frankness that we had spoken of me.

"You've confused me so many times, Yeshu, but never more than when you talk of your father. Yusuf was your father, wasn't he?"

"Yes, dear Avrum, Yusuf was my father. I doubt any father loved his child as Yusuf loved me. I like to think I returned that love. What makes a man a father isn't some physical act; nor does it make a woman a mother. In either case, it is the acceptance of responsibility that makes a parent. Many men and women do what is necessary physically to have a child; sadly, they are not all fathers and mothers. Yusuf was my father, Avi; have no doubt about that."

"You have heard me pray to the God of All Things and call Him 'Father'; maybe that confused you. But he is Our Father, my friend; like all good fathers, He knows how to care for us. He accepts His responsibility, and does so with love."

"That's not quite how our people have seen Him," I replied. "The Almighty as a parent…."

"Oh, but He is, Avi. And He knows each of us as any father knows his child. He knows your heart and your soul. And He is always with you."

'But what if he doesn't approve of what is in my heart and soul?"

I believe I had asked him a question that he had no quick answer for. And he indeed waited to answer. He looked pensive, but suddenly his eyes brightened.

"Tell me honestly, Avi, and think before you answer. Does your father approve of your move to Jerusalem?"

I honored my friend's request. Did my father approve? On the one hand, I knew he was disappointed that his beloved orchard would likely pass from the family. But I also knew he had a particular pride that I had made a difficult decision to be my own person, and to make my path.

I explained the dichotomy to Yeshu.

His smile returned. "Jacob is a fine man; I have

always respected him. But he is just a man. If a man can be of two minds about the same thing, especially when it deals with something about his children, don't you think the Almighty is capable of an infinite amount of minds? Even about the same thing?'

My reason was clouded by the wine, but I could immediately see the truth of my friend's parable. Yes, it made all the sense in the world.

I saluted my friend's ability as a teacher. 'Surely you should become a rabbi."

With that same smile, he responded. "Now you're beginning to sound like James. Perhaps I will. Avi; I've certainly thought about it. But Israel does not need another rabbi; many are called to that noble profession, and most perform it well."

"A preacher, then?"

"Another group Israel has little need of. How many preachers pass through Nazareth a year? Sometimes it seems like a hundred. But I have to admit to you in candor that I admire most of them. And I have thought about joining their ranks."

"Are you going to stay in Nazareth?"

"If I remain within my trade, it is likely. I have a great love for this village, and even though I enjoy working in Sephoria, I would never want to live there. Nazareth is special, Avi, we know that."

"But if you preach…..."

"I would likely travel, that is true. The physician who has a cure for a disease is obligated to share it with the largest audience possible. There is nothing just in limiting it to a few."

"But for the present, I am unsure I have any cure, and if I do not, then I am better off staying within my trade. Those who are well have no need for a physician. Perhaps everyone is well, and I am the one who is ill. I can't answer that question, Avi, at least for right now."

We sat silently for a moment, perhaps contemplating the serious revelations we had shared that evening. In a somber tone, Yeshu began to speak.

"Besides, my dear friend, these are questions for the future, not for the last night, if it is the last night, which we share wine. I must ask you a most important question."

Nervously, I waited for what he would ask.

"Tell me, who is Ephraim courting these days?"

Our mutual guffaws dissipated the tensions that had built. I laughed so long I thought my belly would burst. Yeshu's reaction was the same. And I didn't know whom Ephraim was courting; I feared there were few in Judea he was not courting.

The night had almost passed. Quietly, father and Sophia had returned, and respectively had left us alone, retiring to their bed. I embraced my friend, and he returned the affection. It was a long embrace, as befitted both our friendship and some of the matters that had been discussed that evening. I would remember that embrace for many years; I remember it now as I write these words. Only my death will remove its memory; of that I am thankful.

It was not the last time I saw Yeshu before I left for Jerusalem. There were gatherings given by friends and family. And he attended all of them. But nothing would replace the intimacy of that night. It wasn't a physical intimacy; it was beyond that. It was better than that.

~~ 14 ~~

In a scene often witnessed as a young man from a small village leaves to seek his destiny, I finally did leave Nazareth. This time there would be no caravan or groups to travel with me. Indeed, my only companion would be the two donkeys which carried my provisions. Every night, and often during the day, I thought of turning around and heading back to Nazareth. It was autumn, a strange time for a Jew to be wandering, and the roads and byways I traveled were virtually deserted. Such a journey generates an intense feeling of loneliness. I spoke to no one for days, and had conversations with myself audibly, to convince myself I could speak. Every night I attempted to sleep, I was terrified a highwayman lay lurking in the shadows to steal my donkeys and the silver I carried with me. I did not sleep much.

When the walls of Jerusalem came into view, I felt as if I was a sailor who had spent a year at sea, finally spotting land. My fears about how I would live in the Holy City gave way to delight that I would have a consistent and safe place to lay my head each evening. I entered the city in jubilant spirits.

It was not hard to find lodging. A merchant in the city, a Syrian gentleman, owned a large house almost precisely in the center of the city. He rented space within a large room on a monthly basis. It wasn't difficult convincing him that I would be a good tenant; three months rent in advance accomplished that. I sold the donkeys, unpacked my meager possessions, and moved in.

Six young men, all of us about the same age, shared the bottom floor of a two-story home; the Syrian and his family lived atop. Essentially the six of us each had a small space inside one giant room. My area consisted of a mat to sleep on, a trunk to store my things, and a small table. I would discover the landlord had devised all kinds of way to make additional money. If you wanted a candle, there was a charge; if his wife was to wash your tunic, another charge. And there was no privacy, none whatsoever. Still, it was my first "home", my first time on my own, and I loved it.

I surprised myself by how quickly I became friendly with my roommates. There were two other Jews and three gentiles. The religious differences didn't seem to prohibit companionship; we would play games where the sides were Jew versus Gentile. Our common threads lessened the differences between us; we were young, we were poor, and each of us in his way, was starting off his life.

I was further buoyed by the ease with which I found employment. My thought that scribes would be needed in Jerusalem proved accurate. I presented myself at the Temple armed with two letters of reference. One was from my uncle the rabbi, the other from the Roman praetor for whom I had written the history of Nazareth. I was immediately employed, joining forty or so other junior scribes working in the basement of the Temple. I deemed it a great honor. I was put under the charge of a man called Levi, who himself had emigrated from a small town twenty years earlier. We took an immediate liking to each other, and I found him to be a very agreeable and likable man, especially as a supervisor. Levi put me to work immediately on a translation to Greek of the book of Daniel. Throughout the assignment, thoughts of Yeshu were never far from my mind.

It took some weeks, but I had to admit my transition was going smoothly. I wouldn't say I was happy, but I indeed wasn't miserable. Some aspects of the Holy City amazed me, while others frightened me. There was a lot less animosity between Jew and Gentile, and even Pagan. Assyrians, Greeks, Cypriots, Samaritans, and a host of others intermingled freely. Wine seemed to be the currency of most of the interaction, and I admit that I became too well acquainted with all the varieties available in Jerusalem. Mostly I worked all day and drank all night. But the camaraderie was worth the morning headaches.

The Romans, of course, were another matter. It was a rare time when a Jew could pass a Roman without hearing a disparaging comment. The larger the group of Romans, the more insulting the comments were, and of course, Jews could not retaliate. Romans seemed especially fascinated by our ancient rite of circumcision, and there seemed to be no end to the insults that practice generated. With shame, I admit I found some of the jokes to be amusing.

Jerusalem was also my first real exposure to civil law. The Romans had a codified system of laws and consequences of breaking those laws. The system was anything but perfect, and the laws would change often. With most of the residents being illiterate, they would be unaware of the changes. And as we all knew, punishments were much more severe for Jews, especially Jews, more so than for other occupied nations. I questioned how a system so filled with inequities could ever be called civilized, but as the Romans saw it, their's advanced civilization.

Punishments for transgressions ranged from flogging to imprisonment to legal servitude and ultimately, to execution. Capital punishment was meted out on a stratified basis. A Roman citizen convicted of a capital crime would be given a vial of lethal poison and a week in which to drink it. Like Socrates, many of the condemned were allowed family and friends around as they died at the behest of Mother Rome.

Non-citizens and some occupied members of the Empire would not be allowed all that pomp and circumstance, or that long of a time frame. They would be taken immediately after judgment to be beheaded. It was said that beheading was painless, but I questioned how anybody could know. Painless or not, beheading was a bizarre spectacle.

Not nearly as bizarre as the method of execution reserved for peasants and enemies of the state; Jews, by definition, were both. Crucifixions usually began with a flogging, after which the condemned was forced to carry a crossbar from which he would eventually hang, for a mile to a hill called Golgotha. There the crossbar would be affixed to a planted base, and the condemned man would hang directly on the finished crucifix.

Unlike the swiftness of other executions, crucifixion was a long, arduous and painful death. The condemned man would hang there, often for days; four days was the average. Slowly his internal organs would begin to sag, making the simple act of breathing an ordeal. The condemned would suffer from lack of food and water, and with no protection from the sun, wind, and rain, death from exposure was inevitable. Often the man would beg his executioners to pierce him with a sword, ending his fatal ordeal.

When a Jew was crucified, his clothing was removed, his circumcision revealing to all his faith and nationality. It was a bizarre, excruciating death; certainly among the most brutal ever designed by man. And while most poisonings and beheadings were private affairs, crucifixions were public spectacles. On any given day, condemned men were led to Golgotha to join others so sentenced, and who were likely still alive.

Capital crimes ranged from crimes against the state, such as treason and sedition, to so-called crimes against nature, such as rape and sodomy. I found it ironic that the rapist and sodomite, even the consensual one, were considered to be no different; both likely faced the cross.

Some of my roommates would attend crucifixions, but I found them repulsive. I could not understand what possible interest the entire process could have for anyone; watching the life force drip out of a man by degrees had to be horrifying.

I vowed never to attend or to witness a crucifixion, a vow that would last for many years.

~~ 15 ~~

My religious life in Jerusalem, which you would have thought would have magnified (as Yeshu had said, I was within walking distance of the Holy of Holies), in fact, deteriorated. All Jews were excused from work before sundown on the Sabbath, but to say I kept the day in the manner specified by the Torah would be stretching the truth. My Jewish roommates and I would recite the prayers and perform the rituals, as our gentile roommates looked on, sometimes respectively, sometimes less so. While their occasional ridicule was understated, it was nonetheless uncomfortable.

It troubled me that this was happening. I might not have had the religious zeal of Yeshu, but I did have respect for the traditions of my faith. I explained the situation to Levi, who then insisted that my Jewish roommates and I begin spending Sabbath evening with his family. It would be a blessing for him, he said, although we were expected to contribute to the cedar. I felt comfortable that while I might never experience a Nazareth-style Sabbath, I at least would be keeping the law.

And of course, there was Passover. I so looked forward to that first reuniting with the Nazarenes who would be coming to the Holy City. Perhaps father would come this year; certainly, Yeshu would. I longed for some familiar companionship and eagerly awaited the holiday.

Passover week arrived, and I ran each evening from the Temple to the arriving caravans at the city gates. Each night a new family from Nazareth would come, but it wasn't until the day before the festivities began that I heard a familiar voice.

"Avi, Avi, over here," my uncle bellowed.

He had brought many of my extended family members this time, and his caravan easily numbered thirty. I immediately ran to him.

"Is father coming?"

Uncle shook his head. "I'm afraid not, Avi; you know your father. But he insisted you give me a full report of your doings in the big city, and in return, I will share all of Nazareth's gossip. What I forget, I'm sure your aunt will fill you in," he chortled.

"Oh, and your friend Yeshu is coming with his family; he is but a half day behind us."

I was elated that I would see my friend again, though disappointed I would not see father. Despite that, the family would be the focus of the day and of the evening meal, at which I was the honored guest. I was informed of all that was happening in my native village; who had given birth, who had died, and who was courting whom. As to the last, Ephraim took up most of the conversation.

At the end of the evening, uncle motioned that he wanted to see me privately. "Of course you'll want news of Yeshu." Indeed, I did. "He is well, as are Miriam and James. And his brother Judah's wife gave birth last month."

"Is Yeshu still at the synagogue every night?"

"More than ever!" uncle explained. "His work in Sephoria is done. And every sundown, as I light the candles, I see him. Sometimes he is alone; sometimes Miriam and James are with him. But he is always there."

"Still debating you, of course," I kidded.

"Only every night," uncle said, sardonically. "I will never lose my wits as long as he is there to challenge me."

But suddenly he turned serious.

"I am beginning to worry about him, Avi. I don't know where he gets his ideas. Just the other day, he argued with me about our dietary laws. He asked how we could insult the God of All Things by labeling some of his creatures 'unclean'."

"And then he argues with me, and with Scripture, about divorce. It doesn't matter to him that the Torah allows a man to divorce his wife. And I could go on and on. But enough about Yeshu; tell me about Avrum."

I promised to show him my rooming house and introduce him to my co-workers at the Temple. I spent the night in uncle's tent, bathed in the warmth of kin.

At daybreak, we entered the city. I showed everyone where I lived; my aunt wasn't very impressed ("The wife of this landlord of yours, does she own a broom?"). Then we headed to the Temple. I felt a bit of a celebrity, showing everyone where I worked, the inner chambers of the Temple the public rarely sees. I introduced them to Levi and appreciated the nice things he had to say. In many ways, it was a glorious day.

A day made even more glorious by my friend's arrival. We returned to the campsite to find Yeshu settling in with Miriam and James. We embraced firmly and kissed; I hadn't realized until that very moment how much I had indeed missed him. Miriam insisted that I have the evening meal in their tent, which made the reunion that much fonder.

During the meal, Yeshu and I talked as women do at the well in Nazareth. I don't believe Miriam or James said five words. I gave Yeshu a daily (I'm sure it seemed that way to his mother and brother) accounting of my time in Jerusalem so far. In turn, he told me his side of his "discussions" with uncle.

"I'm sure he has mentioned them to you."

I smiled in reply.

Yeshu laughed heartily. "Ah Avi, you must be doing well at the Temple. You have a newfound talent for diplomacy. The Sanhedrin must have their eyes on you."

After dinner, Yeshu invited me to walk with him; apparently, he wanted to speak to me privately. His first statement surprised me, but only a little.

"I too will be leaving Nazareth, Avi; like you, I'm thinking a few years ahead, but I'm certain that time will come."

"Will you come to Jerusalem?" I asked, both with hope and trepidation.

Shaking his head, he said he wanted to visit other synagogues and speak to other rabbis. He was also curious about some of the sects that had splintered off from mainstream Judaism, and Israel had no shortage of those. He imagined a nomadic journey rather than a relocation.

The following day we attended services. Afterward, I gave him an abbreviated tour of the Temple. Regrettably, Levi was at home that day; I would have liked Yeshu and him to have met each other.

After seeing the lower levels of the Temple, Yeshu said: "Pretty stifling down there; it must be why the Sanhedrin is so stifled."

During the Mick bah, I continued to marvel at the man he had become. He was as handsome as sunrise, with eyes that spoke of sunset. A fellow bather, a man from Capernaum, said to me, "Your friend must be tossing women out of his tent every night." I laughed as I repeated the remark to Yeshu afterward.

"There are many splendid women in Nazareth, Avi; you know that." Then turning oddly serious, he added: "A man should not look at a woman in that way unless there is marriage in his heart. I would make a poor husband; a husband must focus solely on his family; it must be his only joy. But I seek other joys."

"You will have no heirs, then," I said.

Again with that wry grin of his, he said: "Actually, I suspect I will have many."

The perplexing look I gave him must have been obvious; he embraced me again.

"Come. Let us speak of other things. Show me your house."

I took him to my residence, where he seemed very at ease with my roommates (and they with him), fitting in with his good nature. He seemed to be enjoying himself the entire day. We toured the city, and he looked as if he was seeing it through the eyes of a child, yet with the sophistication of an adult.

And I totally enjoyed his company.

Yet a sense of relief swept over me as I bade him and the rest of the Nazarenes goodbye. Perhaps I just needed to return to my Jerusalem routine.

Or perhaps it was something else.

~~ 16 ~~

The following year would be anything but routine. I had promised my uncle I would visit Nazareth in that year, but I would break that promise. I can make several excuses, about some of which I will write. But the truth was that I was entirely caught up with my life in Jerusalem. The Temple, my work, and even the developing friendships with my roommates made me not want to leave, even for a short while. I was enjoying the life I had constructed.

And in that year I would discover a companion.

As with so many events in my life, it happened oddly. I arrived at the Temple one morning to see Levi conversing with a Roman centurion. Few Romans ever entered the Temple, much less a man of that rank. Most Romans considered the Temple an unholy place. A standard joke was that the Roman who entered the Temple came out less of a man, a not so veiled reference to circumcision.

As I began my work, Levi called to me.

"Avrum, I would like to introduce you to Flavius. He is a centurion; one of Caesar's most honored soldiers."

I bowed to the Roman as he began to speak.

"Levi tells me that you are among the best scribes in the temple. Is that true, young man?" I did not want to appear conceited, but I was proud of both my talents and accomplishments. Still, humility was the best course.

"I am honored that Levi feels that way, sir."

"I wish to employ you, Avrum," Flavius said. "I have a son, about your age, who seeks to further his literary skill."

My surprise must have been evident. Literacy among the Romans was only slightly higher than among the Jews. Like many of my people, Romans did not see the use of reading and writing. Moreover, a centurion would have many others at his disposal, whether they were just scribes, or servants or slaves. Why was this one interested in me?

"I am honored sir, but if I may ask...."

"Why employ a Jew?" Flavius had anticipated my question. "Simple, really. Roman scribes see the world as Romans see it and. I prefer my son to have a broader view. That said, I hope what Levi has told me is true; that you are fluent in Roman. I want my son to know the works of his people."

"Of course sir. Levi might have told you that I wrote a history of my native village for the praetor......"

"Yes, yes, he told me," Flavius interjected. I had a feeling that the conversation was ending. But I was curious about one crucial thing above all.

"May I ask the centurion why not just use one of your slaves?"

It was Levi who spoke. "I do not believe you need to know that to be in the centurion's employ, Avrum. If you are not interested in the position, there are others."

"Oh no sir, I have every interest."

"It is done then," Flavius spoke. "You will report

three nights a week and work with my son. You will be paid for your labors. But as I stressed to Levi, your first obligation is to your Temple. If it becomes an issue, you will be discharged."

I had begun to realize that Centurion Flavius was a man of few words, yet very choice words. I tried to answer him in kind.

"I accept your position with great humility, sir."

"Fine. I will gather you this evening and show you to my house. There you will meet Marcus, who I believe will approve of you" With that, the centurion turned and began exiting the Temple. I had a thousand questions for Levi, but he silenced me with one sentence.

"You will heed the centurion, Avrum, and do his bidding. Or he and I will take turns giving you a beating that you will never forget." Levi turned and followed after Flavius, and I was left alone to anticipate the evening.

True to his word, as I suspected he would be, Flavius arrived at the Temple precisely at dusk. Leading me through the streets of Jerusalem, many of which I had never traversed, he demonstrated the shortest route to his house. We began walking down tree-lined streets containing individual, mostly wooden structures, unlike any I had ever seen. Most of the homes I was familiar with were identically built honeycombed stone structures, chiseled out of a mountainside. Each of these homes had its own style.

We arrived at a good-sized structure, which appeared to have its own extra land in the rear. Flavius had said little during our walk, and I followed his lead in kind. He motioned me inside his house, a plain yet obviously well-kept abode. From the outside, I could tell it was much more spacious than any I had been used to. Indeed, it was easily ten times the size of the house I had grown up in.

We were greeted at the door by an Assyrian woman, whom I assumed was a slave. She bowed to Flavius, and then to me. It was the first time in my life I had ever been greeted by anyone with a bow.

The centurion said, "Nilsa will prepare supper for us. Then you and Marcus can become acquainted. No tutoring needs to be done tonight, but I expect there will be rapid results in the future."

I sensed that this was a statement of fact, not desire. I was hoping my nervousness was not showing.

Off the anteroom was a wash area, and Flavius invited me to join him. After washing ourselves, he led me into the dining area, which was complete with an over-sized table and several chairs. Either the centurion had a large family, or he entertained often; perhaps both were true.

He did not have a large family. He introduced Marcus, who had come bounding into the room, as his only child.

Marcus immediately embraced his father. He was built as sturdy as the centurion, at about the same height and weight, with ebony black hair; he had what Jews would call a "Mediterranean" complexion. In short, he was an incredibly handsome young man, as I assumed Flavius had been at that age. The resemblance was striking.

I had the impression that embraces were frequent between the two of them. Nilsa brought out dinner, which was as sumptuous a repast as I had ever seen. If Romans ate like this regularly, I couldn't imagine how they feasted on holidays. I gazed at the plates, wondering if I should begin eating. Suddenly Flavius stood up, and while looking at Marcus and me, said:

"The gods have provided us with a full table. May my son and I and all of the Empire continue to earn their approval."

With that, he sat and began to eat. It was apparent that Nilsa was an excellent cook; the meal was delicious. As we ate, Flavius talked.

"Marcus, this is Avrum, your teacher. I know you have come a long way in your reading and writing, but Levi tells me Avrum is the man to speed it up. Avrum, this is Marcus, whom I hope you will find a suitable pupil."

"Oh, and Avrum, if my intonation at the beginning of supper offended you, I apologize. I believe it is always proper to give thanks."

There I was, literally shaking as I was eating, and my host was concerned about offending me. And that I would find his son suitable. I had already decided Marcus was suitable. More than suitable.

Marcus grinned at me; in addition to everything else, his smile was infectious. "Can you read and write Greek?" he asked, and I nodded. "Excellent, and I want to learn Hebrew also."

Why would a young Roman want to learn the language of my ancestors, I wondered? But this was hardly the time to ask.

'Let Avrum speak, Marcus", Flavius said.

Again I recited my qualifications, this time to the son, as I had done to the father. Marcus seemed excited.

"I'm sure you will be fine. Avrum," Flavius said. "And I see Marcus has no objections. I will instruct Nilsa concerning your dietary needs. How's that, Marcus? Not only will you learn Hebrew from a Jewish scribe, but you will eat as the Jews do three times a week!" Again, Marcus responded with a wide grin.

I remained essentially mute during the rest of dinner. I was more involved listening to father and son discussing their respective days. Clearly, Flavius was deeply involved in his son's life, as Marcus was involved in his father's. There was a warmth here I had never seen between parent and child. My own relationship with my father had improved but was nothing like this. I wasn't sure father and I could ever relate like this. I began to realize the opportunity that we had both missed.

~~ 17 ~~

I was relieved when dinner finally ended. The general uneasiness of being around new people, people with a completely different value system than mine, was added to by the almost constant attention Flavius and Marcus received from their slaves. There was Nilsa the cook, her Egyptian assistant, a Cypriot named Simon (who seemed to be some kind of manservant) and a host of others, including an elderly Roman gentleman; I couldn't imagine what he had done to deserve his fate.

Flavius suggested we first go to the backyard area, and then to his study. That way I could get comfortable, as he said, with his residence. Unlike Jewish homes, where open spaces were the norm, Romans appeared to favor many small rooms, separated by walls. We passed several of them on the way to the patio.

The backyard was neatly trimmed, with an eating area; behind that area stood a stable, suitable for four or five horses that occupied it, with room for more. My first thought was that if all centurions lived in such splendor, it was hardly a mystery why they were so loyal.

Our tour completed we settled into the study,

another small room but entirely different from the others. Here wooden shelves were nailed to seemingly every inch of the walls. Guiltily, my first thought was of Yeshu; this was the kind of room he and Yusuf would have loved to have built. Manuscripts of all types lined the shelves; Flavius had an eclectic collection, ranging from classics to tomes of which I had never heard. I smiled as I saw a copy of the Torah on one of the shelves.

A large table centered the room, surrounded by four to six soft chairs. Clearly, this room was meant not only for intellectual discovery but physical relaxation. It was warm it was cozy, and yet ornate, and I immediately fell in love with it.

Flavius withdrew, and I was alone with Marcus.

"Will you be speaking while you are tutoring me?" he asked with a smile.

"Oh yes" I replied, "Actually I really talk a lot."

"Just not to Romans, it seems." The smile was still there, not a mocking smile, more of one generated by curiosity. And a certain amount of awkwardness.

If Marcus felt awkward, he wasn't alone. While I felt reasonably relaxed in his company, I was confused about what I should be saying or doing. He was able to ease the situation.

"I know your qualifications, Avrum, but what I want to know about is you."

I was surprised by his interest in my personal life and immediately gave him a truncated biography. He seemed pleased and opened a bottle of wine. Perhaps he too had been searching for a way to begin.

"Wonderful, how exciting. I will learn much from you, Avrum of Nazareth. And of your people, who fascinate me."

"Really," I replied. "I never thought Jews were all that fascinating, especially not to Romans."

Marcus paused before he answered. "I know most of your people think all Romans are brutish and arrogant, Avrum. And most of my people have similar misconceptions about Jews. But let me ask you something; does my father strike you as brutish and arrogant?'

I had to respond honestly; moreover, I wanted to respond honestly. "Oh no, not at all! He's certainly nothing at all like I thought a centurion would be."

"And Avrum," Marcus replied, "is nothing like I thought a Jewish scribe would be. We will indeed be learning much about each other." He raised his glass in salute.

I joined him in that salute and was willing to chance that our acquaintance was growing enough to allow more honesty.

"Your father is much more intellectually curious and much more, well, gentle, than I ever thought a centurion would be."

"He is gentle, Avrum, especially for a centurion." Pointing to an impressive collection of ribbons on a shelf, Marcus added, "especially for a centurion who has earned so many awards in battle. And his intellectual curiosity has allowed him to appeal to a wide range of people. Your supervisor Levi, for instance, has dined in this house often. As have people of all nations and beliefs."

"Naturally I'm curious about your father's relationship with Levi," I said.

"It was three years ago when my mother took ill and died. Father sought council from any and every one; that's when he and Levi became friends. Your supervisor helped him deal with his loss. And helped me also."

So, like me, Marcus was motherless. There was more common ground here, I thought, than I could have hoped.

He had become distant as he spoke of his mother's death, and I wanted to bring him back into the moment. Holding his arm, I said: "I too lost my mother years ago. I more than understand."

It worked. Marcus' mood immediately changed. 'So we are like brothers then, both only children, both motherless; it seems like we much in common."

I wanted the conversation to continue in this style.

"And we both have a fascination with Israel."

Marcus grinned and said: "To father's wishes, then, I believe the teacher and the pupil will get along well." Again, we saluted each other with wine.

I was curious about one thing, especially. "Were you born in Palestine?"

"Oh no. I am a true Roman, born in that extraordinary and magnificent city. We came here seven years ago; Augustus had stretched the army so thin that the Senate began recalling troops from here. As a result, many of the legions that patrol Palestine are mercenaries from other lands. They need to be taught the Roman way of battle and soldiering; that's my father's commission, to train and develop them."

"So your father is a teacher, also?"

Again Marcus laughed. "I hope I am a better student than some of father's pupils; his task is significantly harder than yours. Some of his students…….."

"I can imagine the problems," I said. "But it's strange; I never thought that Roman soldiers were, well, not Roman."

It would be my first exposure to Marcus' great wit.

"Oh Avrum, with all the garb they wear and those face guards, you could hide Cleopatra in that uniform, and no one would know."

I roared loudly. The image of the Queen of the Nile in Roman war gear was hysterical.

"Shih" Marcus cautioned. "Father thinks were

discussing Cassius, not Cleopatra." But he said it with a giggle.

The rest of the evening conversation continued in that relaxed manner. Whatever nervousness I had felt at the beginning of the evening had dissipated entirely. I could have stayed talking to Marcus all night. And quite a bit longer.

But the hour was getting late. And I needed to heed the centurion's warning that my first obligation was to the Temple. And, whatever else was happening, Flavius was still my employer, with all that that title entailed.

I prepared to leave, elated that Marcus was as disappointed as I was.

"Too bad you can't stay, Avrum.

"Marcus, you have to understand…."

"I know, I know, but it doesn't mean I have to like it."

We embraced as men who had known each other for years, not hours. But also like men who both knew that something extraordinary had happened that night.

As we left the study, I asked if I should tell his father I was leaving or just the slaves.

"Slaves?", Marcus asked me with a curious glance. "What slaves?"

"The cook, the man-servant, and the rest. They're all slaves, aren't they?"

Marcus shook his head. "No, Avrum, my father owns no slaves. He has never owned slaves, although most centurions do. He believes slavery is an insult to a man's dignity, and an affront to the gods themselves. Everyone you met is a paid servant, who is also given lodging for his work. Father must treat them well; Nilsa has been with him since before I was born, and Simon since right after. I doubt their wages or conditions would be better anywhere else."

So the house was run by servants, not slaves. My

admiration for this centurion was growing. But Marcus was quick to add:

'Make no mistake though Avrum; father may think what he thinks and acts as he acts, but his first loyalty is to Caesar. He is a servant of the Empire, first, last and always."

With that, Marcus bid me good night. I began my walk home in a spirit I had never before felt. I had not only discovered, by fate, a remarkable man, and his son; I had learned something about myself. Marcus obsessed my thoughts on the way home; as I fell asleep, as I worked the next day.

My self-knowledge was now complete. As difficult as it was to imagine, I was in love with Marcus. As I had been before in my life, I was elated and petrified at the same time. It was a difficult place to be. And I minded it not one bit.

~~ 18 ~~

It would be inappropriate to delineate the various phases of how Marcus and I became lovers. Suffice to say that I found in him everything that I had ever sought on every level; physical, emotional, and spiritual. Yes, even spiritual. For Marcus had a great curiosity about Judaism, and I shared his journey of understanding, and as I explained our beliefs and rituals, they became more alive for me. At the same time, I was discovering the nature of pagan religiosity. Marcus and Flavius were as dedicated to Zeus and Jupiter as I was to the God of All Things. Was that surprising to me, that the pagan could have the same religious devotion as the Jew? It was earth-shattering.

I wouldn't want to give the impression that we met and immediately fell in love. A year would pass before we had our first experience, made more special by the fact that it was his first time as well as mine. It was a continual process of discovery, sometimes tricky, sometimes exhilarating, and even at times comical. We certainly did not want any of the residents of the household, especially Flavius, to know what was going on. What Marcus and I had was special. However, it could also get us both imprisoned and worse.

Meanwhile, my admiration for the father was growing as rapidly as my love for the son. This was not the soulless Roman of Jewish description. Flavius was intellectually curious, yet firm in his convictions about justice and dedication to his Caesar. As much as I had begun to appreciate my father, Flavius represented for me all that the word denoted.

And Marcus loved him dearly. This was not mere filial devotion; whatever he did for his father was done with joy.

I continued my life at the Temple, the days made more tolerable by those magical three nights a week I spent with Marcus. Indeed, I was excelling at work. Levi raised my position to his assistant and trainer for his staff. As such, I no longer directly transcribed manuscripts but acted as an advisor to other scribes. Between my success at the Temple and my relationship with Marcus, it was a wondrous time.

I was becoming less a transplant from Nazareth and more a citizen of Jerusalem. Through my association with Flavius and Marcus, I was granted many privileges unavailable to most Jews, and there was little I was denied access to. I was even being teased by my roommates and co-workers that I had become a semi-Roman, with the way I was fitting into the Roman lifestyle. I was told that I would make the perfect Pharisee since we all knew they were in league with the Romans.

Regrettably, I had to keep all these things secret during Passover, when my Nazarene connections came to visit. The motives were both professional (Flavius) and personal (Marcus). I would have loved for Yeshu, his family, and my family to have met them. But the lack of comfort involved was just too large. In that sense, I had not wholly escaped Nazareth.

The Nazarenes would come to Jerusalem twice in the next three years. A drought that had invaded Palestine in the middle year made the holiday a secondary consideration. It was the second of these visits that was the most memorable.

I had finally begun in that year to deal with my feelings for Yeshu. Marcus had helped me with that. I started to realize that Yeshu had been my first love object; and that more importantly, he was unable to return the same type of love I needed. All of that had probably had more of an effect on me than I realized.

But I still loved him as a friend and had begun to pity him somewhat. He was nearly thirty, an age when most men had established their lives; he was still searching, it seemed, for his. I had relocated from my native village and found a mate, and I cared not that my culture would not approve. He was still in Nazareth, living with Miriam and James, cocooned from the outside world. I was growing, open to a myriad of new experiences that were coming my way. He, I was told, was still spending his nights arguing with a small town rabbi. Indeed, my uncle claimed that he was becoming a nuisance.

"All those questions, all that probing," uncle complained to me. "He doesn't want to become a rabbi, doesn't want to learn to read, but he wants to tell the rabbi what to do." In past years, uncle would say things like that with a chuckle, and now there was no longer any humor in his words.

"You know what I think, Avi? I think he's just unhappy. I used to enjoy seeing him at the synagogue and liked the bantering that he would bring. But lately, I admit to avoiding him whenever I can. He's so miserable, so morose...."

"Do you think it would help if I talked to him?"

"It can't hurt anything. If nothing else, try to convey my feelings. Look, I like the man, and I respect him; I respect his family. But frankly, he's becoming too large a load to carry."

I felt compelled to approach Yeshu. Though we had spent a decent amount of time on his previous visits, our conversations, save for that first year, had been superficial. It was the talk of acquaintances, not friends. I was unsure if that was his fault or mine; it was likely both. I vowed that this year would be different.

I met him and invited him to a nice café I had discovered in the city. Within a short while, I could see the changes of which my uncle had spoken. My every attempt to generate a meaningful conversation failed. I even tried humor, pointing out that I had heard that Ephraim was divorcing his second wife to marry a third. Yeshu seemed non-pulsed.

When we walked to the Temple to attend services, he was virtually silent throughout, even as we ascended the Temple steps themselves. Then suddenly he stopped and turned to me. Grabbing me by the shoulders and staring directly into my eyes, as would a madman I confessed to thinking, he said:

"Avi, whom I have known since childhood, how can you see what you see and not be disgusted?"

I was mystified. What was he talking about?

"Disgusted, Yeshu?"

"Just open your eyes and look," he said with a venom I had never heard him use. "This is a Temple, a place to worship the God of All Things. What do you see? Moneylenders, silk salesman, fruit peddlers, games of chance. This isn't a Temple. It's a carnival."

"But are we not to celebrate the Passover?' I objected, albeit meekly.

"This isn't a celebration. It's a blasphemy. Right in front of the Holy of Holies, there is avarice. Our Father must be tempted to send another flood."

I was most taken aback by the manner of his speech. It was vengeful, hateful, and spiteful. This was not the Yeshu I had loved.

"I don't see anything wrong," I said, almost pleadingly. "Many of our merchants need Passover to feed their families. And what harm is there if your mother can purchase her linens here? It's better than paying the peddlers in Nazareth, isn't it?"

"The God of All Things does not exist to facilitate profit; nor for trade or commerce. Women can buy their things somewhere else." He had almost spat out his reply.

With that, he moved away from me, literally and figuratively. What was worse was that he walked in front of me, rather than at my side. I realized he was angry, but what had I done? The Sanhedrin did not consult me when planning the Passover celebration.

During the rest of the day, we barely spoke. It was easily the most challenging time I had ever spent in his presence. Every time I opened my mouth, I was rebuked with a diatribe about the sinfulness of the celebration. Indeed, his sheer annoyance was moving me to anger; this from a man I had thought I could never be angry with. In substantial terms, I was beginning to understand what my uncle had said.

I had wanted a deep heart-to-heart with a good friend. I had even planned to speak of Marcus, and possibly even introduce them to each other. After all, it was Yeshu who had predicted I would find someone in Jerusalem. But by the end of the day, I was frankly glad to be rid of him. We embraced, but only formally, with no warmth. No warmth whatsoever.

I could not let my relationship with Yeshu be defined by this conversation. I had to find out what was happening in his life that had caused this almost radical change in behavior.

I would go to the source. I would talk to Miriam, alone.

~~ 19 ~~

A stroke of luck would make it possible. James had told me that he and Yeshu would be dining in another tent that night. I asked Miriam if I could see her, and with no hesitation, she agreed. Perhaps she wanted to talk to me as much as I wanted to talk to her.

Immediately she chastised me for not visiting Nazareth and solicited my promise that I would do so in the near future.

"But you didn't come to be scolded, Avi; you are here about Yeshu."

I smiled; perhaps this was going to be more comfortable than I thought.

"Tell me, Miriam, what has happened to him? He used to be so full of life, so vibrant; he seemed to enjoy his every step. I spent the day with him today, and found him so sullen, so reserved; it bordered on being depressing. We used to talk as brothers; today, we hardly talked at all. And when we did, all he did was berate the Passover celebration. I felt he was blaming me personally for its gaudiness and commercialism."

Miriam looked very thoughtful as she measured her

response. It was apparent she was choosing her words very carefully.

"I'm sure he wasn't blaming you personally, Avi. But Jerusalem is beginning to depress him. He used to love this city, as you do; this year I had to beg him to come."

"I thought he would get violent at the Temple."

Miriam seemed surprised. "I really wouldn't expect that of him, even as intensely as he feels about things now. But there is much about the Temple that troubles him. And you have to agree that much goes on there that should trouble us all. Do you think the children of the God of All Things, the children of Israel, are behaving in the manner they should?"

Ruefully I admitted they were not, especially around Passover. I agreed that even I got caught up in what Yeshu had called a "carnival."

"We have traveled far from the covenant of Abraham," she continued, "and we have not traveled well. The Sanhedrin adorn themselves with fine robes while their people go hungry. Justice for our people is inconsistent if it's applied at all. The Pharisees fight with the Sadducees with the Skeptics, all over trivial matters. Meanwhile, the children of Israel suffer from poverty and disease. My son sees these things, and they anger him."

"But once we rid ourselves of the Romans......" I answered.

"Then what, Avi? Does the Sanhedrin want to rid us of the Romans or replace them? A man is a slave one week, the master the next, and a slave yet the next. Israel's problem isn't with Rome; Israel's problem is with Israel."

I admitted the truth of what she had said. In many ways, Israel was no less corrupt than the Empire. And I was not one to criticize either; the Sanhedrin still employed me, and a Roman had changed my life.

"But what can Yeshu do, Miriam? It's one man against the sea."

"Abraham was one man, Avi; David was one man, as were Solomon and Elijah. Even Moses himself was only one man."

"Is that it, Miriam?" I asked. "Does he think he's another Moses?"

Her lips grew into a small smile as her mood lightened. "If the God of All Things felt we needed another Moses, He would have sent us another Moses. Don't worry, Avi; Yeshu doesn't think he's another Moses."

"Whatever or whoever he thinks he is, Miriam, it seems to be making him miserable." Perhaps we were getting to the crux of the matter. "He has a good trade, people around him who love him, and while he hasn't married, he admits it's by his own choice. So why is he so unhappy?"

Again, she seemed to be choosing her words carefully.

"I believe my son walks in the steps of the God of All Things, Avi. That journey, while ultimately joyous, can be hard and difficult. I believe Yeshu has confronted his fate; it can be a terrifying realization. I have some knowledge of just how terrifying it can be. As I discovered my fate, there were many tear-filled sleepless nights. Many, many such nights."

"And yet, the will of Our Father must be done. Yeshu has begun his path to becoming one with that necessity."

"But Miriam...."

"I don't mean to confuse you, Avi, although much of what I have said can be confusing, and I realize that. Let me put it another way. We are seeing a very wounded Yeshu right now. But I can speak from experience and say that those wounds will heal. You already realize that the Yeshu you talked to today is not the Yeshu of yesterday. But neither is he the Yeshu of tomorrow."

"So you think he will change…."

She gave me a reassuring smile.

"That I do. But whatever that change brings, whatever path he chooses, whatever decisions he makes, I am his mother. The only love that matters is unconditional love, and my son will always have that from me. And hopefully, from others."

There was no mistaking that she expected me to be one of "the others." That didn't trouble me; short of committing some unspeakable crime, I would always love my friend unconditionally. I told Miriam as much.

"I know you will, Avi, and I know the road you have traveled together has been a difficult one for you..." As she was saying this, her eyes bore directly into mine, indeed passed mine, right into my very soul. I had no doubt she knew that soul; I also had no fear that she knew.

I rose to embrace her. As tears were forming in my eyes, I could see her eyes also getting moist. We hugged each other, and silently stood there for what seemed like hours. I had felt closer to no other woman except my mother in my entire life.

But I could not let the conversation end there.

"He spoke of leaving Nazareth at some point…..."

A sense of melancholy crossed her face as she turned away from mine. But after a while, that wry grin was there again. "I suspect that will be the case. After all, I believe your uncle is beginning to hide in the alcove of the synagogue whenever my son approaches."

Despite myself, I began to chuckle, a chuckle that turned into a hearty laugh with Miriam's next comment.

"But tell your uncle not to worry, Yeshu will find him."

She too was laughing as we embraced again. What a magnificent woman she was! How fortunate Yeshu was to have her as a mother, and how fortunate I was to have her as a friend.

It would be an hour or so before we parted, and as I did, I promised to visit Nazareth soon. I walked home feeling better about Yeshu, and hoping what Miriam had said was true. He was making some serious decisions; from my own experiences, I knew how troubling that process could be. Though I had made them earlier in my life, I sensed the scope of my choices paled when compared to the ones he was making.

Even if I had no real idea exactly what they involved.

~~ 20 ~~

As dramatic as Passover had been, it was only a harbinger of what would be a very significant year in my life. I had returned to my routine, back to the Temple, back to my manuscripts, and especially, back to Marcus.

Our relationship continued to flourish, as did my lover's career. He had developed his literary skills to the point where he found employment as a copyist for the Roman guard. This was a highly responsible position, located in the innermost rooms of the Palace. Marcus was the chief source for all Roman military maneuvers in Palestine, not by command but by communication. He would share that information on a strictly specified need-to-know basis. Of course, he would also share that information with me. I prided myself on knowing all the news of Rome oftentimes before the Romans did. In return, I kept Marcus abreast of Temple happenings, though they were decidedly less juicy.

Marcus and I were growing in our love for each other, and its effect was evident on each of us individually. We often joked that if husbands and wives got along as well as we did, there would be no divorces in Palestine.

But a significant mountain in our relationship had to be climbed. Marcus and I struggled mightily about what to tell his father. I understood Marcus' reluctance to discuss the matter with Flavius; I would have had the same issues, likely more, discussing it with Jacob. At the same time, it was becoming obvious to everyone in Flavius' house that this was more than just a friendship. Nothing was ever said, but both Marcus and I had the sense that the spirit was there.

We debated the issue often, oftentimes with more discussion than debate. We concluded that for the time being the best course of action was no action at all.

As it turned out, no action was needed on our part; Flavius had instead taken the initiative.

After dinner one evening, he invited us to join him in his study. Of itself, this was hardly extraordinary, as we would often discuss matters the day, glass of wine in hand, in front of a crackling fire. The conversation was always very relaxed.

Yet this evening Flavius seemed extraordinarily pensive and strangely distant. So much so that Marcus asked his father if anything was wrong.

Flavius offered us wine, and true to his nature, went directly to the issue.

"Nothing is wrong, Marcus, but the time has come for a conversation I have been mulling for months. You two are no longer boys, Marcus and Avi; you're not even young men any longer. You are men, and I will speak to you both as men. The two of you have been as brothers for several years now, and yet you are not brothers. There is a relationship between the two of you that in our culture, and in Avi's, causes suspicion."

"But father…..." Marcus tried to interrupt.

Flavius motioned his son to silence.

"Please, Marcus, hear me out. Let me say what

needs to be said, then we can discuss it."

Marcus and I eyed each other, our discomfort growing by the moment.

"As I said, many would treat the two of you with suspicion. This is difficult for me, this suspicion, even as your public behavior has been exemplary and perfectly proper. As both of you are aware, my position bears some scrutiny. A centurion must be of the highest moral character and his house the same."

Despite his father's furtive glance, Marcus interrupted.

"But father, we both know men of your station who drink excessively or have concubines, or gamble or do all three. Most centurions are far from being above reproach."

"I will not deny that, son; many of my equals do as you say. But a man is individually responsible for his moral character, not only before Caesar but before the gods."

Resting his hand on his son's shoulders, he continued: "And whatever you may think, while your mother was alive, I never so much as glanced in another direction. I want you to know that. It wasn't that I thought I would be betraying her; I believed I would be betraying myself."

Marcus was quick to reply: "I didn't mean to......"

"I know son; I know; I know you didn't. But I needed you to hear that."

Marcus rose to hug his father. This may not have been the primary substance of the conversation. It was also true that it needed to be said.

Flavius continued. "But let me return to my main point. I don't pretend to know the way of the gods, whether they are our gods or Avi's God of All Things. I stand in judgment of no man or woman. Nor do I pretend to understand the bond the two of you share. It is foreign to me; it is strange to me, it is confusing to me. But since no one is to blame, I will blame no one. A man can only do what feels natural to him."

Marcus' hand found mine as the centurion continued. "While I do not understand your feelings, I will not condemn them. They are both of yours; they belong to you. But know this, Marcus; you are my son, and nothing or no one will stand between us. Nor between me and the one you have chosen for your companion. Know this before the gods."

Tears began to flow from Marcus' eyes and my own. Indeed, they rushed from Flavius also. We rose to embrace the noble centurion. A smile of understanding crossed his lips, as he poured us all some wine.

After a short pause, he continued. "But there are practical considerations to be dealt with." Turning to me, he said "Avi, I would be honored if you left your rooming house and moved into my home, as one of my servants. I apologize for that term, but it must be that way."

I nodded my head with complete understanding. Being his servant was the most reasonable explanation for my living in his house.

"I accept your kindness, sir, and swear by the Almighty that I will never dishonor your house."

Flavius again smiled. 'I know that, Avi. There was never a doubt in my mind. And while you stay with us, I want to learn more about this God of All Things of yours. You can help me with that."

"I'm afraid I may not be His favorite servant," I said.

"That would be for Him to decide, don't you think?" the centurion replied.

The evening ended after more conversation, chiefly concerning arrangements that would have to be made. I would have my own room and have complete access to the house. Flavius said my rent would be paid by teaching Simon to read and write. It wouldn't be long that, encouraged by their employer, the other servants would also become my pupils. Flavius would have the most literate household in Jerusalem, if not in all of Palestine.

And I would have myself a home.

Flavius had generated a plan for my move, expecting it would take about four weeks. Neither Marcus nor I wanted to wait that long. Marcus wanted me to move in that night. But as little as I had, I still estimated it was going to take a week to make it happen.

It would, of course, take three days.

~~ 21 ~~

That wasn't the only moving around I would be doing that year. I returned to Nazareth, albeit tardily, fulfilling the promise I had made to Miriam. It was an easy trip; while I had been teaching Flavius' servants to read, they were returning the favor by showing me to ride. I arrived at my native village atop a well-bred steed; that itself caused a ruckus in the town. Few Jews rode horses in those days; since I was now technically a servant to a centurion, I could ride around unquestioned, a somewhat bizarre perk of my new position.

I didn't explain any of that to father, who just exclaimed, "My son, the Roman Jew!"

It was great seeing him. He was aging well, and Sophia continued to be good for him. He had hired an overseer for the groves and was enjoying the free time that it allowed. He confided in me that he was even attending the synagogue on a routine basis.

"So I can expect you in Jerusalem for Passover," I asked, not quite sure how I would explain my life there to him.

"Well, Avi, I'm not sure…"

Sophia interrupted. "We'll be there, Avi; twelve of those fine steeds of yours won't keep us away. Will they, Jacob?"

I sensed that she had taken over not only my father's house but his schedule as well. Again I found this to be a good thing.

I didn't speak of my new living arrangements, and they did not pry; Sophia seemed satisfied that I was well fed. She did ask about my social life; this time I was sure it was an earnest question, not a belittling one. I answered as truthfully as I could, saying that I was very happy.

Sophia prepared an excellent supper, and I believe we all enjoyed not only the food but the conversation. Though I was fatigued by my travels, it was father who asked me about the rest of my evening. "Of course, you'll be seeing Yeshu." I had my reservations, but decided the sooner, the better, and set off for Miriam's home.

She greeted me warmly. I was fortunate that she, James and Yeshu were all at home. We shared much wine as we got caught up about our lives since Passover. Yeshu had seemingly shed his sullenness, which had so darkened the holiday; indeed, his radiant smile, quick wit, and general good nature had returned. As my visit concluded, he offered to walk me home.

All the nights in Jerusalem could never replace the sheer comfort of a clear, star-lit Nazareth night; the quiet was exhilarating. Nothing at all compared to the noise-filled Jerusalem evenings I had experienced; even Flavius' house was generally busy at night. But here, there was refreshing silence.

Yeshu continued to seem very comfortable, which is why I was taken aback by his opening comment.

"The time has come, my friend; I am leaving Nazareth."

"Now?" I asked. "I know you've talked about it, but you seem so settled now."

"I'm 'settled,' as you say because I have accepted my fate, Avi. The last time you saw me I was struggling with that fate; in fact, it was beginning to overwhelm me. I'm sure you can guess mother helped me through it."

Of that I was sure.

"What will she and James do once you leave?'

He chuckled. "James is coming with me. I think mother wants him to keep an eye on me. She's returning to Sephoria, where her cousins are eager to see her again."

"And where will you and James be going?"

A faint smile crossed his lips. "As the God of All Things is my Lord, I do not know. What I do know is that my time in Nazareth is at an end. I love this village and its people; I can't imagine having grown up anywhere else. But my thoughts are elsewhere now."

"You're sure?" I asked.

"Very sure, my dearest childhood friend, very sure."

"How will you eat?"

Again he smiled. "Ah, Avi, ever the practical one. The Lord God provides for his greatest nomads of them all, the birds of the air. They are well fed by what he provides. If he takes care of them, surely he will provide for His servant."

I couldn't resist my own witticism.

"That's wonderful if your desires end at birdseed, but I've seen you eat better than that."

Yeshu let out a hearty laugh; it was good to see that laugh.

"James and I will carry our tools with us. But the real purpose of our journey will be discovery. The horizon doesn't end at Nazareth; you know that, Avi. There are other towns, other rabbis...."

"Then you do have an interest in becoming a rabbi?"

"You ask questions that I cannot answer, for now, my friend. Becoming a rabbi would not be disappointing to me; perhaps that is how this will all turn out. But the truth is I do not know."

It was his turn to be witty.

"Besides, as your saintly grandfather knew, and your uncle knows now, I lack the humility to be a good rabbi. And you know what the great Hillel said; a rabbi who praises himself has a congregation of one."

"Oh Yeshu," I said laughing. "It's so good to see you in such spirits. When you were in Jerusalem….."

"My childhood friend was so concerned he paid a visit to my mother. Don't feel betrayed, Avi; mother said nothing to me. But James saw you leave our tent that night. It wasn't hard to put the facts together."

"I did go to see your mother," I admitted. "I was so worried; you were so gloomy…..."

"Like all men (and women too; I know this through mother), I would like the path to the wisdom of the God of All Things to be full of lighthearted steps. Perhaps I even believed for a while it would be. But now I know better. I know that His will is sometimes very hard; it's not meant to make your life easy, just meant to make it meaningful."

"You left Nazareth with a cache of dreams, Avi, many of which I can tell have been fulfilled. My journey may be the fulfillment of my fondest dreams, but possibly of my deepest nightmares. Once again, and please, I don't mean to hide anything from you; but I honestly don't know. I have days when both possible outcomes overwhelm me. But I know the path to those outcomes is outside of Nazareth."

I nodded in understanding.

We talked of other things that night; Ephraim was on wife number three, and there was other gossip. It was an excellent evening between two close friends, and I honestly hoped there would be others.

We embraced as we parted. I was happy for Yeshu, perhaps happier than I had ever been for him. He'll be all right, I thought. Whatever voice was motivating him to leave Nazareth had to be heard; I knew that because I had listened to a voice years ago, although I was sure mine wasn't from the God of All Things. But perhaps I was less sure of that after my night with Yeshu.

I wished him well on his journey. As I lay in bed, I prayed that our paths would continue to intersect. They would, of course. In ways neither of us could have imagined that quiet and serene night in Nazareth.

~~ 22 ~~

I remained in Nazareth for three more days, with friends and relatives. I promised to seek them all out the following Passover. And seek them out I would, rather than have them search for me. They did not need to discover the entirety of my life in Jerusalem. I also made a solemn vow to return in the near future.

Aglow in the feeling of what had been an excellent excursion; I rode out of Nazareth early in the morning. I decided I would take my time returning to Jerusalem. Levi had encouraged my holiday, and I knew he would not be upset if I were a day or two late. I ached for Marcus' companionship, both physically and emotionally, but the time I spent by myself would only make our reunion that much more joyful.

I slept, perhaps as well as I ever had, under star-filled skies. My first night was spent along the banks of the river Jordan, a river that had meant so much to my people's history. My dreams were of Marcus, though again they were strangely intermingled with images of Yeshu. While this confused me, it did not concern me.

I was awakened the following morning by some

loud noises coming from the shores of the river. Some twenty people or so had gathered there, and they seemed to be having some sort of celebration. As I walked toward them to investigate further, I saw instead that they were listening to the emanations from the strangest man I had ever seen. And he spoke in a voice that roared. I thought every village in Judea would be awakened by the bellicose sound of that voice.

With some trepidation, I inched in closer. The orator was a tall, sturdily built man, about my age, with a rough beard and even rougher appearance. He was dressed in the coarsest of rags, rags that scarcely covered his physique. I had seen beggars in Jerusalem better clothed. I thought the poor fellow might be mad.

But rather than avoiding him, I saw people listening intently to his ravings. Moreover, they were participating with him in some ritual. Entering the Jordan fully clothed, they approached the man individually. The strange man grabbed each one, man, woman, or child, and submerged them entirely in the water. Through it all, his voice roared, saying words I could scarcely understand. Perhaps I had stumbled onto some strange religious sect, but Jewish, gentile or pagan, I had no idea. Perhaps they were all mad.

Curiosity compelled me to move closer to the scene, being as careful as possible to remain hidden. It didn't work; the man caught sight of me. He began pointing at me, screaming loudly:

"And you, will you receive baptism? Will you be cleansed of your sins before the Messiah comes?'

He was performing an elementary, perhaps sacrilegious form of the michbah. Fortunately, everybody was keeping their clothes on. My primary emotion, I admit, was fear. But then a very attractive young woman approached me. In a very calm and reassuring tone, she said:

"Please join us sir; there is nothing to be afraid of."

"Who is that strange man?" I asked her nervously.

"His name is Yonni, and he performs the right of purification or as he calls it, baptism."

"Is he a rabbi?"

"Oh no sir, he belongs to no synagogue; he is unlike any rabbi we have ever known."

None that I knew of either, I thought. Not that I was unfamiliar with these traveling vagabond preachers; again I was reminded that I hoped this wasn't what Yeshu was preparing himself for. These preachers would wander from village to village, preaching their gospel, which inevitably involved some forthcoming cataclysmic event such as the end of the world. For the most part, they were regarded as harmless, and though few listened to their message, they were in general treated with kindness. They all seemed to be undernourished.

Not this Yonni character, however, who looked remarkably well fed. But was he really purifying outside of the Temple? And who was this Messiah of which he spoke? My people had long since imagined a savior who would come to rid us of the Romans, as they had imagined centuries ago one who would rid them of the Babylonians. Whoever the oppressor of Israel was, they would be ousted by this Messiah. The problem was that centuries had passed, and Israel was still an occupied land. Further, I wondered why any such Messiah would choose this odd man as his herald.

Yonni again spoke directly to me.

"My fine friend, here you are dressed in your fine tunic, with your impressive steed at your side. Surely you are a man of means."

"Surely I am not!" I managed a chuckle." I am from Jerusalem, where I work in the Temple. And the steed belongs to another."

"Ah!" the Baptist bellowed. "From Jerusalem, where you work in the Temple! A man should have no earthly masters, and you have two, the Romans and the Sanhedrin. You are twice cursed."

The gathering appreciated the humor at my expense. I was not offended and laughed along with them. If nothing else, this Yonni seemed genuine.

"You have a point," I replied in a tone that attempted to match his. "But I am only of late from Jerusalem; I was born in Nazareth, and I am returning from there."

"Nazareth?" Yonni said inquisitively, as he looked at me oddly. "Nazareth, you say...."

I almost felt smug that I had rendered him without retort.

But he quickly recovered. "Well, son of Nazareth, do you wish to be baptized?"

I did not want to add to this strange man's sideshow, and his look when I had mentioned Nazareth troubled me. I shook my head and began to withdraw.

But the same woman who had spoken to me earlier stopped me.

"Don't be shy. Yonni is quite wonderful. We believe he was chosen by the God of All Things to make way for the great prophet who is to come. We cleanse ourselves to prepare for his coming."

"Does Israel need another prophet, especially one that would have this man as his precursor?"

"We believe there has never been anyone quite like Yonni. And we are greatly awaiting the Messiah who he says will follow."

The woman seemed to be more than a decent sort, and I felt compelled to warn her.

"Cleansing is a function reserved for the Temple. That has always been our tradition. The Sanhedrin will not be happy if they hear about this."

The woman just shrugged. "I believe we should

obey the God of All Things. The Sanhedrin we must obey also, but above all, the former."

It was quickly evident that no amount of convincing would change this woman's mind nor for that matter any of the others who had assembled. I turned to my horse, and Yonni's voice followed me.

"Be on your way, then. A man with two earthly masters has no room for a heavenly one. But know this, son of Nazareth, that soon your true master will be among us, and Roman and Sanhedrin will both tremble in his presence. Who will you serve then?"

I didn't answer the Baptist's question. Instead, I mounted my horse as quickly as possible and rode off. What a strange and unsettling man this Yonni was. I had no doubt this Messiah whose coming he was foretelling would be equally strange and unsettling.

My urge to return to Jerusalem was hastened. Soon I would be with my two earthly masters, as Yonni had said. But I would relish them both.

~~ 23 ~~

Unfortunately, that relishing would be short-lived, as I would return to Nazareth sooner than I could have imagined.

In fact, it would only be in six months. I would lose my father that shortly after our first reunion. Father had shown no indication of illness during the time I was with him; I had thought he looked healthier than he had in a while. I was told afterward Sophia had begged him to send a messenger to Jerusalem, but father had dismissed her pleas.

"Avi has enough of his own problems. Besides, I'm not all that ill. I will recover, and then you and I will go to Jerusalem. Avi came to us; we should go to him next."

But in fact, he was seriously ill. The downward slope of his health continually grew momentum as the days passed. Finally, Sophia ignored father and commissioned a messenger to go to Jerusalem.

My life has been filled with more than a little irony; this would be no different. The messenger Sophia chose (actually I was later told he had volunteered) was the same Roman soldier who had first engaged me to write the history of Nazareth. He had remained friendly with my family, and when he heard of father's condition, he suggested to Sophia that he could find me on his next sojourn to Jerusalem, which was occurring shortly.

Levi approached me at work one morning, saying a Roman messenger awaited me at the front of the Temple. As I rushed to see him, a myriad of thoughts ran through my mind; none, I confess, having to do with my family. I was expecting news of Flavius, or Marcus, perhaps of Yeshu. My surprise at seeing the familiar soldier evaporated as he told me the reason for his visit.

I had to leave quickly, and Levi agreed. The soldier offered me immediate transportation back to Nazareth. He gave me a questioning glance when I told him I had access to my own steed; the glance became a long stare when I asked him only for transportation to the Palace. Silently we rode; I have no doubt he was wondering why a Jew would need to go to the Palace.

I had to see Marcus to tell him what was happening. He wanted to come with me, but I couldn't allow it. I could scarcely explain our relationship in Jerusalem; in Nazareth, it would be impossible. I cursed the fate my nature had dealt me, denying the most important person in my life being present when I most needed him. Did the God of All Things recognize the impossibility of the situation? Did He even care? Yeshu had spoken of the Almighty as a father; what kind of father so persecuted his children?

These thoughts and others filled my mind as I sped to Nazareth. I rode all day; I rode all night. Exhaustion encompassed both my horse and its rider as we arrived at my native village.

I would be too late. My father had passed while I was en route. Sophia begged my uncle not to inter the body until I arrived; uneasily he had agreed. Father lay prostrate, anointed for burial, as I entered my childhood home.

Sophia hugged me as I broke into tears. As I suspect many do, I cried that my father would no longer enjoy our earthly existence; but I also cried out of guilt. Sophia sensed this.

"Avi, you wouldn't have been able to do anything. And you know your father; he would not have wanted you to see his suffering. That was not his way; he had too much dignity."

She had encapsulated my father's entire earthly existence in that simple sentence. He was proud of his achievements, perhaps even proud of his son. He would not have wanted to be a burden to anyone; he never did.

Sophia and I talked much that night; of father and her love for him, among other things. Jacob had, I mused, achieved something remarkable; he had not replaced mother with Sophia but had found in her the perfect adjunct.

Though the rabbi and the town had respected my needs, our tradition required father to be buried before the next sunset. Almost all of Nazareth joined Sophia and me for the burial march. Father had not only been an integral part of the community when younger, with his olives and figs; his last years had been spent doing much for the village and its people.

We buried him next to mother. I decided at that moment that I would portion off two additional plots; one for me, and one for Sophia. The three most important people in father's life would be at rest with him, shaded in eternity by the orchards which had so defined his life.

The house was full for the next three days, as mourners and well-wishers sat Shiva for the man who had contributed much to the town. I held up pretty well, maintaining my composure as we received all the guests,

I lost that composure only twice; once with Ephraim, as our reunion brought back so many childhood memories, memories of a time when father was a significant influence in my life. And once with Miriam, who traveled from Sephoria when she heard of father's passing.

As always, she comforted my tears as she shed some of her own. More than most, she seemed to realize the unique bond an only child has with his parents; I was now essentially an orphan. There were no brothers or sisters to join with; in my case, no wife or children with which to share my sorrow. I was fortunate to have Sophia; perhaps more so to have Miriam.

She further raised my spirits when she said she expected to see Yeshu soon, perhaps even in a day or two. She had not seen him for months. He and James had set out shortly after I had returned to Jerusalem. It was difficult for me to gauge Miriam's reaction to her sons' absences. She seemed saddened by them, yet accepting of the course they had chosen.

She too was now alone, and while she lived with her cousins in Sephoria, she needed an income to survive. To that end, she had become a seamstress, an occupation that many widows adopted. Men who were alone, without wives or daughters, still needed to be clothed. More than one marriage had resulted from the relationship between seamstress and employer, not unlike what had happened between father and Sophia.

I asked her if anything like that was happening in her life. She was, after all, still young and vibrant, and also still very attractive; she would make a great catch.

Miriam looked at me shyly. "I knew that when I married Yusuf that he would be my only husband, Avi. I knew that as well as I knew anything. The spirit of the man remains with me, almost as concretely as his mortal body had. Yusuf is even now not gone from my life."

Like with Yeshu, I didn't wholly understand Miriam's explanation, but I accepted it. It was a common trait with this family, I mused.

I would have liked to spend more time with Miriam, but both her need to return to Sephoria (Yeshu after all had promised to visit her) and my need to deal with the practicalities of father's passing took precedence. I was now the owner of the groves, with no desire of being so. With a business acumen I hardly suspected I had, I was able to negotiate the sale of the groves to the man who had been father's overseer. Ignoring the documents that made me the sole heir, I divided the proceeds equally with Sophia. The woman who had meant so much to father would not, and could not, ever be in need. Our understanding was that if she remarried, her share would go the synagogue; it would be my gift to Nazareth. Sophia would also have title to the house she had shared with father.

She cried at my generosity, but I did not view my actions as being generous. She deserved everything she received; it was merely the right thing to do.

Even with my gifts to Sophia, I was well provided for and had more than I needed. I would share my inheritance further with Flavius and Marcus, setting aside whatever I thought I needed for my old age. I would not be rich, but I would likely not want for anything material.

My business completed, my stay in Nazareth was coming to a close. I anticipated returning to Jerusalem the next day.

I would be delayed by a visitor I received. It was Yeshu. He had indeed returned to Sephoria to see Miriam, who had told him what had happened. The pain of father's passing would ease as I once again spent a night with my friend.

~~ 24 ~~

As always, we embraced. We spoke for an hour about father. I was gratified Yeshu remembered him warmly.

He had not returned alone. He had indeed become the itinerant preacher that I had predicted. As he traveled from town to town in northern Judea, he confronted rabbis in each synagogue with his unique interpretations of scripture. Some of those interpretations had made him popular with others (the reverse was no doubt equally true), and those others had joined him on his ministry. I was a bit concerned about this new development as many of those who followed preachers around were from the fringes of society. All of them seemed to have this reason or that one for seeking a savior. Most were disenfranchised. All were poor.

Yeshu admitted as much. He had returned for many reasons, one of which was in search of food for his newfound flock. Food was something I had plenty of since Sophia and I hadn't even begun to dent the food that mourners had bought during the Shiva. I offered it, with Sophia's permission (she readily agreed) to Yeshu.

He asked me to help bring the provisions to his followers, now encamped on the outskirts of Nazareth. Without hesitation, and with my curiosity aroused, I consented.

As we set out for the camp, I mentioned my strange meeting with the eerie Baptist during my last visit to Nazareth. Yeshu grinned.

"So you've met Yonni?

"You know him?" I asked, genuinely surprised.

"Oh yes, Avi, many know Yonni."

"He is not a pleasant person, Yeshu. I felt he was mocking me."

Again my friend smiled. "Yonni has that effect on people. But I've never met anyone closer to Our Father. Nor one more unashamed of spreading His word. Tell me, did he baptize you?"

"He wanted to, but I resisted. I get enough cleansing the proper way, at the Temple."

"It's not the same, Avi. Yonni baptizes to demonstrate that everyone must surrender the allures of sin, to repent, and to re-emerge from the waters as they did from their mothers' wombs; in essence, to be reborn. Temple cleansing may prepare you for God; Yonni's is to prepare you for the life you live in order to reach Him."

"Well, whatever he's doing, it's bizarre. He's bizarre. Not to mention he needs to curb his tongue about the Romans and the Sanhedrin, else he'll lose it. And that may not be all he loses."

"Yonni is a messenger from the Lord, Avi. Threats from the Romans or even other Jews will not discourage him."

"Perhaps they should." I stopped and placed my hands on Yeshu's shoulder.

"And you too, Yeshu. Irritating rabbis is one thing, but our people have had enough prophets who have gotten themselves into trouble."

"Oh Avi, you worry like a woman. What possible interest can the Romans and High Priests have in a stone cutter from Nazareth? Besides, my mission is about Our Father, not about Rome or Israel."

"That may be so, but promise me you'll be careful."

"Yes, Avi, for you I will be careful. But here we have arrived."

Immediately James noticed me and ran to greet me warmly. Whatever Yeshu was up to, his brother seemed to be proud of him, almost beaming. As were the others Yeshu had gathered around him; five men about our age. As I feared, they all appeared to be hungry, yet seemed to be in good spirits. Again, I was reminded of Yeshu's influence on people.

"I need to apologize for my friends, Avi. Like me, most are ignorant of reading and writing. This is Levi, one exception to that. Levi used to be a tax collector. He wishes now to be called Mathew. You should have heard what he was called when he was a tax collector."

The men began laughing, and Mathew seemed to enjoy the joke at his expense.

"And this is Judah, who can also read and write. And here is Simon, who has become the leader of the bunch. Simon left his wife to join us; I'm told she is eternally grateful."

Again, the men roared, and again, the one called Simon appeared unperturbed.

After introducing me to the others, Yeshu said, "Friends, this is Avrum, whom I have known since his birth. Please, welcome him." They all surrounded me with handshakes and embraces. Clearly, they regarded Yeshu with great warmth and were willing to transfer that fondness to me.

"And Avi has brought us food. Unfortunately, his father, a good man, has recently passed. He owned some olive and fig groves in town, and Avi brings both, with the remains of the gifts of food he received at the Shiva."

The one named Judah snarled, as all gathered around the food.

"Humph, a landowner's son."

"Judah, Judah, whether a man works the land or owns the land, Our Father makes no distinction. We are indeed reminded on this solemn occasion of Avi's father's death that the serf dies, the landowner dies, and all must face the end of their earthly days. But glorious are the days to come in the Kingdom of Our Father."

"Besides, Judah," Yeshu said wryly, "I see you have no moral issue with the food."

Again the men roared, and even Judah forced a smile.

"Well, I'm hungry," he said ruefully as the men chuckled.

After we ate, Yeshu turned to me and said, "Come, my friend, no doubt you have lots of question. Let me walk you home."

We began to walk, and indeed I had questions. But first I needed to compliment my friend.

"They seem to have great affection for you."

"And I for them. They are good men, Avi, strong men. I would cast my lot with any of them." He paused briefly and added, "Even Judah, whom I noticed you took a dislike to."

I smiled. "You are perceptive as ever, Yeshu. He seems a bit… I'm just not sure that his agenda is the same as yours."

Again, Yeshu paused. "He has a basic distrusting nature, and I'm working with him on that. Your grandfather and uncle would like him; he's not always fond of how I interpret scripture. I'm resigned to the fact that I have that failing."

I smiled as my friend continued.

"But in his way, Judah might be the most pious of the group, and he has a keen sense of social justice, which I admire. The more you get to know him, the more you may get to like him, Avi. And he distrusts the Romans and Sanhedrin equally."

"I can't see myself ever liking him," I replied, "But I'll respect your judgment on that one."

"Accepted with gratitude," Yeshu said with a grin. "But enough about Judah the Iscariot. I imagine you want to know more about Yeshu the Nazarene and what has happened to him since he left his native village."

"Absolutely!" I replied. It was a comment I would rue by the end of our conversation.

~~ 25 ~~

"So you began preaching as soon as you left Nazareth?'

"No, Avi, not immediately. James and I wandered, without any real direction. The best part of those first few days was the knowledge I gained of my brother. Maybe it was because he was away from Nazareth for the first time, but he began to speak to me as he never had. He talked of the feelings he had for Miriam, and for Yusuf, and for the woman Agatha who had given birth to him, and yet he never knew. I discovered perhaps for the first time what a wondrous man I had for a brother."

"After about a week, we arrived at the river Jordan and saw Yonni baptizing. It was so strange; Yonni stopped what he was doing, and pointed directly at me. I was drawn to him, Avi, by a force I could hardly control. He grasped me, and stared directly into my eyes."

"'The God of All Things has fulfilled His promise,' he said, as he grabbed me and immersed me into the river."

For a brief moment, Yeshu paused. When he continued, it was with a solemnity that I had never seen in him before.

"It was if not only my body was being washed, but my entire being, my entire essence, my entire life force. When I rose from those waters, it was not Yonni's face I saw, but a collage of colors, some of which I didn't even recognize. It was as if this collage covered the entire universe; even more, as if the entire universe was this collage. I couldn't distinguish either people or things, just the enormity of color. I began to tremble; I feared I was near death."

"But exactly at that moment, a profound calm overtook my spirit. The colors began to unite, joining and meshing into something I can only call beauty itself. It was beyond wondrous, as all those colors came together into one entity. I stood dumbstruck as I looked at it."

"And then I heard a voice, the most calming, reassuring voice I had ever heard. It was the entity, Avi, and it was talking to me, to me alone. It said:

'Know that you are my son, with whom I am well pleased."

"And then the entity collapsed, directly in front of me, merging and morphing itself into a dove. I reached in vain to catch that dove, but my hand instead was grasping Yonni, who again stood there, peering into my eyes. Again, he said:

'The God of All Things has fulfilled His promise.'"

I stopped walking as my friend concluded his fantastic epiphany. Thousands of questions swirled inside my head, and thousands of emotions. It was my turn to look directly into Yeshu's eyes, as he said Yonni had. Who was this man, I thought? What did he think he was?

"It all sounds fantastic, I know, Avi, and believe me, I forgive you if you don't quite believe it. Judah doesn't; he admitted it to me. He thinks I hit my head on a rock when Yonni baptized me. So don't feel guilty if you don't accept an experience I know I had. Because there's more."

I was feeling no guilt. But in my stomach was churning and my head was throbbing every second that Yeshu was revealing his "experience" as he called it. I was utterly unsure I wanted to hear any more.

"Yeshu ………" I tried to interrupt; it would go unnoticed.

"I did not mention my revelation to James; I was afraid it would compromise the closeness we had achieved. He would hear of it only later. So we left the Jordan, and I asked him to be left alone for a while. I settled him into a campsite and began to wander into the desert. I walked and walked, with no idea why I was doing so. I ate fruits and berries that violated my stomach; I was without water for days. I began to feel that rather than being reborn by my baptism, as Yonni had proclaimed, I was again being led to my death."

Pallor came across my friend's face. "It is when a man is suffering like that that the Evil One makes his attack. And he did attack me, Avi. I confronted Has Satan himself, The Accuser, The Prince of Darkness."

My sense of awe began morphing into one of terror. I stared at him in total disbelief, and not without a considerable degree of horror. Every Jew knew of the Evil One, the fallen of God's spiritual beings, who is in constant battle with the Almighty for men's souls. The mere mention of his name was forbidden by our beliefs. And now Yeshu was claiming that he had met this being personally. For the very first time, I feared my friend had crossed into madness.

"For days and nights, he tempted me, Avi. Many times I felt close to surrender. He offered me a Paradise, and though I knew it masked the darkest of places, I felt drawn to it. Then he showed me an image of all human suffering, blaming the God of All Things for all of it. 'This is what your God has done to his children, Nazarene,' he said. 'And you wish him to be your father, this vindictive, sadistic monster of a being? Is that what you desire?'"

"I was more tempted by that image than by any of the Evil One's offers of Paradise. And yet I knew that at essence he is a deceiver, a liar. I prayed to the God of All Things to remove those temptations; I did more than pray. I begged."

Suddenly Yeshu's face brightened. "And He answered, Avi. It was as if all of heaven was marshaled behind me as I confronted the essence of the Evil One. I found the strength to repel him, to cast him and his images away from my soul. And he retracted; his power to terrorize was nothing compared to Our Father's power to love. Has- Satan knew he was defeated, but he did not go quietly. He cursed me; he cursed my family, he cursed my friends. Then he stood brazenly, looking directly into my eyes and said, 'Nazarene, you will accomplish nothing'."

"Then he was gone, Avi. The God of All Things, Our Father Himself, had saved me. There was so much joy in my heart I felt like singing. It was then that I realized I had indeed been reborn, reborn into the joy and love of Our Father. I was sated with that joy and love."

Yeshu's face had brightened so much it seemed to possess its own aura. Whether anything he said had happened, it was clear he thought it had.

Had it happened? The question gnawed at my soul as we reached my home. Was it a spiritual awakening, one whose seeds had been sown in his childhood in Nazareth? Or was it my friend had succumbed to the illusions of the Evil One? Or was it that he had imagined the whole thing, the entire experience a product of the fruits and berries he had ingested.

I was at a loss for words as our walk ended. Much more importantly, I was frightened that my friend was now so self-possessed that only harm could come from it.

And I admit I was more than just frightened. The entire conversation was utterly unsettling. I had never wanted a conversation with Yeshu ever to end; I was always sad when it did.

But not this one. I had so much relief when we arrived at my house I could hardly express it. I was completely confused about my friend's revelation; it was the most uncomfortable I had ever been in my life.

We embraced and said farewell. He had said I would see him soon, likely in Jerusalem during the next Passover. But I would not eagerly anticipate the reunion as I had all the others. Impossible as it was to imagine, I went to bed that night regretting that I would, in all likelihood, see him again.

It was unfathomable that I felt that way. The night had been that disturbing. It would take months for that feeling to change, months in which I would not set eyes on Yeshu. I would not be troubled by that.

~~ 26 ~~

I could not return to Jerusalem fast enough, and I rode back in that style. Whether I wanted to place as much distance possible between me and my sadness at father's passing, or between Yeshu and me, I could not say. But I suspected the later.

I discussed much of what had occurred with Marcus, delaying any talk of Yeshu. Marcus realized, of course, the financial ramifications of father's death. He also knew that, as an only son, he too would be in line for such an inheritance. We kidded ourselves often about what we would do as old men, walking the streets of Jerusalem with pockets full of silver. What was the going rate for a young man's company, Marcus asked wryly? About thirty pieces of silver or so?

I continued at the Temple, and I continued my relationship with Marcus. It was a year of what I would call gentle discovery. I tutored Simon into literacy, and then Nilsa and the other servants. I continued to introduce Marcus and Flavius to the ways of the Jew, ways that seemed to fascinate them endlessly. In return, I learned much about Roman religiosity, about Zeus and

Jupiter, and the many sub-gods they ruled.

At Marcus 'and Flavius' insistence, I proudly held a Sabbath service witnessed by father and son. Both were enthralled by the solemn beauty of the chanting of the prayers and lighting of the candles. I had always felt our rituals were beautiful; demonstrating and explaining them to non-Jews reinforced that feeling.

Most evenings were spent discussing a variety of topics, focused chiefly on Roman and Jewish politics. Flavius and Marcus spoke freely of the intrigues of court, be they in Jerusalem or Rome itself. While devoted to their Caesar, I had the impression that neither father nor son thought much of the new governor of Judea, a man named Pontius Pilate. In his unique way, Marcus described Pilate as a "wash woman," more concerned with art and music and the trappings of power than with the affairs of state. Pilate spent most of his time in Caesarea, his seaside resort, coming to Jerusalem only for special events like watching the Jews at Passover.

Flavius speculated that Pilate was disappointed with his new assignment. Caretaking for an occupied people paled in comparison to the romance of battle, and Palestine was certainly not an attractive locale. Flavius had heard a rumor that Pilate had crossed the wrong member of the Roman army, and had been de facto exiled to Palestine.

As for Jewish politics, Flavius was especially interested in the happenings at the Temple. I was reminded of his friendship with Levi. He knew about the strife within the Sanhedrin, between the liberal Pharisees, the orthodox Sadducees, the philosophical Skeptics, and the mystical Essences.

We all agreed that no matter what their religion or national belief system, The Roman senators and the Sanhedrin priests were both essentially politicians, as greedy for power and silver as their counterparts. Flavius warned Marcus and me against becoming involved. Nothing good could come of it, especially considering our natures.

There was another particular reason why I was interested in events at the Palace. Despite our last conversation, and perhaps because of it, Yeshu was never far from my thoughts. Word would come to both the Temple and the Palace about this new prophet or that one, this healer or that one. I always paid close attention at the Temple and asked Marcus to do the same at the Palace. Occasionally it seemed the preacher might be Yeshu, but it was difficult to discern.

In all, the emptiness I had felt at father's passing and the uneasiness I felt at Yeshu's epiphany, were both being replaced by the love I felt from my adoptive family. The God of All Things had taken time from his battles with the Evil One on behalf of Yeshu to provide significant benefit for his insignificant servant Avrum. I mused at which was the greater miracle.

I would finally breach the subject of my last conversation with Yeshu with both Flavius and Marcus. I wanted their opinion as to what I had heard.

After I had explained entirely everything that Yeshu had said, both of them sat silent. It was Marcus who broke the group contemplation.

"The man Judah might be right; I wonder exactly how huge the rock was that your friend hit his head on."

Grins appeared on all our faces. Maybe the answer to Yeshu's revelation was that simple. Or perhaps it was not.

"He wouldn't be the first holy man to speak of a vision, Avi. It happens in our religions also", Flavius said. "Years ago, a man stood in the center square of Rome itself, describing a vision he had where Augustus Caesar and Julius Caesar were having dinner. Quite a trick, since Julius had been dead for a century."

"Julius couldn't have been much of a conversationalist," Marcus quipped.

We all laughed. But it was up to the centurion to focus the conversation, which of course he did.

"You have spoken only indirectly of this childhood friend of yours, Avi, so it's hard to make a full judgment. It seems to me, if you allow me, that you do think he is very special even if it's not in the way he thinks he's special.

To form, the centurion was right on the mark.

"That's probably exactly right, Flavius. I don't doubt for a moment that Yeshu has a deeper understanding of Scripture, and maybe even of the God of All Things than most Jews, including rabbis. But the leap from thinking he is inspired to believing the Almighty has singled him out among all the world is a pretty huge one. And that imagery…."

"Is perfectly consistent with a myriad of mystics from the past," Marcus contributed. "There's always some spiritual event that propels them to do what they do. Whether the event ever really happened seems almost irrelevant. It's the person that comes out of the event that's important."

"And you can't deny the possibility," Flavius added, "however small you think it may be, that this Yeshu of yours is indeed involved in a special relationship with your God. Your people have been waiting for this, what have you called him, Messiah? For ages, they've been waiting, and perhaps Yeshu is the one."

I recognized the sound counsel of my lover and his father. But the idea that Yeshu, whom I had known as a boy, whom I had seen grow up in a way so like other Jewish boys; the notion that he was the Anointed One, was just too much to fathom. Yes, he was pious; yes, he was obsessed by our religion and yes, to my knowledge he had led an exemplary life. But the Messiah? Yeshu?

And the image of the gentle Yeshu astride a steed, leading a revolt against Rome, sword in hand, was just too unbelievable. More than that, it was bizarre.

We continued to talk of him through the night. I feared I might be boring them with my constant chatter about that one singular subject. But both seemed so fascinated by my descriptions. When our talk ended, I knew it was not the last time Yeshu of Nazareth would be discussed at our table. Flavius even mentioned that I should feel free to invite him to dinner the next time I saw him.

Clearly, both father and son found Yeshu interesting, and Marcus would ask many questions over the next several weeks about him and my relationship to him. In many ways, the extent of Marcus' interest troubled me.

I anticipated the next Passover with a sense of anxiety. What would I do if Yeshu came to Jerusalem?

~~ 27 ~~

My anxiety was unfounded. Yeshu did not come for the next Passover. But Judah did.

Of all of Yeshu's friends, Judah, of course, was the one I least wanted to see. I still felt resentment at his mockery of my recent dead father's wealth. And, as Yeshu had noted, I had taken an instant dislike to the Iscariot.

But as I wandered the caravans in search of Yeshu, it was Judah who yelled at me. Beckoning me over, he greeted me.

"Hi Avrum, remember me?"

I was civil. If nothing else, he could give me information about Yeshu. Judah sensed that my interest was not with him.

"He's not here."

"Where is he, then?" I asked.

Judah said he was unsure, that Yeshu likely was in Sephoria, visiting with his mother. Wherever he was, Yeshu had told him not to expect him in Jerusalem this holiday. Judah explained that he himself had never spent Passover in the Holy City. Despite my dislike for the man, I agreed to be his guide, motivated by my need to know about Yeshu.

"So you knew the Master since you were children?" he asked as we entered the city.

"The Master? I didn't realize that's how you men had begun describing him."

"Some among us do; some call him rabbi. I think Simon thinks he's more than that, but then Simon has a very childish imagination."

"You have me at a disadvantage, Judah. You know much about me while I don't know anything about you. How was it you met Yeshu?

"Unlike you, I did not grow up in splendor," Judah said with his usual air of condescending. "I am from a nomad family, going town to town looking for work; sometimes looking for bread to eat. I only learned to read and write out of the kindness of a family in Judea, who employed my family for the harvest. As part of his payment, the husband offered to tutor me. My father readily accepted; he always felt I was destined for greater things."

"Once when we in Capernaum, I heard Yeshu speak at the synagogue. I admit I was taken in at once. I felt as if he was speaking to me directly. I may not have agreed with everything he said; I still don't. But he moved me, and I felt compelled to join him."

"Until Levi, the tax collector came along, I was the only literate one, which the Master certainly found useful. As he does even now; Levi's knowledge is limited."

"So tell me," the Iscariot continued, "has the Master always been as he is now?"

Judah had caught me without a ready explanation. Had Yeshu always been this way? Yes, there were signs when he was younger and more as he grew older; the bizarre happenings at the Temple, for example. And he indeed was pious and devout.

"He always spent a lot of time at the synagogue," I answered. "He has a great interest in Scripture."

"Why?" Judah asked almost sneeringly. "So he could learn all the laws of Moses in order to ignore them? He must have been a treat for the rabbi."

I chuckled, trying to ease the mood. "I wouldn't exactly call it a treat. My grandfather, and then my uncle, was the rabbi, and I heard their irritations frequently."

"I'm sure they had those with the Master. As much as I love and respect him, he says things to madden me. Imagine, we should love the Romans! Bah!." Judah almost spat out the words.

"The Romans aren't all that bad," I said, almost defensively. "You might even like some of them."

"I doubt it. All Romans are scum. Occupation is a sin; slavery is a travesty. The God of All Things expects us to spread his words, then denies us the tools to do so. If He knew we were going to be so politically inept, why did he choose us?"

"I'm afraid that's one for Yeshu to answer, Judah. But tell me, since you disagree with him on many things, why do you continue to stay with him?"

The Iscariot stared at me. "Avrum, friend of Yeshu, I ask myself that every day."

We were at the Temple, and I showed Judah around. He was impressed, but also questioned all the ornaments while the people of Israel went hungry. It was strange; Judah was echoing what Miriam had said months earlier.

"You ask me why I follow him," he said suddenly. "I think most of it is how he speaks of the Almighty as Our Father. That appeals to me greatly, for reasons not worth going into. I like to think Yeshu is right; that the God of All Things is not too busy to care about a poor peasant nomad. That would give meaning to my struggles. But at the same thing, some of the other things he says and does…..."

"Such as?" I pried.

"He seems not to care about our traditions. He is a healer; there's no doubt of that. I have seen him exorcise spirits myself. But he does so on the Sabbath, which Moses himself forbade."

"You have seen him heal, then?", I asked.

Judah nodded his head. "As I said, I've seen it. A man who had been born with a crippled leg approached him on crutches; he was able to walk away free from them. A woman possessed by so many demons she was mad; Yeshu spoke to her, and her madness disappeared. There is no doubt he is a healer."

"Have you asked him how he is able to do these things?"

"His power to heal, he says, is from Our Father; directly from Him. Quite a claim, isn't it? As for healing on the Sabbath, he rebukes me, saying the Sabbath was meant for man, not man for the Sabbath. I'm pretty sure Moses and David would disagree."

"You're probably right about that one," I agreed.

We were completing our survey of the Temple. Judah asked if I minded if he purchased a dove to offer in sacrifice. Watching him make the sacrifice, and stand in quiet observance of the prayer, it was easy to see the pure honesty of his devotion. With no question, Judah had great respect for the rituals of our faith.

After his time alone, Judah continued his exposition, "Still the most irritating of all, Avrum, is the way he speaks of Rome, or, more aptly, how he doesn't speak of Rome. From listening to him, you'd think that our bondage is our doing. He criticizes the Sanhedrin more than he does the Romans."

I had to reply. "I told you earlier that I work inside these very walls. I assure you that you would think less of our leaders if you saw them up close every day."

As usual, Judah had a biting reply. "So you labor for those your friend attacks. I guess we all have our quandaries about Yeshu."

"Put that way, perhaps you're right. And maybe that's what separates him and me."

"Mm-mm, perhaps that and other things," Judah responded. "Yet he is not particular; many of his followers are undesirables; it doesn't seem to bother him."

The tone of that last comment signaled for me the end of our conversation. We parted, both of us with the sense that we would meet again.

I remained uncomfortable about Judah; the day had nothing to ease the feeling. Whatever sympathy I might have had for him was undone by his parting jibe. I discussed all of this with Flavius and Marcus, who both agreed that Judah would be one to keep an eye on.

I didn't mind doing so, as long as it was from afar.

~~ 28 ~~

In three months I would see Judah again. The good news was that this time he was accompanied by Yeshu, and Yeshu's other followers, some of whom were new ones. I was assisting a young scribe one day, and I felt a tap on my shoulder. It was my childhood friend, who had brought his band to Jerusalem for the celebration of a minor holiday. I was caught completely off guard, yet immediately agreed to spend the evening at his campsite.

I spent the entire day debating whether or not to bring Marcus along. A useless worry as it turned out since Marcus had sent word to Nilsa that he would be working late at the Palace that evening. So I loaded my horse with food, anticipating that Yeshu's gang would be hungry.

But arriving at the campsite, I discovered my concern about Yeshu's nutrition was unfounded. His followers, who now looked to number twelve, surrounded their leader as he carved a freshly slain lamb. My surprise must have been apparent. Yeshu rose with a smile on his face and said, "Don't worry, Avi, we have not pilfered any of this feast. I'll introduce you to the source of our fine repast, and to the others, later. For now, please join us."

As we ate, I sat mute as the twelve discussed with Yeshu what had been happening. He had gained in popularity. He was drawing significant crowds wherever he preached. He had also honed his skills as a healer; I heard stories of the lame walking, the blind seeing, and the deaf hearing. I wasn't sure how much of it I believed, but I wasn't about to spoil the party.

After the meal, a fine wine was served, and Yeshu introduced me to the new members of his flock. Like the first ones, they were all about our age and seemed enamored of their leader. Motioning me outside, Yeshu invited me to walk with him. It was as always a beautiful evening. The star-lit skies of Palestine always seemed a suitable backdrop to our conversations.

"Had enough to eat, my friend?" he asked.

"More than enough; it was delicious. But how….?"

"Has a poor preacher come upon such a wealth of food? Come; let me introduce you to the two Miriam's." He led me to another tent, where two women, perhaps fifteen years older than Yeshu and I, sat weaving new tunics.

"Avi, this is Miriam of Bethany and her friend Miriam of Magalda. They have joined our circle and added a much needed feminine touch to it. I admit that without them we would be both hungry and naked."

The two women chuckled Speaking to them, I immediately noticed how nice they seemed. They were also both obviously of means. It appeared that Yeshu had found himself sponsors for his ministry, something I teased him about as we left the tent.

"You always chided me about being the practical one. But these women are providing you with assistance, aren't they?"

"That they are, Avi and both are gifts to our tribe

from the God of All Things. Both pious women, and eager to learn; their arrival has been perfect for us. But tell me, my friend, how are you?"

"I'm well, Yeshu. And you?"

"I have been blessed by the God of All Things, Avi. He has taken this lowly tradesman and made him His herald, that all might know Him."

"So you are the Almighty's herald, Yeshu? He has selected you to spread his word to every Jew in Palestine?"

"Not only to Jews in Palestine, my friend. The good news must be delivered to Jew, Gentile and Pagan alike. The covenant of Abraham must be expanded and made fresh."

I shook my head. "You're speaking heresy, Yeshu, and you more than most must be aware of it. To say that the gentile stands before the God of All Things as does the Jew……"

"As does the Syrian, the Egyptian, the Cypriot, and yes, even the Roman. Even those in lands not yet known are His children."

"And you are preaching this throughout Palestine?"

"I preach little else."

"You know the respect I have for you, Yeshu. I love you as a friend and even more than a friend. But many would say you are preaching blasphemy."

"There is no blasphemy in what I preach, Avi. None at all. How can the God of All Things not be the God of All People? Do you think it matters to him that a man is born in this woman's womb, or that one? In this nation, or that; of this heritage or that? Man has made those distinctions, not Our Father. What a man's place is in the world means nothing, only his place in the kingdom of Our Father matters."

"And Avi, the woman is equal to the man; there is no difference."

"This kingdom, Yeshu, where would it be? Where could I find it? Where would I see it?"

My friend smiled. "Can you see love, Avi? Can you see music? Can you see the wind? You cannot see any of these things, and yet you know when you are in their presence. Like love, music and the wind, the kingdom is here. It just needs to be felt."

"Oh Yeshu, you speak in a way I can hardly understand." I looked away and said, "They say you can cast out demons, and cure the sick."

"Only Our Father can do those things, Avi. I can only channel his power."

"So you are a prophet, then?"

"Many will see this Son of God as a prophet, many as a heretic. Many will see more, many less. Our Father sends us what we need. Many see this and say 'Glory to God.' Others deny the gifts. Has this not always been so?"

Again I shook my head. "I cannot speak to all the things you say. You speak of the God of all Things as Our Father, and you say that you channel Him. Then you say you are the Son of God. Are you sure your philosophy is the true one?"

Yeshu paused and looked directly at me.

"So you think I may be the False Prophet? The one the Torah warns us of? Or am I merely confused? Or am I even mad?"

"Have those possibilities ever occurred to you?" I asked earnestly. "If you have some doubts, perhaps...."

"For ten years, while you were in Jerusalem and I was in Nazareth, all I had was doubt. Especially doubt about the revelation which had been given to me, Avi. My mind was constantly at odds with itself. I know now that the bickering was the battle between Our Father and the Evil One inside me. I believe that the battle wages within every man and woman. It was not until I confronted the Evil One himself that the war was won. I knew then what I know now to be true, that I was born to become what I have become."

An uncomfortable thought was forming in my mind.

"Are you the Messiah, Yeshu?"

He smiled. "Do you see me leading legions of soldiers against Rome? Or calling the wrath of the Almighty down on our other oppressors? Do I act in the manner that Scripture demands the Messiah acts?"

Now it was my turn to smile.

"No, not at all."

"There may come to Palestine a Messiah someday, to free Israel from the chains of Rome. This Son of God comes to free Israel from the chains of Israel."

I didn't have time to respond. Simon Peter had joined us.

"Judah needs to see you, Master."

Yeshu smiled. "Judah, Judah, Judah; he always needs to see me. I am beginning to realize what a pest I must have been to the rabbis in Nazareth."

We both roared at his comment and walked back to his tent. It was good that humor invaded our conversation. I needed the respite to digest what my friend had said.

The night was over, and it was time for me to leave. Curiously, I felt better about my friend than I had in a while. Even if he had some grandiose ideas (and decidedly anti-Jewish ones) about himself, it all seemed relatively harmless. He was, after all, only a stone cutter from Nazareth. He might influence a few people, but what harm could come of it?

And, most importantly, he seemed happy, happier than I had seen him in a while. That thought gave me pleasure.

As we embraced, I asked him about the next time I would see him.

"Next Passover I will be in Jerusalem."

~~ 29 ~~

Marcus was still awake when I returned home. I opened my heart to him about Yeshu, more than I ever had. My lover just listened, as I continued on and on about my childhood friend.

Marcus had his own surprise for me.

"I have seen him you know."

My mind began to race. "Seen him! Where? When? Why didn't you mention it before?"

"Calm down, Avi, I was just waiting for the right time to tell you. Have a glass of wine, and I'll tell you all about it."

I indeed poured myself some wine and some for Marcus. Nazareth was about to collide with Jerusalem.

"Two weeks ago, when I joined father for that reconnoiter in Capernaum, you remember it , don't you?"

I certainly did. It was one of the few nights Marcus and I had spent apart, aside from my trips to Nazareth.

"Anyway, on my way back, we saw a crowd surrounding a preacher. You know father, Avi; he's always curious about those things. So we stopped to listen."

My shock was sufficiently recovered to ask: "What was he saying?"

"My first impression was less what he was saying than how he was saying it. You've described him as a natural orator; you understate it, my love. Roman senators would give their first-born to have Yeshu's oratory skills. The entire crowd was enraptured."

"I was enraptured, so was father. I recognized him immediately from your previous descriptions, and occasionally he referred to his childhood in Nazareth. It took me no time to conclude that this was your friend. So, of course, my curiosity was peaked, and father's also when I identified Yeshu to him."

"He was speaking about a kingdom; a place I suppose where your God of All Things lives. And how that kingdom was based on love. And, maybe most importantly to me, is how your God was inviting everyone into it. I felt that I, a Roman, would be as welcomed into this kingdom as anyone else. I was amazed at this message as I was by the messenger. Father was also; he kept moving closer as if to ensure he wouldn't miss anything."

"The two of you must have been quite a sight."

"I doubt anyone was paying much attention to us; your friend so fixated them. I immediately understood all the feelings you have for him. And how you could be captivated by him."

Marcus said this with a certainty of purpose, as if to grant a certain absolution for my lifelong obsession with Yeshu. Perhaps he had felt uncomfortable when I spoke of Yeshu; I could understand that. As close as we had become, there had been a life for Avrum before Marcus, as there had been for Marcus before Avrum. Perhaps he was simultaneously forgiving himself for whatever doubts he had.

"In any event, his sermon ended, and the crowd

began to surround him. It was as if they felt a need not just to hear him, but to touch him. Father felt it was best if we left, and I agreed, though not without hesitation. I would have liked to speak to Yeshu personally. But father was right; it would have been inappropriate. But I tell you, Avi, Yeshu was all father talked about on the ride home. I think he wants to meet him, though I realize that may be uncomfortable for you……"

Uncomfortable indeed, I thought. Yeshu and I had never formally discussed my nature, and he had never expressed any desire to meet the companion he had predicted I would find. I was okay with that, as I assumed he was. Perhaps that time had come.

"That may be possible, Marcus. He told me tonight that he will be in Jerusalem next Passover."

"To preach in the Temple?"

I chuckled at my lover's naivety; the wine was having its effect.

"Probably not. Our Sanhedrin may not take kindly to his message."

"How can they be offended by such a wonderful preacher?" Marcus asked innocently.

"Oh my love, the Pharisees and Sadducees can be offended by the rising of the sun."

"Sounds like the Senate to me."

Flavius had entered the study in time to respond to my last comment.

"Father, Avi just spent the evening with his friend Yeshu, and I told him we had seen him."

"We owe you an apology, Avi; we should have mentioned it to you sooner. But that aside, that friend of yours is a remarkable preacher. I find myself thinking of his idea of the kingdom often, even at night; maybe especially at night. I felt like he was inviting Marcus and me into that kingdom. Me, a Roman centurion, and Marcus, a Roman scribe, both of us invited into the kingdom of the Jewish God of All Things! Very bizarre, yet very captivating."

The wine had set me very much at ease.

"I think the self-described Roman centurion and Roman scribe may understand this Jewish preacher better than most Jews," I said wryly.

"I wouldn't go that far, Avi; I still have much to learn about your faith. But I can appreciate Yeshu's overall appeal and why you care for him."

The wine was having its effect. "I do care for him, and intensely. I think Marcus has always known that. But I worry about him also."

"Because he says some worrisome things," Flavius responded. "I can see that. I find myself wondering what would happen to a Roman orator who suggested a Jew would be as welcome at Zeus' table as Caesar. I believe he would find himself a galley slave in no time."

We all chuckled at the centurion's remark. But then his tone turned serious.

"I would like to meet him. I would like Marcus to meet him. I would ask you to set aside your apprehensions and introduce us."

I could not deny he who had made so much possible in my life. For Flavius, I would do anything.

"As I told Marcus, he will be here for Passover."

"Mmmm, Passover," Flavius mused. "Pilate will have the entire guard on duty then, and I doubt I will have much time. But I will make time; if Passover is the only time I can meet him, I will do so."

As usual, this was said with the certainty I had seen him utter several times; the decision was made.

"But there are months before your holiday," Flavius added. "Perhaps I will hear him preach again."

We talked of Yeshu for the rest of the night. To my surprise, Simon joined our conversation; he too was curious about the new prophet who preached the equality of all. I marveled at Yeshu's appeal to Jew, gentile and pagan alike; to the oppressed and the oppressor. His message was for all men, and, I was reminded, for all women.

It would not be the end of the involvement between my adoptive family and my childhood friend. Instead, it would only be the beginning.

~~ 30 ~~

Only a week later Flavius would see Yeshu again. On assignment in southern Judea, the centurion heard him preach. That evening I had no sooner entered the house when he told me all the details. His narration would continue through dinner when Marcus joined us.

"Remarkable, Avi, the way he preaches. He would have a brilliant career on the Roman stage."

"He has many natural gifts," I replied, unwilling to admit that I feared those talents might be more unnatural than natural, perhaps even demonic. Yeshu's so-called battle with the Evil One came to the forefront of my mind.

"Did he talk about the kingdom again, father," Marcus asked.

"That and a whole lot more, son. He intoned a type of prayer, unlike any I had ever heard before. He spoke to his God as a father, pleading with him, as a child might, to forgive his sins. More remarkable, he prayed with equal earnestness for his father to forgive those who had sinned against him and caused him harm. How extraordinary. Pleading a case for forgiveness of those who had hurt him. In fact, half of the prayer celebrated the act of forgiveness itself. It was exceedingly powerful, yet very touching at the same time. I can't describe how the crowd reacted. It was a mixture of awe, respect, and even joy."

"Any more about miracles and healings," I asked, not without some trepidation. While Yeshu's intellectual approach would appeal to those like Flavius, healing the sick would draw much more massive crowds to him.

"Many in the crowd spoke of them. It seems apparent your friend is indeed a healer. Understand my thoughts about healers, Avi. The Romans have them too. I remember engaging one, Marcus when momma took ill. The healer, a woman, was well-known with a strong reputation. She had had many successes, I was told. But we would not be one of them. I've come to believe that the major weapons healers have are time and luck. So I don't pay much attention to healers."

"But it's his words, Avi, not his supposed actions. The way he addresses his God, the relationship he has with Him. And he speaks of the relationship we should all have with this God of All Things. I can't imagine having this type of relationship with Zeus or Jupiter."

"Our God of All Thing has always been a personal one," I answered. "Though not as personal, I fear, as Yeshu would have Him be."

Flavius continued. "It's just so intriguing that a man could speak to his god like that. Intriguing and refreshing."

"Did he say anything that would offend Pilate?" I asked.

"I don't think so, but then Pilate is a strange one," Flavius responded with a certain distance in his eyes. "You can never be too careful with someone like our new governor. His reputation is developing towards rashness and political expediency, rather than for intense deliberation about the facts. He is a lot more political than his predecessor."

"Didn't he have a Jewish preacher arrested just a while ago?" Marcus asked.

Flavius' laugh seemed a bit odd but made sense once he explained it.

"Well, that one should have been arrested, son. He was going village to village suggesting that Caesar's testicles be boiled in oil. I think Pilate made the right decision on that one."

Marcus continued the lighthearted mood. "Didn't the preacher also suggest that Caesar should still be attached to them?"

We all laughed heartily, but the conversation quickly turned serious again after I asked what had happened to the preacher.

"I don't know, Avi; after his arrest, he was never heard from again. And nothing was ever said."

"In any event," Flavius continued, "Yeshu is not of that ilk. It seems Rome has nothing to fear from him, though I suspect Avi's higher-ups in the Temple might."

"They are as vindictive as any Roman, Flavius," I responded.

"Have you heard anything about your friend from them?"

"No, not a word," I admitted. "But the Sanhedrin does not confer with lowly scribes about such things. Now that you mention it, though, I may ask Levi about it tomorrow morning. He will know."

"Likely he will, and Levi is an honest man," Flavius agreed.

The time had come to ask Flavius about his relationship with Levi, and I did so. "How is it that you know him so well?"

"Two reasons actually, Avi. In the first case, I've confessed to you my interest in your people. Unlike many, I could not dismiss off-handily the beliefs so many hold so dear. I always wanted to discover the nature of those beliefs. So, through various channels, I sought someone at the Temple who wouldn't recoil at the thought of explaining Israel to a Roman. Levi's name was frequently mentioned as a man I should get to know. He's liberal enough not to let my position trouble him. So I made it my business to get to know him."

"His explanation of your beliefs was clear and concise, as was his explanation of why your people believe as they do. Knowing Levi has provided me with a window into your world, a way to better understand that world."

"Then Marcus' mother took ill, and Levi was the first to come to my aid. It may be hard for you to believe, Avi, but Levi is a thoughtful and caring man. And open-minded enough not to allow my rank or station to interfere with that care and compassion."

Flavius was right. It was a side of Levi I was unfamiliar with. But my supervisor's constant encouragements to me at the Temple, his providing a place of worship in his home and other similar actions began to make sense to me in light of Flavius' explanation.

"See him, Avi. See what he knows. I can't shake the nagging suspicion that Yeshu has more to fear from his people than he may realize."

I wanted to see Levi and talk to him, but I also decided I wanted to see Yeshu. And I didn't want to wait until Passover.

"Do you know when or where he will preach again?" I asked.

"No Avi, I have no way of knowing. Nothing was said of it today. I wish I did know. I would like to hear him again."

Flavius would see Yeshu again, and quicker than any of us could have imagined.

~~ 31 ~~

I went to the Temple extremely eager to talk to Levi. Based on the way he had treated me for many years, and how Flavius felt towards him, I looked forward to the conversation.

I could not have been more wrong.

Levi first surprised me by knowing much about Yeshu.

"I haven't mentioned it to you, Avrum, though I know he is from your home village and the two of you are about the same age. But I also know that you have a peculiar relationship with that Roman family I introduced you to. Are you a servant to the centurion, or is something else going on?"

I was ill prepared for this frontal assault, made worse by Levi's calm and unobtrusive tone. What had motivated Levi to make such a comment? I was entirely taken aback.

I recovered quickly enough to respond: "I am Flavius' servant, and I continue to tutor his son, along with other members of his staff. Beyond that, I have no idea what you are talking about."

"Really?" Levi's tone remained calm. "To some, my assistant, that alone would be considered treason. Romans have their world; we have ours. The less they mingle, the better."

"But Flavius told me of your friendship," I objected. "Above all, it was you who recommended me…...."

"What's in the past is best left in the past. Flavius is a good man, perhaps even a noble one. But he is not one of us."

I longed to know what had happened to Levi. Had he been rebuked at some point for his friendship with Flavius? I vowed to discover the reasons behind what my supervisor was saying.

"But Yeshu is!" I retorted.

"Yes, he is, though he seldom preaches as if he is one of us. He has some troubling ideas; ideas he should have kept with him in Nazareth. Pilate has had his fill with these bizarre preachers, and they do nothing to keep the uneasy peace we have achieved with Rome."

"But I'm told he never attacks Rome."

"I have no idea who or what he attacks," Levi responded. "All I know is that the Sanhedrin has developed a sudden interest in this friend of yours. In fact, they are sending some men to follow him, to hear exactly what he is saying. They know of a gathering in Galilee two days hence. They will report all they see and hear when they return."

Levi peered at me. "I shouldn't even be telling you this, Avrum; I am breaking a confidence from the highest of my superiors. But you have been an excellent assistant and an excellent mentor for our younger scribes; I have duly noted all of this. If that were not so, your other life might well cost you your position, if not more. My advice to you is to ignore this prophet, even if you are friendly with him. Keep your distance; he can do you much harm, and little good."

"One more thing. I continue to value Flavius' friendship. I hold him in high esteem and assume his son shares those same qualities. If you have any interest in this strange preacher, give them the same advice."

With that remarkable statement, Levi motioned that our conversation was over. I spent the rest of the day numb from that conversation. Not only did the Temple powers know of Yeshu, they knew (apparently) way too much about me. I had spent my entire time in Jerusalem deliberately, and with great difficulty, hiding my personal life. It now appeared that those efforts were fruitless. It wasn't just what Levi had said about Yeshu; it was what he had told about Avrum.

But first things first. Yeshu must be warned about the Sanhedrin's interest in him; that was without doubt. But how could I possibly warn him? Any absence from my duties, especially now, would cause suspicion. I could not risk it.

I explained the situation to Marcus immediately after dinner that evening. His first comment was cutting and disturbing.

"Now you know why Romans don't trust your people. I have heard the man preach; he poses no threat to anyone. The whole notion is ludicrous."

"I have to reach him, Marcus, to warn him. It doesn't matter that what the Sanhedrin believes is false. Just like with Romans; if Pilate gets a notion that someone is treasonous, what difference does it make if it's true or not. You know the answer to that as well as I do; no difference at all, It's just not a trait of my people."

He sensed my anger immediately and realized his error. Apologetically he replied:

"I didn't mean it that way, Avi; I'm sorry if that's how it sounded. I'm as much upset by what this is doing to you as anything else. You are being torn between the faith you grew up in and your faith in your friend. No matter which way you turn, you will suffer, either personally or professionally, and perhaps both. It's not fair."

Though I had not formulated the complexity of my situation or all that was happening in quite that way, I had to agree that my lover was right. It was more than just my private life and Yeshu's effect on it; my friend was challenging my faith, the faith of my ancestors. Moreover, though I sometimes rued admitting it, it was a faith I accepted as valid. I would never claim to be a devout Jew. But I was a Jew.

And based on today's conversation, my livelihood was being threatened. I took Levi's warning very seriously; I was convinced he had delivered it in that tone.

But despite all my problems, the issue of Yeshu and the Sanhedrin was my primary concern. Levi had been right about one thing; Marcus showed this evening that he had inherited his father's abilities, especially the one that allowed him to diagnose a situation and react quickly to it.

"I will go to Galilee," he said. "I can tell my superiors I have business with my father there; they will not question it." Then, with a smile that belied the solemnity of the conversation, he added: "If Yeshu does not listen to me, perhaps I will throw him over my horse and bring him back to you."

I was reminded (as if I needed to be) of why I cherished this man; the humor was much needed.

All that was left to do was to inform Flavius of our plan. We feared he might think it was rash. After quietly deliberating all we had to say, in the manner I had seen so many times, he agreed with his son's thoughts; indeed, he took them a step further. Flavius said he would accompany Marcus to Galilee; that gave me a confidence I had not felt before.

Flavius also wanted to know more about Levi; I could not provide him with any more information than I had.

"I'm disappointed in him, Avi; I thought his recent coldness toward me was my fault. But now it appears he has surrendered to pressures from above. I would have thought him better than that."

"Perhaps it is his age, Flavius; he is not a young man, and he has been at the Temple a long time."

"Maybe you're right, Avi. Still, it's disappointing, and not a little bit so."

"But so much for Levi," Flavius concluded the conversation. "Marcus, we need our rest. We will see Yeshu."

~~ 32 ~~

They left at daybreak two days later. As they rode off into the sunrise, I couldn't help but realize how bizarre the whole situation had become. A few short weeks ago I was reveling in how my life was turning out. Now it was a kaleidoscope of fear, a Sophoclean drama of spies, counterspies, and informants. I was afraid for Yeshu, afraid for Marcus and Flavius, and, yes, afraid for myself. And I was convinced that tragedy, while not imminent, was nonetheless unavoidable.

I spent the whole day in total apprehension. That my lover and his father did not return until past sunset only added to it. When they finally did arrive, they eschewed their suppers and beckoned me to join them in the study.

"We found him quite easily, actually," Flavius began. "The crowd today must have been twice the previous one. Yeshu began with the same prayer, inviting his audience to pray with him."

"There was no objection to two Romans in the crowd?" I asked.

"Oh, there were more than two Romans, Avi. We weren't the only ones," Marcus interjected. "Yeshu's followers seem no longer limited to Jews."

"After his prayer," Flavius continued, "he walked through the crowd, answering their questions and challenging them. Some tried to trick him, but he was too quick for them. He made them look silly."

"I'd wager they were spies from the Temple," I suggested.

"I believe you'd win that wager," Flavius replied. "But they were no match for him." Flavius then said pensively, "That should worry your Sanhedrin."

I asked if they were able to speak to Yeshu.

"Sadly, I just had a moment at the very end of his interaction with the crowd. I asked if he was aware that parts of his preaching might be considered troubling to those of his faith."

"He paused for a moment, Avi. I think my centurion's garb had something to do with that. I also think he appreciated the full scope of what I had asked. He peered at me with those eyes of his that you have described as penetrating. Again you understate the case, my friend. Those eyes are indeed remarkable."

"In any event, he answered. 'No child grows without shedding his childhood skin, and often that shedding is troubling, indeed, even painful. And yet the God of All Things provides new skin, does He not? No one gains without giving up that which is old. And yes, Centurion, I'm aware that I, as you say, troublesome of my faith. But the kingdom is theirs also if they simply accept it'."

"I think he appreciated my warning, but I also think he is not too overly concerned. It appears he's willing to accept certain risks to get his point across. I admire that, Avi, and frankly, I'm beginning to admire the message as well as the messenger. He says things that truly appeal to me. He continues to open my eyes."

"Mine also," Marcus chimed in, with a seriousness that I found troubling.

"A kingdom where there is neither Roman nor Jew, rich or poor, master nor slave; nor even man or woman; just the union of the God of All Things with His creation. I am beginning to believe those words, Avi."

"But whose words are they?" I cautioned. "The words of the God of All Things or the words of Yeshu."

Marcus had a short answer. "I don't believe he thinks there's a difference. As far as he is concerned, they are one."

"Either way," added Flavius, "this is an attractive ideal. Very attractive. I may someday accept that ideal."

"Someday?" Marcus asked earnestly.

Flavius looked at both of us carefully. "I've long ago tired of all of our gods, son; forever at war with themselves or with mankind. Too many gods, too much hatred, too much violence. Can the heavens be filled with beings as aggressive as we? Shouldn't they be better than that?"

He shrugged as he continued. "One God, a caring and loving God, is an ideal to be admired and be worshipped. It just seems to make so much sense…..."

There had undoubtedly been indications that Flavius was heading in that direction with his beliefs. But this was the first real statement that he was ready to accept the God of All Things as his own. There was no question that Yeshu was channeling this acceptance

"Does that disturb you at all, Avi?" he asked.

It was my turn to pause before answering. "That you are accepting of the God of All Things? Quite the contrary. In that, I rejoice. But I'm concerned that the version you are accepting may not be the one that exists."

Flavius smiled. "I've been paying attention to you, Avi, as you told us about your God, and showed us the rituals you performed in His name. This change in my thinking hasn't happened in one day. It's been there for a while. Perhaps it's the reason I desired friendship with Levi, perhaps even why I wanted you to tutor Marcus. Maybe Yeshu has just brought it to the surface for me."

We sat silently for what seemed like hours, though I'm sure it was barely minutes. This wasn't some minor change for Flavius. A thinking man of his ilk did not take such matters lightly. He could never be a Jew; he lacked the heritage. Yet he had committed to our God. In the end, that seemed more important.

I ask the question fermenting in my mind.

"And you, Marcus?"

It took him no time at all to answer. "Yes, Avi, yes. I may not accept all your faith claims, but I know that neither do you. And I have some issues with some of the things Yeshu preaches, again as I know you do. But is there a fatherly God of All Things, who loves His children as any father would? Yes, Avi, yes!"

So father and son were now converted. I would have liked to take credit for their respective revelations, but despite what Flavius said, I knew better. It was all about Yeshu.

Those conversions obsessed my thoughts as I retired; sleep would evade me. After a short while, Marcus came to me. Lying next to me, he said:

"What are your thoughts, my companion?"

"Oh Marcus," I said with frustration. "I don't know! There are so many things running through my head I feel it might burst. Who is this man, who I knew as a boy, who has had such an effect on the two most important men in my life? Is he a seer? A prophet? Or is he something else. Does his power to persuade come from the Almighty, or from some nefarious source? My people have been waiting for a Messiah for generations. Is Yeshu that man? I, who once loved him, and in a different way still do; can I ever understand him?"

Comforting me, Marcus said with a smile: "That's an

awful lot of questions for this time of night, and especially for this Roman."

The comment served its purpose. I returned the smile.

Immediately Marcus again turned serious.

"I've realized all along that Yeshu occupies a place in your heart, a place I will never have. It doesn't trouble me. I truly believe that if it weren't for your unrequited love for him, you would have never left Nazareth, my love, and we would have never met."

I had never thought of it in quite that way, but I knew at once Marcus was right. I could only admit it, this evening, at this point in my life.

"But he is not like us, Marcus. Of that I am sure."

"I agree, Avi. But that doesn't change anything, does it?"

"No, I guess it doesn't."

Marcus rose: "So it has come to this, Avrum bar Jacob of Nazareth. What do you say of Yeshu? Who is he? Just a preacher or a prophet? Or is he the living Son of the God of All Things, able to transform even this pagan scribe into a member of the kingdom?"

I knew he was asking me this not only for me but for him also. I formulated my answer with care.

"I'm sorry, my love, but I still don't know. The Son of God? How can he say such a thing, claiming a relationship Moses never claimed, David never claimed, Abraham never claimed?"

"He once told me he wanted to save Israel from Israel. Sometimes I think Israel may have to be saved from Yeshu."

~~ 33 ~~

I was not misleading Marcus; I just did not know what to make of Yeshu. Sometimes I even resented knowing him as I did. Perhaps if I wasn't so familiar with him, I could have more readily accepted or rejected him. But every time I wanted to see him as misguided or mad, I saw the boy Yeshu studying at grandfather's knee, or dutifully carrying his father's toolbox, or strolling in the evening air of Nazareth with Miriam, Yusuf, and James. How could this boy become what he had?

I saw the adolescent Yeshu more and more take over Yusuf's business, challenging the rabbi at the synagogue, even playing and fooling around with Ephraim and myself. This ordinary, average teenage boy now claimed to be the Son of the God of All Things?

I could not escape the quandary I was in anywhere. Every time Levi looked at me, I knew it was because of Yeshu. At home, few nights passed that his name (or latest rumored adventure) wasn't mentioned. He enthralled Flavius and Marcus; for me, there was no break from the specter of my childhood friend.

Meanwhile, Flavius continued to ask me to find out

any information I could, especially about Yeshu's whereabouts. Flavius' position allowed a specific mobility and flexibility of schedule; he wanted every opportunity to see the prophet.

Nothing had been said in the military about Yeshu, Flavius reported. Marcus fortified this information when he told us he had never seen Yeshu's name on any correspondence, originating from Palestine or elsewhere. As of now, Rome was paying no attention to Yeshu of Nazareth.

I knew Flavius was right in being concerned about the interest the Sanhedrin was paying. So I became a mole, looking for any tidbit of information I could find out at the Temple. But I couldn't be too obvious, and both Flavius and Marcus knew it. A curious Avrum might become a uniformed Avrum; worse, an unemployed Avrum.

Somewhat timidly, I approached Levi.

"I thought you were going to mind your own concerns," he said immediately.

"I am, Levi, but naturally I'm curious. I've known him for so long…..."

My mentor shrugged. "Well, he seems to have disappeared; maybe he's returned to Nazareth, never to be heard from again. That would be fine by us."

But Yeshu had not returned to our childhood home. Instead, he was in Bethany, a town not twenty miles from Jerusalem. I discovered this through a junior scribe, who told me in the strictest confidence that his mother, a woman of some means, was providing lodging for Yeshu and his followers. As soon as dusk arrived, I raced home with the news.

As I entered our home, I knew immediately that something was horribly wrong. The house was full of strangers, not the kind of people Flavius usually entertained. These were older, non-military men. Nilsa greeted me at once, a look of grave concern on her face.

"These are medical men that Master Flavius knows. I'm sorry, Avi, but Marcus collapsed this morning as he was ready to leave for the Palace. The fire in his brow is burning, and he is barely conscious."

I do not doubt that anyone reading this text has had the type of reaction I experienced; shock, panic, and complete dismay. Marcus had never even been remotely ill; now it appeared he was seriously so.

I rushed into my lover's room to see Flavius kneeling at his stricken son's bedside. The look on the centurion's face spoke volumes.

"Why didn't you send for me?" I cried, regretting immediately that I had said it.

"I'm sorry Avi, but everything happened so quickly," Flavius said in a hushed tone. "When Simon came to inform me about Marcus, I ran looking for physicians. These men are among Jerusalem's best; Octavo here has served Pilate himself."

He pointed to an older man who was placing cold cloths on Marcus' brow. The physician looked at me quizzically; who was this Jew speaking in such a tone to a Roman?

"It is I who should apologize, Flavius; forgive my selfishness," I immediately said.

Flavius just nodded as I turned to look at Marcus. His face was completely devoid of color, his pallor so pale that it frightened me. He was indeed only barely conscious, his body trembling slightly.

Octavo was speaking to Flavius. "We will continue to bring down the fever. I believe that once it breaks, your son will be healthy."

"And how long should that take?" the father asked.

"A day or two. But you do your son no service by staying here and ignoring your own well being. Have you eaten today, centurion?"

Flavius' non-response was treated by the physician as an affirmative.

"I will remain with him," Octavo continued, "or one of my assistants. I want you to take care of yourself."

Flavius could not have been more resolute in his answer. "He is my son, my only child. My health means nothing, his means everything."

Octavo seemed resigned. "I have seen your devotion before, Flavius, with your wife. But this is not this type of illness. I expect your son to recover."

"As you expected her to recover," Flavius replied distantly.

Octavo shook his head as he left the room, leaving his assistant to care for the patient.

For the next two days and nights, either Flavius or I was at Marcus' bedside. We would relieve each other from our vigils, though neither of us would sleep much. Octavo returned often, yet frighteningly there seemed to be no change. In his suspended state of consciousness, Marcus was unable to eat or drink, thus denying his body the tools it needed to fight the fever. I was no physician, but I knew that much. Octavo claimed the situation was "improving"; neither Flavius nor I could concur.

Simon went to the Temple to explain my absence, telling Levi that it was I who was ill. Levi seemed skeptical. "Indeed, his friend is nearby, and all of a sudden he is taken ill. Curious, isn't it, Cypriot?"

So Levi had lied to me; he knew Yeshu was in Bethany. I wondered how many more lies my supervisor had told me.

On the third day, there was still no change. Octavo shrugged, claiming he was still optimistic, but I knew he had seen the fever take many lives. An acute sense of depression took hold of me. Not only my companion seriously ill, but his father was also undergoing a terrifying agony only few could understand. There is nothing more unnatural than losing a child; it was unspoken that Flavius would change places with his son in an instant. Losing one's parents or mate was horrific enough; no words could describe the loss of an only child. I could not know it then, but I would witness this agony again, and very shortly.

Again, the military mind of Flavius would suggest an action.

In the middle of the third night, he approached me. "I have to act on a thought I have, Avi. It's said that Yeshu is a healer. Do you think he would help Marcus?"

The suggestion seemed bizarre, but when men and women are so ensconced by such stress, the bizarre seemed possible. If what Judah had said was right, and Yeshu could heal, why not ask? As far as I was concerned, Yeshu's power could come from the God of All Things or the Evil One; I didn't care. I would bargain with Has Satan himself for my lover's life.

"He is in Bethany," I replied. "I will leave at once."

"We will both go," Flavius countered. "I am useless here, and I cannot sit idly by."

Within minutes, we informed Octavo and the household we were leaving. Questioning looks were on their faces, but we were in no mood to explain our actions. Flavius and I rode off together, thankful that at that hour few in Jerusalem would notice the strange sight of a centurion and his servant galloping at full speed out of the city.

~~ 34 ~~

Bethany was usually three hours away. We arrived in two. I said to Flavius that the God of All Things Himself must be with us. The centurion had not lost his sense of humor: "May He be with our horses first."

It was scarcely daybreak when we arrived, with the townspeople awakening to their daily responsibilities. We saw a farmer in his field and approached him about Yeshu's whereabouts.

"And what would the centurion want with the Nazarene?" he asked. Pointing to me, he said:" And the Jew who rides with him? I will need some explanation."

Flavius was quick to react: no doubt he had anticipated this response.

"It is this man, Avrum of Nazareth, who seeks Yeshu. I ride with him as a favor to his generous family."

This the farmer could understand. A Roman protecting a Jew, but for a fee. Despite the severity of the situation, I suppressed a smile.

"If you could tell us where the prophet is," Flavius continued, "I'm sure his family would be equally generous." Flavius' hand held a small bag that jingled; he had come prepared.

The farmer looked at him stealthily; few farmers possessed Roman silver.

"His friend Avrum of Nazareth seeks him, you say."

"Avrum bar Jacob of Nazareth, yes," Flavius replied.

"Remain here, both of you," the farmer said, as he took his bag of coins.

As he walked toward the village, I was tempted to chase after him, but Flavius shook his head and remained calm. After a while, I was beginning to doubt his strategy. The farmer seemed to have disappeared. More than a half of an hour passed. As I watched, Flavius rested his brow on his horse I could scarcely conceive what his thoughts were.

Suddenly the farmer reappeared. This time he was accompanied by three men. As they neared, I saw that it was Yeshu and Judah with a third man. I did not recognize him, yet he seemed oddly familiar.

I ran to embrace Yeshu. He stared at me first, then at Flavius. His eyes narrowed.

"Avi, what is it?"

"Yeshu, I.... I......I ". I was having trouble putting words to my thoughts.

Flavius immediately interjected. "I have heard you preach, sir."

"Yes, you have, centurion. I remember you. And now I am blessed by the presence of my beloved Avi, whom you accompany. You will allow my confusion......"

I was able to speak. "It's Marcus, Yeshu, the son of this centurion, Flavius. He is very ill, and we fear he may be......dying." The last word escaped my mouth, and I immediately regretted it. Neither Flavius nor I had ever spoken it, never describing Marcus' condition in that manner. But we both knew it was what we feared.

Yeshu nodded his head in understanding, but it was Judah who spoke.'

"So, the Roman comes to the Jew for healing. Are all the Roman healers busy this day?" he scoffed.

"Illness knows neither nationality nor religion," replied Yeshu. "Avi is a friend, and he has brought a friend in need. That is all that's important. Andrew, inform your brother we will be leaving for Jerusalem."

The one Yeshu called Andrew said, "But Master, shouldn't you talk it over with Simon first?" So this man who looked familiar was Simon Peter's brother; perhaps that was why I thought I recognized him.

"Your brother will want to spend hours discussing it, and I don't believe we have that kind of time. Please tell him."

Flavius surprised me by speaking up.

"But sir that may not be wise."

Judah was quick to answer. "Why is that, Roman? Why should the Master stay away from the Holy City?"

"There has been talk," Flavius replied. "Avi knows more than I. Much of the talk has been at the Temple."

Before I could reply, Yeshu interrupted.

"Always there is talk, centurion, and most of the time, it is empty."

Flavius spoke again. "Still, perhaps this is not the time. It may indeed be inappropriate for you to come."

Then he continued. "Besides sir, I am not of your faith, nor worthy of your presence in my house. If you could just pray for my son, I believe he will be healed."

I stood shocked and mute at this display of the faith Flavius had shown. Yeshu looked at him, perhaps as surprised as I was. He turned from us and began walking toward the town. Suddenly, he turned back to us.

"The faith of this man I have not seen in all of Israel. Go, centurion Flavius, return to your son." With that, he turned again and began walking back to Bethany.

I ran to intercept my friend.

"Yeshu, I have to tell you, his son is my.... I mean, he's the one...."

"I know who Flavius' son is, Avi. Return with his father; they will both need you."

Judah and Andrew stopped me as I returned to Flavius. Andrew spoke:

"We have to know how you two knew where the Master was, Avrum."

I wanted to rush off, but they deserved an answer.

"Some in the Temple knew."

"And how did they know?" Judah asked, obviously agitated. "Maybe they sent you and your Roman watchdog to verify our whereabouts. Maybe this whole business about his son is made up? Are you in league with the Romans now? So-called friend of the Master?"

"Judah, stop it!" Andrew said sharply. "The Master has no need to fear anything from the Temple. And if he did, we are here to protect him. Let Avrum on his way, as the Master bade."

Andrew turned to follow Yeshu into the town. As did Judah, but not without giving me a final sneer.

"You may one day have to choose between your friends, Avrum bar Jacob. I hope you can make the right one."

Judah chased after Andrew and continued to harangue him. I was curious but had no time to watch their argument.

Flavius was already aboard his steed. "We will return home, Avi." We rode swiftly, leaving Bethany with Yeshu and his apostles behind us. Again we rode as rapidly as the horses would allow. I had no idea what awaited us in Jerusalem, and we were silent on the way home. There was simply no time to talk. Moreover, Flavius was so deep in his thoughts I did not want to interrupt them.

It was before midday when we arrived home. Nilsa and Simon were waiting for us the moment we dismounted. Before we could even ask, Nilsa said, "Marcus is awake, and he is asking for both of you."

We raced into Marcus' room, where we were immediately amazed. Sitting up drinking nectar was Marcus. He was still pale and looked fatigued, but he was awake. And very much alive.

"Father," he whispered hoarsely. "Avi...."

"Stay still, my son; you have had the fever," his father told him.

Octavo filled us in. Marcus had opened his eyes a short while ago; the fever had broken. Octavo began explaining the various rubs and herbs he had given his patient, undoubtedly convinced that was his therapy that had brought about the cure. Flavius quieted him, saying that we all needed rest. He hugged his son and motioned to me to follow him out of the room.

I ached to hold my lover in my arms, but the physician's presence precluded it. I began to walk out, where Marcus rasped:

"Avi!"

I turned to him as he said, "Avi, I had a dream, a dream about Yeshu...."

His father subtly rebuked him. "I need you to rest, Marcus. There will be time later to discuss your dreams."

With that, Flavius and I left the room. Utterly spent, we went to our respective rooms. Flavius was used to sleeping during the day, as his military duties often required odd hours. I had no such experience, but it made no difference. I fell fast asleep, my dreams once again filled with images of Yeshu and Marcus in alternating scenarios.

This time though, they were anything but restful.

~~ 35 ~~

Flavius and I both awoke at dusk. I was disoriented but focused enough to realize my first steps had to lead to Marcus' room. I arrived at the same time as Flavius.

Neither of us could believe what we saw. Hours earlier my lover had been at death's door. Now he was wide awake, feasting on a sumptuous meal.

"How do you feel, son?' Flavius asked, almost timidly.

"Like a newborn, father. I doubt that I have ever felt better. Simon tells me I was asleep for three days. I still can't believe it."

With all that had happened, it occurred to me that Simon had been at Marcus' bedside throughout the entire ordeal. I glanced at the Cypriot to express my appreciation. He merely nodded. Flavius' thoughts echoed my own; as he walked toward Simon, tears were forming in his eyes, and he embraced his servant. Again, Simon nodded, though I noticed a look of appreciation cross his face. As he left the room, I marveled at Simon's dedication, little knowing that it would not be the last time I saw the man perform almost heroic service to someone in pain.

We joined Marcus in his repast. We too were famished after our ordeal. Nilsa as always was up to the task; the food kept coming, and for Flavius and I, so did the wine. Marcus stared at the wine, but a quiet shake of his father's head told him there would be no wine for him this night.

The three of us spoke as three men who had just scaled the highest mountain, and reached its apex. Flavius did not mention our excursion to Bethany, and I followed his lead.

Marcus began to speak. "Whatever else happened, I had the most incredible dream. I was laying on a bed of hot embers; I wailed out to the God of All Things to take my life and end my suffering. Then from a distance, a figure began to approach me. I couldn't believe my own eyes; it was………it was momma."

At the mention of his deceased wife, Flavius flinched and looked away.

"She looked so beautiful, father. Just like she did before the illness. As she neared me, she put her fingers to her lips, as if to quiet me."

"' Don't cry, Marcus," she said, 'we're here to help you.' I didn't understand what she meant."

"Who else is here, momma?"

"You know who else is here, son. It is He."

"Somehow I understood who she meant; it was Yeshu. I had sensed him from the beginning. I couldn't see him, but I knew He was there."

Flavius and I stole a glance at each other.

Marcus continued. "Then she hugged me. You don't know this, Avi, but momma always hugged father and me every day. Once, when I was little, she woke me up in the middle of the night; she had forgotten to hug me that day."

At that moment Flavius looked away distantly as he

said, "I remember that night. Go on, son."

"As she hugged me, a great coolness swept over my entire body. I began to sob, so much that everything began to shake. 'Oh momma, I cried, 'I'm not going to die!'"

"Of all things, momma began to laugh. Tilting my head to hers, she said quietly: 'Of course, you are going to die' Then with a huge grin, she said, 'but it won't be today, my son.'"

Flavius buried his head in his hands. Looking up with his eyes damp from tears, he said "That was momma, all right. That humor, no matter what else was happening......"

I knew now the source and origin of my lover's quick wit. Marcus continued:

"I said to her,' I miss you so much momma, and father....'"

"' Neither of you should miss me, my son, for I am never far from you. He makes all things possible; the two of you are beginning to realize that now. Please promise me that you and your father will continue along that path.

"Suddenly she began to fade from me; before I knew it, she was gone. The next thing I knew Simon's hand was in mine; my eyes opened, and I saw his face. Never was I so glad to see anyone, and I mean that with no disrespect to either of you. Then I just began to feel so good...."

Neither Flavius nor I could damn our tears. I knew he was crying for his son and his wife; as was I. Yet I also had my reasons. Marcus' dream of his mother had strangely brought my own mother to mind. If his mother was somehow near him, could mine be near me? Above all, was it Yeshu who really made this all possible?

Flavius recovered and interrupted my reverie.

"There is much we need to tell you, Marcus, but it

will have to wait. For now, I want you to rest. I would love to spend the night talking to you, as I'm sure Avi would. But you have suffered a great ordeal; rest is called for. And the time for that rest is now."

His son smiled. "As you wish, father. And, truth be told, I am exhausted. Tomorrow, you will tell me what you need to tell me; that I know. And I also know that I will see both of you tomorrow; momma told me."

Flavius rose and embraced his son firmly. Now it was Marcus' turn to shed tears, and he did so freely.

"But father, I need to see Avi for a moment. Alone."

"Of course. I had anticipated you would want to. Avi, when you are finished, I'm sure Nilsa has another batch of food prepared. I don't think it will trouble you to join me." I smiled my appreciation as he left the room.

"What did you think of my dream?" Marcus immediately asked.

How could I respond? I didn't want to offend him, but I owed him my honesty.

"A lot of people put great stock in dreams, my love, but I cannot say I am one of them."

Turning very serious, he said: "My people also speak of their importance. Pilate himself is said to make major decisions based on his dreams, and his wife's also. But there is more."

"Oh?" I said, looking directly into my lover's eyes.

"I know you and father went to see Yeshu."

"How could you know that? Did Simon…?"

"Not Simon, Avi; momma told me. She moved her hand, and I could see you and father, Yeshu, and some other men. I couldn't hear the words, but I knew all of you were talking about me. I know the two of you were going to pick the right time to tell me, but I want you to realize that I already know."

I didn't quite know how to respond. Whatever I felt about dreams, this pronouncement stunned me a bit.

Not nearly as much as his next comment would, however.

"I want to follow him, Avi. I want to be his disciple. I believe he is who he says he is."

"Marcus, you've been seriously ill. Sick people imagine all sorts of things and have all sorts of visions. You can't make the kind of leap you're making based on a dream."

I had never seen my companion so resolute.

"Yes Avi, I can. And I have. I believe in the God of All Things; I believe Yeshu is His son; I believe in his kingdom and his reign."

There wasn't much for me to say. Marcus had made his declaration with such certainty and conviction that it was beyond discussion; certainly not on this night.

I hugged and kissed him as deeply as I ever had.

"Get some rest, my love. I promise before the Almighty we will discuss these things when you are up and well."

Again with the same resolve, he said," Yes we will, Avi; yes, we will."

~~ 36 ~~

Marcus' revelation had startled me, but it was just a branch of a trinity full of shocks I would endure over the next two days.

That night, I told Flavius of his son's newfound beliefs, and of his decision to follow Yeshu. Neither seemed to surprise the centurion. He admitted to having the sense that Marcus knew of our sojourn to see Yeshu, and to having an understanding of his son's resolve. Both continued to trouble me, and I said as much.

"Too much has happened in the past few days to truly grasp it all, Avi. I am due back, as is Marcus. And your continued absence from the Temple might be garnering suspicion. Don't you think it's the best case that we all return to work, and discuss these things later?"

As he often did, Flavius had formed what was the obvious thing to do in the form of a question, a question that had only one answer. I agreed, and we all set off for our duties the next morning.

My day started routinely, but shortly Levi motioned that he wanted to see me privately. Wasting little time, he asked about my illness, then added:

"Apparently you were well enough to spend the morning in Bethany."

That would be my second shock; my ploy had failed.

"I…, I was ill," I stuttered, "and even you admit to Yeshu's healing ability. Why shouldn't I go to see him?"

"You're being defensive, Avrum, I'm not telling you this because I was upset by your absence. I've said before that your attendance has been exemplary. I only wish you to know that we are aware of your friend's movements. You might want to remember that in the future."

Levi spun and walked away. As before, a hundred questions emerged in my mind. How could Levi know about my about my trip? It had been nearly dawn when Flavius and I met Yeshu. Even a spy lying nearby would have had a difficult time recognizing anyone through the early morning mist.

More terrifying was the possibility that Levi's spy was one of Yeshu's followers. Only Judah and Andrew saw us together, and although I didn't trust the Iscariot, I found it impossible to think he had any connection at all with the Sanhedrin. Hadn't he admitted to me that he had never been to the Temple before the time I had acted as his guide?

Of Andrew, I knew very little, besides that he was Simon Peter's brother, and that I had a nagging suspicion that I had seen him somewhere before. But doubtless, the two men had discussed what had happened that day. Was one of those who had heard the conversation the informant?

The questions reverberated through my mind throughout the day. On the way home, I debated telling Flavius what Levi had said. But it would not be the main component of the evening's conversation. The third and final shock awaited me as Flavius, Marcus and I met in the study.

It was typical Flavius. In short order, he listed the series of events that had led him to their only possible conclusion, that Yeshu indeed was the Son of the God of All Things.

I sat nursing my glass of wine. It had become utterly bizarre. I, the Jew, would be the only non-believer in a house where two former pagans had annunciated Yeshu's divinity. It was beyond bizarre.

Marcus again showed his flair for using humor to diffuse the situation.

" Lighten up, Avi. It's not like father and I are about to run off and get circumcised, or live in the desert eating gnats!"

My lover smiled at his witticism, and Flavius and I joined him. To some extent the tension was eased, but only in a small sense.

Flavius wanted to reassure me.

"Exactly right, son. Please, Avi, have no thought that my newfound belief in Yeshu will affect my position. I remain a servant of the Empire, my life dedicated to it and my Caesar. There is no disconnect here. Hasn't Yeshu told his followers to cede to Caesar what is his, and to the Almighty what is his? In my case, I continue to give Caesar my professional life, and if it becomes necessary, my earthly existence also."

"But I also will give to the God of All Things that which is His. I believe I can do both of these things. In fact, by remaining in my position, I may be of special service to His son."

Marcus continued his father's theme. "The same holds for me, Avi. I believe I can be both a loyal Roman and a follower. It may not be easy to do, and someday I may have to choose between the two of them. Please understand, my companion, that I have no desire to stop being a Roman. I know many of your people see us as only brutal conquerors, but hopefully, you of all people understand the beauty of Roman art, the integrity of Roman scholarship, and the fairness of Roman justice. Our contribution to the advancement of civilization is huge, and I have a pride in that."

Flavius nodded. "Well said, son. I too have pride in our heritage, and cannot denounce it. And I will not. And with Yeshu, I need not."

I spent some time digesting what the two of them had said. "I love both of you, in different ways; this you know. Neither of you has let my faith interfere with what we have shared. I will not let this development stand in the way."

"At some point, Avi," Flavius said, "I would like the opportunity to discuss exactly what you find so troubling about what Yeshu says."

Marcus spoke up. "Oh, it's really easy, father. Despite all his denials and criticisms, Avi remains a loyal Jew. Don't be embarrassed by it, Avi. It's one of the things I have always loved about you."

"Either way," Flavius again spoke, "this cannot come between us. Families have survived bigger differences than this, and I have always considered us a family."

I was moved to hear those words, almost moved to tears. But there were other matters to discuss.

I updated my family (how amazing for me to have thought of us like that) about my conversation with Levi. As he had done before, Flavius analyzed the situation militarily.

"I don't believe there is much to do just yet. Sometimes the soldier rushes into battle; sometimes it's best to let the battle come to him. I've said before we would have to keep our eyes on both the Palace and the Temple. Those eyes must now be narrowly focused. If Yeshu is in any danger from either, it's crucial that we are aware of it. Perhaps that is why the God of All Things has revealed the truth to us, Marcus. If you look at the three of us, we are in a unique position to protect His son. Duty demands that we do so. We will attempt to save the Son of God from those who would do him harm."

My thought at the moment was simple. And who will protect the man who calls himself the Son of God from himself?

I had witnessed my lover and his father journey from paganism to monotheism to believe in the man from Nazareth. While I loved the travelers, I questioned the journey. But true to their word, their conversions would generate no distance between us over the next several months. We continued with our eyes and ears opened, but the fact was that not much was happening.

However, Passover was approaching, and I knew Yeshu was coming this year. I may have hoped his plans had changed, but those hopes would be dashed four days before the beginning of the solemn feast.

~~ 37 ~~

Levi wanted to see me; I could easily anticipate it was about Yeshu. Still, he surprised me with his opening question.

"Your friend is planning something, isn't he, Avrum?"

Immediately I turned defensive. "I haven't seen Yeshu in months, Levi. I have no idea what you are talking about."

"No idea, huh? No idea about his planning to make a grand entrance into the city at Passover? His followers, or apostles, or whatever they call themselves, are here now setting it up. We've heard that he intends to speak at the Temple'"

"So let him speak," I said almost timidly. "He'll gain some supporters and likely generate some detractors. Why are you so afraid of him?"

"Don't be as naïve as he is, Avrum. We're not afraid of him; it's he who should be afraid of us. His gospel of heresy has to be stopped; it's gone too far already."

"Gospel of heresy?" I replied incredulously. "What's so heretical? Love your neighbor? The God of all Things is a compassionate, forgiving father? Are you calling that heresy?"

"You don't know everything he's been preaching, do you?' Levi responded. "Imagine he takes it upon himself to reduce the Ten Commandments to two. Then he tramples through the teachings of Moses, about the Sabbath, about divorce, about our rituals, and just about everything else. He tells stories about the goodness of Samaritans, a people who have belittled Israel for ages. And he socializes with every type of degenerate, telling them they are welcomed into the Almighty's kingdom. And this 'Son of God' business; who is he to claim such things?"

"You question that these things are heresy? You of all people, my most talented scribe, you question it? You know better, Avrum. You above all should realize how dangerous he is."

"Dangerous to whom," I retorted. "The Sanhedrin? The High Priest? A bunch of politicians you yourself have mocked?"

Levi looked at me with contempt. "The Sanhedrin has protected Israel and our faith for generations. They have their issues; you think others like them do not? But those others have not been charged by the God of All Things to enforce His will. Through many attacks, they have remained strong and true to that charge. We are at one with the Almighty because of them. What would you like to see happen? The shattering of Israel into small splinter groups, each confused about what the God of All Things demands? What would happen to Israel then? The man preaches heresy and blasphemy; if I had my way, he'd be stoned."

I was astounded. "You're serious!"

"Nevermore, my scribe. I've seen dozens of these false prophets come and go, but none as dangerous as this one. The Romans are laughing at us, as Yeshu teaches to love our oppressors and pay homage to Caesar. They'd be happy to see the traitor gain power; they'd be euphoric if he became High Priest. I can see it now; a king of the Jews who mocks Moses and preaches the very destruction of Israel."

"He says none of those things, Levi; that's not true. And he seeks no power."

"Sure of that, are you, Avrum? Coming to Jerusalem at Passover, among the throngs of our people? He has a flair for the dramatic, doesn't he; he knows how to work a crowd. His lust for power has no limit."

"So ultimately" I challenged, "this is all about power, about the terror the Sanhedrin has that they might lose it. Politics!" I spat.

Levi grew strangely silent. A moment passed, and then he peered into my eyes. With a controlled and steady voice, he replied:

"Yes, some of it is about politics. But there is so much more about it. Are you aware of your friend's grandest pronouncement? That he is the new covenant, the new contract between the Almighty and His people? Do you know this, Avrum?"

"That's crazy," I cried "Who has told you these things? Who has been spreading this scandal?"

"Fool!" Levi yelled back; his control and steadiness had evaporated. "Do you think I make these accusations based on rumor and hearsay? We have more than one source traveling with the blasphemer. The evidence is overwhelming, and it's been verified."

I was stunned by Levi's implications. If what he said was true, Yeshu had crossed into a territory not visited by any other prophet in our history. The covenant between the God of All Things and Abraham remained the nexus of Jewish belief; without it, there was no Israel. Had Yeshu gone that far?

"Silent now, huh, Avrum? You didn't know what

your friend was up to, did you? You thought he was all about love and the kingdom and the acceptance of all. You didn't realize how greedy for power he is, greedier than any Pharisee. Replacing the High Priest wouldn't come close to satisfying his lust for power; he wants to replace Moses, to replace Solomon, to replace Abraham. I tell you as sure as David slew Goliath, Israel must rid itself of the Nazarene."

I was trembling as I asked:" What are you going to do, Levi?"

"I'm saying that he must be eliminated. I don't know how, since his popularity seems to be growing. Stoning him would turn him into a martyr, and cause unrest; that we cannot have. Rome will do nothing; they'd love to see Yeshu become the leader of Israel, the King of the Jews. That way, they can beat us senseless while we stand there and turn the other cheek. An answer must be found......"

I turned away from him; I wanted to vomit.

"Why are you telling me these things, Levi? What makes you think I won't run off and tell him of your plans?

"It's my fondest hope that you do just that, Avrum. Go to him; tell him to go back to Nazareth and break his stones. Tell him to take his left-outs and miscreants with him and hide in a cave somewhere. Tell him that if he values his life at all, he will never come close to Jerusalem, this Passover or any other Passover."

The full scope of what Levi had said began to affect me. I was to be the Sanhedrin's conduit to Yeshu; as they have conduits working the other way, I did not doubt Levi's sincerity, no doubt at all. He was not a man who threatened idly.

I also did not doubt that Yeshu was in mortal danger.

Levi was hardly finished. "They know about you, Avrum, and most in the Sanhedrin are not as liberal as I.

I became friendly with Flavius years ago because we are both tolerant men, willing to admit that we ourselves are far from perfect. I was drawn to him because he seemed so willing to see the other side of things, and I pride myself on being of that ilk."

"But do not fool yourself that either he or I would ever surrender our basic beliefs without a battle."

Levi could not know how wrong he was.

"You're wrong, Levi, very wrong," I said quietly.

"That's what you think," he replied. "But it wouldn't change anything. It would be in your best interest, my scribe, that Yeshu never comes to Jerusalem. You are a man with a decision to make; I pray you make the right one."

Levi began to walk away.

"But what if he won't listen to me?"

Levi stopped walking, turned, and looked directly at me.

"You knew the answer to that question before you asked it."

~~ 38 ~~

I was able to gather from Levi Yeshu's whereabouts. He told me with no hesitation that Yeshu and his apostles were camped in Galilee, awaiting their sojourn to Jerusalem. I raced home with the news.

Both Flavius and Marcus sat silently as I repeated my conversation with Levi. Marcus spoke first.

"I'm not sure what your superior is up to, but it seems as if he wants you to inform Yeshu."

Father agreed with son. "Levi is brilliant and very dedicated to his faith. He may be attempting, in his way, to ward off what he sees as a dangerous situation. From my view, there's only one thing to do. Tomorrow morning first thing, we ride to Galilee."

And so it was another daybreak ride, but this time four of us rode out. Marcus and Flavius were aboard Flavius' horse, Simon and I aboard mine. Before midday, we were at Yeshu's campsite; again, it had been easy to locate. Unfortunately, he was not the first to see us arrive.

"The Master is very busy, too busy for this…. this collection", Judah said, almost spitting out the words.

He was no match for Flavius. "We will see Yeshu directly."

Judah snarled. "Listen, Centurion, your armor and your decorations mean nothing to me. The Master saved your son, and you may ride with the scribe from Nazareth, but neither gives you pass."

"Please Judah," I implored. "It is really important."

"Why?" Judah demanded. "Is someone else ill? Maybe your Cypriot friend would like to change his skin tone?"

We were saved from any further barrage by the appearance of Miriam herself. I was shocked to see her there.

"They will see my son, Judah." The Iscariot just grumbled as we followed Miriam through the caravan.

Entering his tent, we saw Yeshu lying on a mat, his hands folded behind his head. Staring at the ceiling, he seemed to be in a meditative state. Miriam withdrew. As I grasped her hand, she shook her head; I would have preferred she stayed.

Yeshu arose. "Avi," he embraced me. "And the faithful centurion. You honor me with your presence." Looking at Marcus, he said: "And this of course is…."

"My son, Lord, whom you have saved. This is Marcus."

Marcus ran to Yeshu and embraced him in an almost childlike fashion. His eyes teemed as he said: "You are my Lord; I owe you so much."

"This Son of Man is owed no debt, Marcus. The debt is owed to the God of All Things. It was He, together with your father's faith, which healed you."

Flavius pointed to Simon, who had remained respectively by the entrance to the tent. "And this is my servant Simon, who has heard your word."

Yeshu walked to embrace Simon, who seemed to be embarrassed.

"Many have heard the word, Simon, and yet few have listened; fewer still have understood. Indeed, many of those who have camped with us do not see or hear what their eyes and ears tell them. But come all of you and sit, I can tell that much troubles you."

He needed no supernatural power to discern our fears. It was understood that Flavius would speak for us.

"My Lord," he began, "Avi and Marcus have been acquainted for years. It is through Avi have I heard of you. But yesterday he discovered distressing news. There are forces within the Temple that wish to interfere with your ministry in general and your entrance into Jerusalem in particular. I fear that those forces will use their influence with Rome to cause you great trouble."

Yeshu sat silently listening to the centurion, a sense of melancholy crossing his face. I had seen the same look on Miriam's face months earlier.

Finally, he spoke. "I am warmed by the concern, Flavius, which I know is shared by each of you. But I have spent my entire adult life following the will of Our Father. Many times it was difficult. Many times I prayed that He remove the cup filled with my destiny from me. I also have little doubt that you are correct in your thoughtful assessment of the situation."

"But be assured I fear neither the Sanhedrin nor Rome nor the two of them in unison. Their power to harm is nothing compared to Our Father's power to heal. You know this to be true, Flavius; as does your son."

"At the same time, despite Avi's fears, I have no desire to suffer at either of their hands. I am a man, and as a man, I fear being harmed. But I also knew that this day would come. I am prepared; I am at one with Our Father as to what that destiny will bring."

"But Yeshu," I interjected. With a smile, he silenced me.

"I have broken no Roman law, Avi. If I had, I should

be subject to them. But I have not. As for those in the Sanhedrin, if they cannot hear this Son of God's words, I fear more for their fates than for my own."

"Your nobility and dedication are unquestioned, Lord." This time it was Marcus who spoke. "Both Israel and the gentiles would suffer if your voice was silenced. All we would like you to do is consider the possibility of postponing your entrance into Jerusalem. There will be other Passovers, and in years to come other Jews, gentiles, and pagans to inspire with your words."

"The proud and caring Roman has raised an equally proud and caring son. There is no greater tribute to a man than that his son so mirrors his character. Avi, you have chosen well."

Perhaps with a clarity of vision I had never before had, I said," The choice was made for me, Yeshu. As you said, I just had to see what was right in front of my eyes. And I believe you knew it all along."

Yeshu's brow furrowed. "You have always been unhappy with the way you are, dear friend, and perhaps angry with Our Father. And yet in no small part, because you are the way you are, you sit in front of His son, offering counsel and comfort. Many are the ways of Our Father, and foolish is he who cannot understand them. More foolish are those who deny those ways."

"But you did not come to discuss Avi; nor Marcus nor Flavius. You have come to discuss Yeshu, to warn him of the coming storm. I cannot repay the kindness the four of you have extended; such kindness is beyond compensation. And if I do not heed your warnings, do not think it is because you have failed. Understand that I know the risks of what I am about to do, but I also know the rewards that will come from it."

"And Marcus, don't be discouraged if this Son of Man is silenced. His word has already spread throughout Israel, and even beyond. Like a mustard seed, it has been planted in the firm soil of men's hearts, to spread throughout the land. If I a silenced, my followers will not be."

"There is a clear path Our Father has shown me, and that path leads directly through Jerusalem at Passover, this Passover. You remember, Avi, it was during another Passover years ago that I first heard Our Father's voice. I could not ignore it then; I will not ignore it now."

With an unmistakable air of resignation, Flavius spoke. "It is settled, then?"

"Twice now you have warned me of danger, Flavius. Your faith continues to shine throughout Israel and the Empire. But if the Evil One himself cannot dissuade me, neither can men, whatever their motivation. Yes, it is settled."

Flavius' reply would remain with me to this day.

"When you enter the city, would you do me the honor of dining with us?" It was apparent to all of us that Flavius wanted to remain as close to Yeshu as possible.

"Nothing would give me more pleasure," Yeshu replied "But my followers and I are due at the home of an old friend, whom I suspect is as concerned with my welfare as you are. I owe him my attendance."

"Very well, Lord. At some other time, then?"

Again that look of melancholy crossed Yeshu's face.

"Yes, my friend, some other time."

Yeshu embraced us all warmly, with me being the last to receive his affection.

"You will take care of yourself then, Yeshu?"

"Our Father will take care of me, Avi."

~~ 39 ~~

We were all silent on the way home. But true to form, Flavius' mind had been working; he motioned us to the study immediately after we had dismounted.

"I would like to propose a plan for Passover," he began. Yeshu's insistence of coming to Jerusalem would focus our efforts on that arrival. That was the path Our Father (Flavius actually said those words) had laid out for us. Again, the Temple would be my assignment; the Palace, Marcus'. Flavius would act as a source for any military information and act as the communication conduit; Simon would assist him.

The following morning, we set out on our tasks, as soldiers do approaching their duties. We were resolute, we were determined, and each of us was more than a little frightened. But nothing would happen for two days. I began to suspect (and hope) that Yeshu had heeded our advice. All those hopes were dashed the next day.

Slightly after midday, the object of our concern arrived in Jerusalem. Word had begun to spread that Yeshu was headed to the Temple, accompanied by perhaps one hundred of his followers.

He arrived, the crowd around him seemingly twice that number. He saw me and gave what can only be described as a wry smile.

"Keeping an eye on me, Avi? Worried about what I will do? Don't worry, my friend, all that I do is my Father's bidding."

He allowed me no time to respond. He began to climb the Temple steps rapidly; I fell in with his followers who were trailing directly behind their leader. Suddenly, someone grabbed my arm.

"Do you know what he is going to do?" Judah yelled at me.

"How could I!" I cried. "Don't you?"

"He has said nothing, not even to Peter. But he warned us...."

The Iscariot's words began being drowned out by a cacophony of sounds, all emitting from the first level of the Temple. I ran up the steps to see Yeshu and some of his followers causing a riot among the vendors and the money-changers. He was screaming at the top of his lungs about how a sacrilege was being allowed, calling the vendors a "den of thieves." I had heard it all before, but now Yeshu was shouting it shrilly to everyone. As he walked around, he upset more and more tables; coins were everywhere, and animals meant for sacrifice were running or flying wildly about the campus. It was unlike anything I had ever seen before; unlike anything anyone had ever seen before.

A group of the Sanhedrin heard the clamor and had begun to form on the outer fringes of the melee. Yeshu peered directly at them, screaming:

"The Temple was built so that all nations could worship Our Father. Is this how Israel shows its worship? Is this what the God of all Things wants from his people?"

The priests stood mute, but the vendors certainly did

not. A massive fight broke out between them and Yeshu's gang, a row that he paid no attention to as he continued to peer directly at the priests.

Abruptly, he turned and began to walk down the Temple steps; everybody was screaming at him, many of them using words that would be inappropriate to repeat. All the while Yeshu kept staring at the Temple hierarchy, a look of fierce disgust on his face. They returned the gaze in like manner. As he descended, only a scant few of his followers joined them, many of their numbers still being involved in the fisticuffs.

I tried to follow him as he exited the Temple grounds, but the noise and confusion made it all but impossible. I yelled at him, trying to get his attention, but either he couldn't hear me, or he was ignoring me. I couldn't say at the time which it was; I can't say now which it was. But I would come to rue that I did not make more of an effort.

I had no desire to continue to watch the riot Yeshu had inspired. Instead, I searched wildly for Judah or Peter or James; anyone who could tell me what was going on. I recognized no one as Yeshu's band left the Temple grounds. I began to lap the campus, running spot to spot in a vain search for someone to give me information. Every place I stopped, someone was commenting, most of them unkindly.

I couldn't begin to fathom what Yeshu was trying to accomplish. As quickly as all the fighting had erupted, it was starting to subside. Within an hour the money lenders and vendors would be back at their tables, their Passover profits perhaps diminished, but certainly not eliminated. By the next day, I reasoned, it would be as if the riot had never taken place.

But there was no doubting the effect it had had on the Sanhedrin. The collective look on their faces as Yeshu had descended the steps was menacing and frightening.

I said as much to Simon, whom I saw riding toward the Temple as I stood outside its walls. Neither he nor Flavius had heard of the breakout; Simon was just checking in with me. As he listened to my description, he did not comment but asked some pertinent questions. He said he would immediately inform Flavius and that it was probably best that I remain where I was. The centurion's servant was beginning to take on the same analytical air as his master. We made plans to meet at dusk and ride home together.

I spent the rest of the afternoon vainly searching for any of the apostles on one side, or for Levi on the other. As much as I wanted to see any of Yeshu's followers, it was more crucial, I thought, to get as much information as I could from Levi. But the afternoon ended with my frustration that I could accomplish neither.

Simon and I arrived at our home. Marcus was already there, and he explained that his father had gone to the Palace as soon as Simon had told him about the events at the Temple. Yeshu's outburst had indeed been reported at the Palace; Marcus had heard all about it, to his knowledge, there had been no Roman reaction; but only to his knowledge.

Flavius arrived home an hour later. One look at his face told me of his concern.

"For the first time in a long while, I saw some Jewish leaders at the Palace. Levi was not among them. But they all seemed to be men of some rank. They met with some members of the High Command. Unfortunately, none of them were men I know, so I have no idea what they were discussing. But there's more."

Marcus and I listened attentively.

"Pilate arrived from Caesarea about the same time, and immediately joined the meeting. They met for the rest of the afternoon, Avi; that's not an especially good sign. I have no idea what to make of it, but I think something may happen over the holiday."

Flavius' words terrified me. I knew he would not exaggerate the situation. We spent the evening examining all the possibilities, including a scenario where the Romans would take Yeshu into custody "for his protection." Those words sent a shiver down my spine.

We went to bed, each of us with our thoughts, our concerns. If Yeshu was indeed dining with an old friend that evening, as he said, I hoped he was enjoying himself, I thought almost with rancor; certainly, his old friend from Nazareth was not enjoying himself. I lay on my bed seeking a night of sleep that would never come.

~~ 40 ~~

In the middle of the night, Marcus came rushing into my room.

"Avi, Avi, get up! They've arrested him."

"Arrested him?" I cried incredulously. "For what?"

"Father doesn't know. He's leaving for the Palace immediately and wants us to join him."

It took little time for the three of us to reach the Palace. The streets were deserted; it was past midnight, and most of Jerusalem slept as the drama was unfolding. As soon as we dismounted, Flavius instructed us to wait. Only he was authorized to enter the Palace at this hour.

Only thirty minutes would pass, but it seemed like a year. On this cloud-filled night, if not for the torches lighting the Palace, Marcus and I could scarcely see each other. Roman guards were passing to and fro, but the starless sky hid our presence. If there was anything to be thankful for, it was that, since we could never explain what we were doing there. Especially me.

Marcus and I talked in hush tones incessantly, but I can't remember a word that was said. Our eyes were fixed on the Palace, at the entrance Flavius had used. It was so difficult to see, but I thought I saw a woman who may have been a prostitute using that entrance.

I may not remember anything Marcus said, but I will never forget every word Flavius spoke as he rejoined us.

"Yeshu is before the magistrate. There are allegations of criminal conduct and testimony is being given."

"Testimony about what," I cried. "What can they possibly be accusing him of?"

Flavius insisted that I quiet down; nothing could be gained by calling attention to ourselves. His next words would have the effect of melting my very soul.

"I want the two of you to digest everything I'm about to tell you. No screaming, no dramatics. What I have to say is as difficult for me to say as it will be for you to hear. But there is no choice, and neither is there any time."

Marcus and I stood silent.

"Yeshu was arrested in the Garden of Gethsemane," Flavius began, the difficulty of his words noticeable. He paused.

"They have charged him with being a.... Sodomite."

Marcus and I recoiled in shock and horror. I began to babble incoherently and shook so violently that Marcus held me as tightly as he ever had, Flavius in no uncertain terms ordered me to silence.

"Let me finish, Avi. There is evidence. Yeshu was found with a young man. The young man was naked under a linen cloth that covered him. Someone had led the Roman guards to the exact spot where the two of them were. As the troops approached, the young man jumped up, trying to flee. One of the soldiers grabbed at him, but all the soldier could grasp was the cloth itself. The soldier has given that cloth to the magistrate as evidence. The young man escaped, naked, but Yeshu was still standing there, and the soldiers assumed he and the young man were…together." I had pledged silence, but silence was impossible. I fell to my knees and began to moan. I could hear myself mixing shock, horror, and terror in my words.

"It isn't true, it can't be true," I repeated over and over again.

Marcus held me by the shoulders, he himself weeping, as I tried to control my emotions. But the cascading effect of Flavius' words was overwhelming. I began to tremble violently. If not for the darkness of the night, I would appear to a passerby to be possessed by demons.

"Avi, Avi," Marcus said, "You have to control yourself. Yeshu's life is in danger."

Those words brought me back to my senses. Yeshu's life was indeed in danger; we both knew that the crime of which he was accused was a capital offense under Roman law. Now was not the time to fall apart. I would have to be strong, stronger than I have ever been in my life.

I was able to stand and vocalize the questions forming in my mind.

"Who made the accusations? How did the young man know Yeshu? Who is he? How did the soldiers know where Yeshu was? Flavius, this is just so incredible…..."

"It may be incredible, but it is being sworn to in front of the magistrate. I cannot answer any of your questions, at least not yet. I'm going to return inside, and I want both of you to remain here. When I find out more, we'll have some idea what to do."

With that, he reentered the Palace. While my entire being ached to chase after him, I understood his reasoning.

Marcus spoke rapidly. "It has to be a plot, a plan……someone with enormous influence. And you know what else, Avi? Where are all his followers, his apostles? Why are they not here defending him?"

"I don't know Marcus. I just don't...." My answer was interrupted by the sound of horns approaching from a near distance, piercing the night air. They frightened Marcus and me as we blended further into the darkness.

"It's Pilate!", Marcus gasped.

It was indeed the Roman governor, now marching toward the Palace entrance. He was familiar to Marcus, but I had never seen him before. Pilate appeared to be diminutive, almost dwarfed by his escort.

"Why is he here?" Marcus asked, with resignation.

I was about to begin speculating when I heard a whisper not ten yards behind me.

"Avi, Avi, its James."

I turned to see Yeshu's brother motioning me further into the shadows. I embraced him, and as my eyes adjusted to the deeper darkness, I saw Miriam. I ran to embrace her.

James was first to speak. "I was there when they arrested him, Avi. I ran to get mother. Where are the others?"

I shook my head and saw the disappointment in his eyes.

"I've seen no one, James. I'm only here because of a centurion....

"Yes, I remember him. But Avi, what about Peter, Andrew, Judah, and the rest?"

I shook my head.

"None of them are here, James. Not one."

Miriam approached me. Her eyes, those beautiful penetrating eyes, were filled with a range of emotions I could not begin to comprehend, much less describe.

"Please, Avi, tell me what has happened to my son."

I had to be honest. "He is in Roman custody."

"Oh Avi," she cried, clutching me. We held each

other, neither knowing what to say.

It was Marcus who would vocalize my thoughts.

"James, were you with him tonight?"

"Yes, I was. We had dinner at one of Yeshu's supporter's house. After we ate, Yeshu asked to be left alone with the twelve of us. He was acting so strange, Avi, so eerie. First, he told us someone in the room was going to betray us, and yet another would deny him. None of us believed what happened next. Judah rose and flung his wine glass right at Yeshu. He yelled, 'Tell them who it is, Yeshu! Go ahead. Tell them, tell them now, you sick, sick, blaspheming man'. Then Judah ran from the room."

"Judah," I exclaimed, looking at Marcus.

"We all began to talk, but Yeshu silenced us. He picked up some Passover bread and began breaking it, handing pieces to each of us. Then he poured wine into each of our cups, saying that the bread and wine were his body and blood the blood of a new and everlasting covenant. That's exactly what he said, Avi. It was so confusing to all of us…..."

Miriam sank to her knees as James finished, and buried her head in her hands, "Yeshu," she cried. "My son, my son!."

I knelt to embrace her, but my thoughts were with Levi. Had he been correct? Was Yeshu indeed calling himself the new covenant with the God of All Things?

I continued to hold the trembling Miriam, but James' revelation was causing me to tremble also. Yeshu had set himself above Abraham in his proclamation to his apostles; I began to sense the depth of the Sanhedrin's dismay.

"Are you sure he said those things, James?"

"Yes, Avi, I'm positive. I still don't understand what he meant…."

Suddenly Miriam surprised all of us. Rising to her

feet, she was more controlled than I could have ever imagined. Quietly she spoke:

"Go to the campsite, James, and gather Miriam of Bethany and Miriam of Magalda. I will need both of them."

James sped off into the Jerusalem darkness.

"I must know what will happen to my son, Avi."

"We'll know more when Flavius returns," was all I could think of to say.

"Until he does, will you and Marcus pray with me?" As she said this, she knelt, and Marcus and I joined her. We repeated her words, the prayer Yeshu had taught his followers:

"Our Father, who is in Heaven,
Blessed is Your name.
Your kingdom come, Your will be done,
On Earth, as it is in Heaven.
Give us this day what we require
And forgive us our sins,
As we forgive those, who have sinned against us.
And lead us not into temptation, but deliver us from the Evil One.
For Yours is the kingdom, the power, and the glory,
Now and forever."

~~ 41 ~~

After the prayer, we knelt in awkward silence. Marcus wanted to see me privately.

"Should we tell her about the young man?"

"No!" I replied empathically. "It's all a lie anyway. I know that now for sure. And I know who has orchestrated the entire charade. As soon as we hear from your father, I'm going to leave. There's someone I have to see."

Marcus began to object but was cut short as Flavius emerged from the Palace. His face was drawn and concerned; my deepest fears were about to be confirmed.

"Flavius," I said, but he interrupted me with a wave of his hand. He had seen Miriam and walked directly to her.

"Dearest woman, I don't know…."

"Please, centurion, you once showed faith in my son. I need you now to show the same faith in his mother. The news is…..very bad, isn't it?"

Flavius just nodded, and Miriam fell to her knees, her hands clasped in silent prayer.

The centurion turned to us. "The magistrate has found him guilty of …. the charge. Pilate joined the magistrate in sentencing him to the cross."

Marcus turned away and began sobbing. My response was based on my earlier conclusions. I turned to Flavius and told him the essentials of what James had said. I quickly explained what my next action would be.

"I'm not sure," he said with hesitation. But this time it would be me who was resolute.

"I have no greater respect for any man's judgment than yours, but I must see Levi. He knows exactly what's going on. He's the key, or at least he knows the key."

Flavius responded to my comment with a look of respect.

"I will find Levi" I continued. "In the meantime, Marcus can take Miriam to the outer wall where her friends are waiting for her."

Quietly I asked him when the crucifixion was to begin, referring to the condemned 's walk to Golgotha.

"That's the problem, Avi. It's to begin immediately; they aren't even going to wait until daybreak. Pilate insisted on that part."

The immediacy of the sentence set me back; there was no limit to the Sanhedrin's treachery.

"Then I must leave now."

I approached Miriam. She looked at me, those wondrous eyes pleading for any answer I could provide for her suffering. But I had none, at least not at that moment. I embraced her, turned and mounted my steed.

I galloped to the Temple guessing I would find Levi (and doubtless his cohorts) there. It was less a gallop of hope than it was one of anger. I had never felt such anger in my life, and it satiated my entire being. I had an allegiance to Israel; no matter that I did not agree with all its proscriptions. Marcus was right; in the end, I was a Jew. And now the leaders of my faith were conspiring to commit an atrocity. How could they!

It didn't take long to find Levi.

"What do you want?" he asked as he separated from some men he was speaking with. "Never mind, I know. Your Roman friends have told you what happened. Interesting, my Nazarene friend, you never mentioned the prophet was a degenerate."

"That's a bold face lie, Levi, and you know it. Somebody set this all up; it was all arranged. And it was arranged in this building."

"Set up? What are you talking about? You're so blinded by the heretic that you can't see the truth. Fortunately, older and wiser men can."

I was gaining strength, my anger like a burning cauldron.

"Who did this, Levi? Was it you? Your superiors? The High Priest? Which of you is so poisoned that they came up with this scheme?"

"Me? Are you blaming me? I am just a scribe, like you, Avrum. There is no plot. Your friend was caught in the act. The Sanhedrin has nothing to do with it. It's a Roman matter now."

"You made it a Roman matter" I replied, my voice beginning to rise. "How did you devise this particular fiction? No, let me guess. You couldn't frame him for murder; nobody would have believed you. You couldn't frame him for theft; you know he has no desire for possessions. So you had to pick the one crime that violates the sensibilities of Jew and Roman alike. That 's how it came about, isn't it, Levi?"

His anger and voice level were beginning to match my own. "And what if we did? We are men whose families have suffered for our faith, a faith that the blasphemer was out to destroy. My father died for this faith; my brother taken captive for this faith. The sacred covenant Israel has with the Almighty has been purchased and protected by the blood of its sons. The spirits of those who have died call out for the elimination of this man. By destroying him, we honor our covenant. We honor Israel."

I had never experienced the venom with which Levi spoke to me. I would accomplish nothing continuing in this tone; accomplish nothing by escalating it. I had to soften my approach.

"What about justice, Levi? How can you face the God of All Things, who demands it, and claim you are doing the right thing? 'You will not murder,' isn't that what Moses said?"

"So now you defend the man who tramples over the teachings of Moses by invoking the teachings of Moses. Is that the kind of logic you learned from your friend? Because you certainly did not learn it here."

Levi himself had calmed down. Looking at him, I didn't see a conspiring cadet of the Sanhedrin; I saw a weary old man. Perhaps he had struggled with the decision that had been made.

I was myself becoming weary, as the magnitude of all that was happening enveloped my being. Levi spoke again, in an almost gentle way.

"I know you loved him, Avrum; you have always loved him. It's best you remember the boy Yeshu, even the adolescent Yeshu. Forget the Yeshu that he became."

I shook my head. "You won't silence him, Levi, even by crucifying him. By daybreak, his followers will hear of what you've done; they will storm the Temple and demand he be taken down from the cross."

Levi shook his head. "You have an optimistic opinion of his followers, Avrum. They will hear of the crime of which he is accused; there will be no clamoring."

He bent forward and almost in a whisper said: " Besides, those possibilities have already been prepared for."

I stared at him with a look of despair and

resignation.

"Go to Golgotha, Avrum. Go and make your final peace with your friend. Then forget you ever knew him."

I began to sob, and Levi put his arm around me.

"You have to accept that the Sanhedrin acts for the greater good of Israel. Years from now, when you will need your faith as you approach death, you will appreciate what has been done this Passover."

"That I will never do" I sobbed. "He is innocent; all the other things you say may be true, but it doesn't change that fact. You are committing murder, and his blood will be on the hands of the very Israel you claim to protect."

Levi looked away. "Go to Golgotha; go to your friend. After the …business… is over, return to your position, return to your Romans, return to your life."

He turned to walk away. I was so spent that I could not follow him, so exhausted that I feared I lacked the strength to leave the Temple. I just sat and cried.

Eventually, I did find the strength to leave, not knowing, as I descended the steps of the Temple, that it would be for the last time.

~~ 42 ~~

Through the darkened streets, I galloped to the path the condemned take to Golgotha. I was able to quickly spot Flavius, who had been joined by Simon. Marcus had not yet returned. Flavius greeted me. "He has not passed by yet."

The cobblestone path was deserted. Did no one in Jerusalem know of the travesty that was occurring? Again, where were the apostles? Were they as cowardly as Levi had suggested?

Flavius interrupted my thoughts. "Marcus will bring Miriam and her friends to Golgotha. There is no need for her to see what is happening here. What did you learn from Levi?"

I told him of the conversation, his disappointment evident as I spoke. Perhaps like me, he was hoping against hope that I would accomplish something at the Temple.

"What else could they be planning?" he wondered aloud. We began discussing the possibilities but were interrupted by a string of torches becoming visible in the distance. Flavius held my arm as he warned me:

"Make no movement as they pass, the guards will not tolerate any interference. And Avi, don't be shocked by what you see. I've been on this path before, and you have not. I know it will be hard but maintain your composure. For everybody's sake, including Yeshu's."

But no words of warning could have prepared me for the procession I was about to witness. Eight Roman soldiers, in full battle armor, had formed a moving box around a man I knew to be my childhood friend, who was carrying the crossbar of a crucifix. As the procession neared, I could see him struggling mightily with the large wooden object. Yeshu was being pushed and prodded by the guards, each brandishing a large stick or lash. It was impossible to clearly see Yeshu until the march was directly in front of us. As it approached, vomit began forming in my mouth.

Yeshu was bound with ropes around his midsection, upper thighs and shoulders; walking itself must have been a significant exertion. On his right shoulder rested the crossbow, which was already bloodstained from both previous usage and Yeshu's fresh blood. His entire torso was covered with welts and open wounds, his back a series of marks seemingly attempting to scab, but still bleeding. With every step, a trail of blood was left in its wake.

Although the three of us could scarcely be seen from the road, a glimpse of recognition crossed Yeshu's face as he neared us. Whether from that glance or exhaustion, he fell, the entire weight of the crossbow landing on his back.

I cried and lunged toward the procession, but Simon grabbed me and held me back; the Cypriot was just too strong. Instead, disobeying his command to me, Flavius emerged from the shadows as the guards were about to strike Yeshu.

"There is no need for that," he yelled.

Recognizing the centurion's rank, the soldier who appeared to be in command yelled back, "You take liberties because of your position, centurion. This is none of your affairs, and we have our orders."

"And I will not interfere with them," Flavius replied. "But Rome does not require barbarity, only efficiency, and beating this man is not efficient. You can execute your assignment without doing so."

Either because of the logic of the argument or the superiority of Flavius' rank, the guards collectively lowered their lashes. Yeshu began to rise, slowly, and again he glanced at me, or at least in my direction. I saw fear in my friend's eyes. I saw pain, I saw confusion, I saw resignation, and I saw horror in those eyes, all at the same time. I could only stand mute, my only response a sobbing that came from the inner guttural reaches of my soul. Simon had released his grip, yet I was too weak-kneed to move. My eyes turned to Flavius, pleadingly, but he, with his own resignation, shook his head.

To my astonishment, Simon himself walked directly into the procession. Silently he walked right past the stunned soldiers directly to Yeshu. With a grunt, the Cypriot hoisted the crossbow onto his shoulders.

The guards, acting as one, raised their lashes and sticks, yelling "What's this?" and "Stop that man." But Flavius' voice would drown out the others.

"Stop! This man is my servant, and he is doing my bidding."

I watched in awe as Flavius commanded the guard to let Simon aid the condemned man. Objections about procedures and regulations filled the air, but none of the soldiers made a move. My eyes were riveted to the scene unfolding before me. Simon and Yeshu began walking, the crossbow resting on Simon's shoulders. With his right arm, Simon was holding Yeshu up as the two continued down the path of the condemned. Through it all, despite the taunts of the guards, Simon remained stoic and quiet, possessed of almost a serene dignity. Yeshu was staring at Simon, holding onto him tightly, and crying.

The macabre march was passing ahead of us. Flavius returned to me.

"Quickly! Go to the outer wall and find Marcus. Miriam and her friends should be with him by now. Tell them what has occurred, but do so with a mother's sensibilities in mind. I will ride directly to Golgotha. The commander of the execution is Leonitis, a man who is known to me."

"Above all, Avi, be careful."

He needn't have reminded me of that necessity. I was still a Jew, riding in the middle of the night through Jerusalem. Flavius handed me one of his insignias. If I were stopped, I would claim I was on business for the centurion.

I reached the outer wall and after a short while was able to locate Marcus, James, and the three Miriams. Flavius had calculated the execution procession would take thirty minutes to reach Golgotha and begin the ascent up Calvary Hill. I delayed the group, wishing to spare Yeshu's mother any unnecessary suffering. I had brought Simon's horse with me so that we all could travel on horseback.

And so we rode, Marcus and James in the lead, the two Miriams in the middle, and Yeshu's mother and I in the rear. We were all silent on the journey, sensing the tragedy in which we were about to play a part.

~~ 43 ~~

And yet I rode with hope, hope that Yeshu could still be saved. If Flavius was correct, we had about thirty-six hours before Yeshu's body suffered irreparable damage. With dawn approaching over the far horizon, the Romans (and Sanhedrin) would be forced to carry out their travesty of justice in broad daylight. And that I felt they wouldn't be able to do. I hoped against hope news of the crucifixion would reach Yeshu's followers at daybreak.

We met Flavius at the base of Calvary. Though the erected crucifix could be seen from that point, the early morning haze prevented witnessing any detail. Flavius wanted Marcus and me to wait, as he conferred with the three Miriams. I knew he would be gentle with his description of what they were about to see, but that could scarcely lessen the horror.

Returning, he spoke to Marcus and me. Simon had indeed carried the crossbow the length of the journey to Golgotha, surrendering it only when the guards forced him to, on top of Calvary. The soldiers then fastened Yeshu too the cross and hoisted it between two other crucifixes. Leonitis, the man Flavius had said was the commander of the execution squad, told him that it was all very routine. Still, Leonitis was also aware of the strange hour and had taken the precaution of posting additional guards around Calvary, in anticipation of daybreak. Perhaps he too was thinking of what might happen if Jerusalem discovered what was happening on a nearby hill.

We began our ascent. As we climbed, Yeshu became more and more visible with each step. Miriam began trembling, and as we advanced, it became more pronounced. We arrived about fifty feet from the cross itself; the soldiers would let us no closer.

Matched against the lightening sky, Yeshu looked eerily peaceful. Flavius had warned us not to be fooled; the condemned, having endured the beatings and horrific march to Golgotha, often felt relieved when the execution preamble was completed. And the Jerusalem sun had not yet risen to exacerbate the pain of the inflicted wounds.

We need only to look at the other two condemned men to see a preview of Yeshu's fate. Both had already succumbed to delirium (I later discovered both were in their third day), caused by exposure and lack of water. They were babbling incoherently to each other and to Yeshu; it was impossible to make any sense of what they were saying.

Flavius had correctly anticipated one other detail. The other men were apparently Roman criminals, allowed the final dignity of a loincloth. Yeshu had been entirely stripped, and was naked, his Jewish-ness exposed for all to see.

We gathered in the area specified by the guards. Miriam and James fell immediately to their knees, the two Miriams flanking them. Flavius, Simon and I stood a few feet behind them. Either because of the hour or that the others apparently had no families, we were the only onlookers. Where again were all of Yeshu's followers, his apostles, his chosen ones?

Yeshu looked directly in our direction, his face an array of confused emotions. "Mother....... James...." he rasped; the words themselves seemed to require a Herculean effort. Then, with an almost childlike innocence, he said: "Momma, I'm sorry, I'm so sorry......" Miriam's friends had to hold her as she collapsed under the strain of her anguish.

He then peered past them, his eyes settling on the four of us; he looked almost quizzical; I believe he was trying to mouth our names, but the effort was futile.

Suddenly Yeshu's body began to tremble and spasm, pushing against the ropes that held him to the cross; the momentary peacefulness that we had witnessed was now replaced with great anguish. The crucifix literally shook from the force of that anguish. In a loud guttural voice, Yeshu yelled out: "My God, My God, Why? Why have you forsaken me?"

The lament rang out through the early dawn mist; all of us, including the soldiers, were startled by the cry. Then, just as suddenly, his body came to a rest. His head drooped, saliva falling freely from his mouth. Shaking his head again, as if to free himself from a daze, his eyes looked at the rising sun, as he said: "My Father, forgive them, for they know not what they do."

`The two pronouncements, said so close to each other, unsettled every witness. Flavius stood in the middle of our gathering.

"Remember, he's lost a lot of blood, and is in shock; he may not realize what he is saying."

A certain lucidity seemed to return to Yeshu's eyes as he looked directly at Miriam and James, now huddled on the ground beneath him. "Mother," he said, "behold your son; James, behold your mother." Instantly I was reminded of the circumstances of James' birth, as they had been recounted to me, especially the death of his natural mother Agatha in childbirth. Just as instantly, I witnessed perhaps the last miracle Yeshu would perform, eliminating the chasm that had existed between Miriam and James. It had never been overt, that chasm, but everyone always knew it was there. Now, Yeshu had closed it.

For what seemed to be an eternity, Yeshu stared out over the landscape. It was as if he was a newborn, seeing the world for the first time. The beauty of the Jerusalem sunrise framed the sickening scene of two men almost dead, a third beginning to die. I looked at Miriam and James as they clung to each other. And at the two Miriams; what deep devotion they had to Yeshu and his family. Behind me, tears formed in my eyes as Flavius, Marcus and Simon knelt, solemnly reciting Yeshu's prayer. The entire scene could only be described as bizarrely beautiful.

But all my reveries would be shaken by the sudden appearance of a horseman cloaked in Roman garb. Riding directly to the crucifix, he withdrew a sword and announced in a large voice: "This man, if that's what he was, has suffered enough." As soon as Flavius heard those words, he leaped up, shouting "No! No! No!" as he ran to the cross. But he would be too late. The horseman had plunged his sword directly into Yeshu's chest, piercing his heart. As he withdrew the sword, fresh blood gushed from Yeshu's chest cavity, a bright red river that showed through the haze.

As quickly as he had appeared, the horseman galloped off. Only the onrushing Flavius stood between the executioner and his escape. As Flavius neared him, the horseman kicked the centurion, sending him sprawling to the ground. In a heartbeat, the murderer had gotten away.

Within seconds, Calvary turned into bedlam. Marcus raced to his fallen father; I followed, my sandals making a sickening sound as they trudged through Yeshu's freshly spilled blood. Flavius was screaming "Stop him!" as Marcus and I helped him stand. Leonitis had already mounted his steed, waving at some other soldiers to follow him, as he pursued the executioner.

Yeshu was writhing, gasping for breath, the ropes that bound him twisting and turning as his body contorted on the cross. His skin turned a hideous shade of ashen pale; his face turned toward the sky, and with a final gasp, he cried "It is finished."

~~ 44 ~~

Miriam hugged the cross as the blood of her only son pelted upon her. She moaned Yeshu's name over and over again, punctuating her sobs with, "As Our Father knows, I loved you as much as any mother ever loved her son." The other two Miriams, themselves in tears, hugged her tightly. Flavius walked toward them and suddenly stopped. Dropping to his knees, he said in a voice that rang throughout Calvary Hill, "Truly this was the Son of the Almighty." Arising, he embraced the mother of that son.

Within minutes, the sun broke through the haze and shown directly on my fallen comrade's face. No artist could paint the scene, utterly tragic yet utterly magnificent at the same time.

But the seemingly endless chain of bizarre events hadn't yet ended. We were jolted by the sight of four Roman soldiers, who silently had placed ladders on either side of the crucifix. Climbing to the top, they began to unfasten Yeshu.

"What are you doing?" cried Flavius. "By whose authority…..."

"Captain Leonitis has warned us that you might try to interfere. We have our orders, centurion, to remove this man from his cross. Preparations have already been made."

"Orders from whom?" Flavius replied angrily. "What preparations?"

"It's none of your concern," was the answer. "You will step back and let us proceed, or you will be reported to your superior."

Marcus and I rushed to Flavius' side. What could be happening? Yeshu was barely cold, yet the soldiers were removing him from the cross. That was in direct contradiction to Roman custom.

"Out of the way, Centurion; your friends too, especially the Jews. Do you want them to appear before the magistrate?"

We knew this was no idle threat. Interfering with an execution was itself a capital offense. The guard ushered us all back to where we were standing.

Suddenly a new face emerged from the shadows. I immediately recognized him. Yusuf of Arithmethia was an influential member of the Sanhedrin and a leader of the conservative Sadducees.

"I know you!" I cried.

"And I know you. You're Levi's assistant and a friend to the executed heretic. Kindly ask your friends not to interfere. We are doing what is best for all concerned. I own a small burial crypt, not a half mile from here. I offer it now to his mother for the proper burial of her son."

Miriam stood silently at the offer Yusuf had made. I was convinced that in her condition, she could not appreciate what was evident to Flavius, Marcus and I. This was apparently the Sanhedrin's attempt at assuring Yeshu would be forgotten much quicker than other executed Jews. They had made him disappear. Now they wanted to do the same with his memory.

"Wait!" I cried out. "Wait! Miriam, this man offers

you no service. It's another trick."

Yusuf looked at me menacingly. "Let the woman decide for herself, scribe. She is his mother." Turning to Miriam, he said: "It is either he is buried in the crypt I have purchased, or he is left to rot with the remains of others in the pit on the other side of Golgotha. Surely you do not want your son's final resting place to be in such a dreadful place."

It was Miriam of Magalda who answered.

"You would not even allow us to anoint the body?"

"Of course you may anoint him. But you all have suffered enough this night. Let me entomb her son. There will be time for anointing later."

I began to object when Miriam grasped my arm. "No, Avi, I appreciate what you are saying, but this man offers me a kindness, a gift that I am prepared to accept."

"Kindness," I replied incredulously. "Gift? This isn't either. This man is a lackey for Yeshu's enemies. They mean to hide Yeshu."

"Watch your tongue, scribe," Yusuf spat back. "Who are you to even express an opinion on the matter. She has made her decision; pay it the respect it deserves."

He neared me and said in a voice close to a whisper: "Besides, Avrum of Nazareth, we all know of your relationship to the man, and some of your other curious associations. It's best for you if no one thinks of you and the heretic in the same manner."

No remark I had heard during those terrible days would focus my plight more than that one. My friend had just been grossly executed for a crime of which he was not guilty. But I was. If the Sanhedrin had enough power to end the life of a popular preacher, it would be little trouble to dispatch an unknown scribe.

"You won't get away with it, you know," I gathered

enough courage to say. "News of what you have done will spread throughout Palestine. Israel will demand answers."

The Arimethean smiled. "Levi told me you were a naïve fool; he understated that part of you. We will give Israel all the answers it needs. The heretic's words will soon be forgotten. He will be forgotten. Nothing that has happened this Passover will ever affect anything. It cannot. For it is we who are Israel."

I had never before struck a human being in my life, but the urge to throttle this sanctimonious Sanhedrin flowed through my veins. Sensing this, Flavius pulled me aside.

"Avi, we need to speak to Miriam." We walked away from the now-smiling Arithmathean.

"There will be time for retribution for those who are responsible for this," Flavius said quietly. "For now, your friend's mother is in great grief. She deserves our attention."

Grudgingly I had to admit he was right. Nothing would be gained and perhaps much lost by attacking Yusuf, as much as I desired it. But Miriam did need our help. Flavius also added in a sardonic tone: "He is an old man, surrounded by protectors. There will be another time."

The Romans had finished removing Yeshu's body from the cross and had at least the decency to cover his body with a sheet of linen. It was further evidence of the Sanhedrin's treachery. Even the funeral procession would be a well-orchestrated travesty. I looked at Yeshu's body. Less than a day before he had been violently attacking the money lenders at the Temple. He was alive, vibrant, consumed by a spirit of righteousness. Now his bruised and battered corpse lay beneath my feet. I cried deeply.

Yusuf's servants carried Yeshu the distance to

Yusuf's tomb with Yeshu's mourners in their wake. The tomb itself had been hallowed out of rock with a small entrance covered by a massive stone. The servants rolled back the stone, revealing a small room where Yeshu's body would lay. They wanted to make quick work of it, telling us we could enter the crypt to pay our final respects, but to do so quickly.

Miriam entered first, supported by her friends and James. The rest of us would wait for them to finish. I worried about my reaction as I would see my life-long friend for the last time. In the end, it was weariness and depression that overtook me. I knelt in front of the shroud-covered corpse, crying. I kissed him, sadly with more emotion than I had ever kissed him my entire life; I was always so stupidly worried. But this kiss was long and fervent, as I knew, in regret, the others should have been. Marcus held onto me as I rose and exited the tomb, my knees quivering and my entire body trembling.

In the last of the strange events of the night, two soldiers arrived. As Yusuf's servants rolled back the stone to close the crypt, they explained to Flavius that they thought it was prudent for them to guard the tomb in order to "protect" Yeshu's body. Flavius scoffed at their explanation.

The business of the burial done, Miriam invited us to her tent, an invitation we respectfully declined. I believe she was relieved we did so. We would all visit her later, but she deserved her privacy, and in reality, we were all utterly exhausted. We provided transportation to the three Miriams and James and then headed for home.

A mere eighteen hours had changed my entire life. Left to be seen was the effect those hours would have on others.

~~ 45 ~~

None of us would sleep comfortably, me less than the others. Images of my entire life morphed into images from the night before; bizarre twists of time and space, where I'd be talking to my mother and father (who were both physically there), at the base of Yeshu's crucifix. Even after those times, I did doze, I awoke in cold, clammy sweat, complete with a sense of impending doom.

Dusk brought Marcus into my room; I could tell at once he also had slept very little. We had little time to talk, however; he told me I had a visitor waiting for me in the courtyard. Shaking his head, Marcus said Levi was waiting for me.

I was quickly reminded of my supervisor's friendship with Flavius; the two shared a table, a flask of wine opened between them. Flavius motioned to the wine, but I had no interest. As Marcus joined us, Flavius began to speak.

"Before you say anything, Avi, Levi has come here as an act of kindness, not ridicule. Please hear what he has to say."

"Kindness!" I spat. "There was certainly a lot of kindness last night, wasn't there, Levi? Oh great scribe, tell me, how many high Priests does it take to trample the Seventh Commandment?"

I expected Levi to react in anger; instead, he listened to my diatribe with a dismissive air. "I didn't come to discuss yesterday, Avrum, but today and tomorrow. Nor to discuss Yeshu of Nazareth, but Avrum of Nazareth. What has been has been. What had to be done was done. And the Sanhedrin broke no Commandment. Your friend was executed by the Romans, for violation of Roman law."

"But I am a respectful man, as you know. If you wish me to leave, I will do so."

Flavius shot me a look of disapproval; he wanted me to hear Levi out. Marcus grasped my arm as if to ally himself with his father. I repressed my desire to ask Levi to leave. "Have your say then, and be on your way."

"I spoke to Yusuf of Arithmethea," Levi began, " about your conduct. He is a rich and influential man, not given to suffering the insults of someone in your position. He feels it would be, to quote him exactly, 'uncomfortable' for you to continue at the Temple for the present."

If I was physically able to suffer shock at the moment, I might have. As it was, I was incredibly stunned.

"So I am no longer your assistant? Can't I work at the Temple anymore?"

"You are still my assistant; you are still employed at the Temple. But I think it's best for you to leave for a while. You certainly have cause; you have suffered a great loss. It would not be uncommon given the circumstances."

"Out of the Temple for a while...." I said with resignation.

"Out of Jerusalem entirely, I would think, would be even better. Your presence here can do no one, especially yourself, any good. And your presence at the Temple could do you much harm."

"You want me to go away, like Yeshu; that's it, isn't it Levi. Out of sight, out of mind?"

"Curb your sarcasm, young scribe; you are not that important. You may return to Jerusalem, to the Temple, to your position, to the splendor of your generous host, and the companionship of his son. But an interval would be wise, and is best started immediately."

I rose from the table and paced the room. This wasn't even a suggestion; it was a command.

"And if I don't?"

"I prefer not to think of that. Given your nature, your native village, and your friendship with the executed heretic, you would be under suspicion. To use Yusuf's word, it would be 'uncomfortable.'"

"Because of my nature, Levi? Have your years at the Temple made it impossible to speak frankly?"

Levi sipped some wine. "Your youth continues to betray you. I am going to allow for that. You overstate my concern with your nature; you are not the first of your kind, you will not be the last. You chose to follow a certain path; it is for the God of All Things to determine the consequences of that choice, not I."

Marcus surprised me by speaking up. "There is no choice in the matter, Levi. A man such of you knows this to be true", he said wearily.

Levi paused thoughtfully; he appeared to appreciate the interruption.

"Your point is made Marcus, and it is a sound one. But the Almighty gives us guidelines; I can only live by them."

With that, Levi rose. "But it is not a discussion for today. I came here whatever you may think in friendship. You are a free man, do what you will. If you decide to stay, I will see you after Passover. If not, Flavius can inform me when you return. Either way, Avrum, believe it or not, I do wish you well."

Flavius escorted him to the gate, the two of them speaking in hushed tones as they walked. The bottle of wine suddenly grew in appeal; I poured myself a generous portion.

Returning, Flavius did likewise. "I'd like to discuss what Levi had to say, if it's all right, Avi."

Marcus spoke up. "You can't agree with Levi, father."

"Whether I agree or disagree is not the issue, son. I've known the man for a long time; he would not come here to speak idly. I believe Avi will have a difficult time if he returns right now to the Temple. I can't see the harm in taking a few days away. If it's a matter of finances, Avi…..."

Marcus interrupted with a thought that hadn't occurred to me. "Does this have anything to do with me, father? Are you concerned about what would happen to me because of Avi?"

Flavius' sheer honesty showed in his answer. "I will not deny that aspect of my agreeing with Levi, Marcus. If I owe you an apology for that Avi, I offer it. But it is far from my main consideration."

Earnestly, I answered, "You owe me no apology, sir. The heavens could not repay the kindness you have shown me. If it is your wish that I do as Levi has suggested, I will do so, and without reservation."

The centurion answered me with an embrace. "You have been a friend and so much more to me, Avi, in addition to what you have meant to my son. My only wish is that you do what is best for you. I am of course by your side no matter what you decide to do."

We sat quietly for a while, father and son respecting

my need for precisely that. I told them I would see no harm comes to either of them and that I understood that harm could indeed come to them. Because of me. I would follow Levi's suggestion; in fact, I would leave at the next daybreak.

"I want to go with you" Marcus aid suddenly.

I found the strength to chuckle. "I will be returning to Nazareth; how exactly would I explain you? My Roman servant, perhaps?"

The tense situation had been erased. I repaired to my room to make preparations. Marcus would come in to talk, as would Flavius. To my surprise, Nilsa and Simon and other servants would also. Flavius' description of us as a family ran through my mind; in many ways, I felt closer to all of them than I ever had,

I needed to rest; I would leave at daybreak, to avoid the crowds exiting Jerusalem as Passover ended. But I had a stop to make, a commitment to honor.

~~ 46 ~~

Intentionally I rode to a spot about a mile from the Temple. Walking my horse through the streets of Jerusalem at Passover, I knew that I would blend in unnoticed, in the crowd. I wanted to hear if anyone was speaking of Yeshu. Whenever I heard his name or any reference to a Nazarene preacher, or to a crucifixion, I made it a point to listen.

Most of the comments disheartened me. Many had not even heard of the events of the past two days. Some were expecting to hear Yeshu speak at the Temple.

But a few had heard, although their knowledge was either incomplete or worse, entirely in error. He had been arrested, some said, not knowing any other details. Some thought he had fled to Nazareth after his arrest. One man claimed with certainty that Yeshu had been detained by the Sanhedrin and scared into leaving the city. "He's held up in some cave somewhere with those nutty friends of his." Another remarked, "I heard he is a Sodomite," to which the first replied, "That doesn't surprise me at all."

Those who claimed knowledge of the crucifixion

were mostly ignored. An elderly man scoffed when someone spoke of it. "That's nonsense. Only two men are hanging at Calvary, and neither is a Jew. The whole crucifixion story was made up by his followers. They're trying to make a martyr out of him." A woman, apparently the man's wife, said, "Perhaps then we can hear him speak. I've heard he preaches that men and women are equal in the eyes of the God of All Things."

"That's because he does with men what most men do with women," her husband retorted. With sadness, I noted that the people around them were laughing.

Leaving the crowds, I felt that the Sanhedrin had won. They had accomplished every last thing they had intended to do. They had removed Yeshu from the scene, his disappearance bathed in ignorance, half-truths, and innuendo. The words of Levi and Yusuf the Arithmithean resonated through my mind as I rode to visit Miriam.

I was surprised to find her alone. She explained that James and her two friends were purchasing oils with which to anoint her son's body. Again, none of Yeshu's followers were anywhere to be found. Miriam was forced to mourn in solitude.

I would not make matters worse by describing what I had heard in the streets. Instead, we talked of her son and our individual relationship to him. At times we smiled, at times we cried. As we spoke of the horrible night that had just passed, I wanted Miriam to know what I had discovered from Levi, and so I recounted the conversation I had with him.

"Your friendship with my son has cost you, Avi."

Before I could object, she continued. "I know you loved him. You always did, even in our days in Nazareth. You have always accepted the cost of that love. That is what the God of All Things requires, to accept the sufferings in our lives in this world. But there is a reason for that suffering. The glory of the kingdom of Our Father will result from them. Yeshu often told me that the wine earned from our labor is sweeter than that which is given at no cost."

My mind raced back to the night, so many years ago, that Miriam had lost her beloved husband, Yusuf. Truly the God of All Things had, in Miriam, His most obedient servant.

'But this news of your leaving upsets me", she continued. "Are you sure it's the right course?"

I answered with a strong affirmative. "It's the right course. Best for me, best for those dearest to me, maybe even best for the Temple. I'm so sickened by what has happened, the very smell of Jerusalem makes me ill. I can use this time away, especially from those I work with. Yeshu would want me to forgive them, even pray for them. But I cannot, and I will not. They should be the ones crucified...."

Miriam stared at me, thoughtfully.

"So you would answer the violence done to my son with a violence of your own? How then would you expect them to respond?"

I had to make the admission. "With more violence, I suppose."

Miriam nodded her head.

"But there has to be justice, Miriam; justice for Yeshu, and justice for his murderers."

"Our Father has not given this mourning mother of a wrongly executed son the wisdom to determine that," she responded with resignation. With a smile, she added, "Perhaps He reserves that ability for scribes."

I was forced to myself smile, despite the solemnity of the occasion. But that solemnity framed my next remark.

"I cannot forgive them, Miriam. And I can't believe that you do."

"No, I do not, Avi, I definitely do not. If vengeance could easily be had, I would demand it. That is why I remain imperfect before Our Father and imperfect before myself. Yeshu was my son; I believe he preached the truth. That doesn't mean I don't struggle with it. I am that human."

"Whatever your son preached, he was wonderful, Miriam," I said, my tears returning. "No matter what else, he was wonderful."

An appreciative smile crossed her face, and she embraced me. With that embrace, I sensed our conversation was ending. I wanted to know about her plans.

"Will you also be returning to Nazareth?" I asked hopefully.

"I cannot say, Avi. After they anoint my son's body, both Miriams have invited me to their respective homes. They have been so dear to me. I don't know how I would have survived without them. So I will go to Bethany for a while, and then to Magalda. After that, I really can't say......"

"I need to celebrate Yeshu's life more than I mourn his death. They will help me do just that."

"If you ever return to Jerusalem," I said, "and I will understand if you don't, please find me," I stuttered. "I want you to know that after my mother passed......"

"I did nothing for you and your father that Rachel would not have done for Yeshu and Yusuf. That is how Our Father arranges it, Avi. What we need is always close at hand, we just need to see it."

Again we embraced, and we said our farewells. Her son may or may not have been the Messiah or the Son of God. But the mother was uniquely touched by that God. Miriam was blessed within the world the God of All Things had made.

Leaving Miriam's tent, I saw James approaching. He

greeted me warmly and walked me to my horse.

"His disciples, the apostles, they have not come?" I asked.

James shook his head. "I don't understand it, Avi. I don't. Not even Simon Peter. I'm so discouraged."

I looked at him knowingly. If justice was due to the Sanhedrin, it was also due to Yeshu's chosen ones. Their crime of desertion was, in my mind, equally hideous. How could they leave their Master, his brother, and especially his mother? It was inexcusable.

But I said nothing of this to James. He had enough on his mind. I explained, in general detail, my sojourn back to Nazareth and asked what his future would hold.

"I will be with my mother," he said with an air of loving pride. Yeshu's proclamation from his cross had worked, and I had no doubt James would be as devoted to Miriam as Yeshu had been.

I said goodbye to James and climbed aboard my steed. I did not know if I would ever see either of them again. I vowed to myself to make every attempt. Each in their way carried a piece of Yeshu's spirit; each in their way was magnificent.

But it would be that last time I saw them together, the last time I would see one of them at all.

~~ 47 ~~

I was successful in avoiding the Nazarenes returning from Jerusalem. Between the early hour and the circuitous route I took, I saw no one on my journey. I spent my nights under the stars, nights filled with the bizarre dreams that had filled my last few days. But remarkably, they were less frightening, less horrifying. It seemed that the more miles I put between Jerusalem and myself, my general state improved.

I arrived at the outskirts of my native village not sure of where I would go. I would see Sophia, certainly; moreover, I wanted to see her, perhaps even needed to see her. Beyond that, I had no idea how I would spend my time in Nazareth.

Our reunion was joyous. I had indeed missed her and sensed that she had missed me. One of the questions about my return home was quickly answered; Sophia would not hear of my spending my nights anywhere but in my former house (which of course was now her home). "You will sleep in your bed, Avi; nowhere else. This is still your home."

And sleep in my bed I would, more fitfully than I

had slept in days. My dreams were no longer nightmarish; indeed, most were harmless, focused more on Marcus and my love for him than of the horrific week I had just spent. For the first time in what seemed to be an eternity (though it was in fact only five days), I awoke refreshed.

Over the morning meal the next day, I began to open up to Sophia about what had happened. Until then she had not pried, I had not volunteered. While sidestepping many of the particulars (especially Marcus), I explained my need to leave Jerusalem based solely on my friendship with Yeshu. A hint of understanding and recognition crossed her face when I mentioned the crime of which Yeshu had been accused. I appreciated that she did not pursue the matter.

Perhaps because of the relaxing nature of the day (in truth, I did nothing but lounge around in the backyard area), I decided I would pursue it myself. After the evening meal, Sophia and I sat, speaking of father.

"It's fitting that we do, Avi," she said. "Many nights he and I would sit here and speak of little but you."

I smiled. "Naturally, I'm more than a little curious about what he had to say."

She sat silent for a while and then spoke. "He felt guilty, I think."

"Guilty?" I asked. That surprised me.

"There's a part of you that you have always kept to yourself, Avi. He felt guilty that you did not feel he was the kind of father you could confide in."

It was my turn to remain silent, and appreciate my guilt in the matter.

"He always suspected that was the reason you left Nazareth," she continued; "to find more like yourself and live your life privately. It may shock you, Avi, but he was ultimately happy you had made that decision. He did confess to me that originally he thought Yeshu was responsible for the way you felt. By leaving Nazareth, you'd be leaving the grip Yeshu had on you."

"But he came to understand that Yeshu had little to do with it. He came to respect your decision even more. He said:' I have raised a son capable of making his own decisions, and accepting the consequences of those decisions, without concern for the opinions of others. That independence is a son's greatest gift to his father'."

I sat shaking my head. I was disappointed, disappointed with my self for my lack of perception. I had been so immersed in my struggles at the time; I had neglected the man who could have and would have, helped me with those struggles. Yeshu was right about one thing, I mused; the answer is so often right in front of us.

Sophia spoke of father most of the night. She spoke chiefly about how father admitted to her that while she could never replace Rachel in his heart, she had added tremendously to that life. He could not forget Rachel, but couldn't let her memory interfere with his and Sophia's love. Sophia was satisfied that it never did; in this, she found great comfort.

By the end of the night, I realized that in Sophia I had found an extraordinary friend.

But it was an old friend who would shock me from the comfort I had achieved in Nazareth. The next day at the well, musing over the revelations of the night before. I heard someone shouting my name. It was Ephraim, whom I had not seen since father's death.

We embraced and got caught up in each other' lives. He resided now in Sephoria; he had found the glamour of the capital city much more to his liking than the simplicity of Nazareth. He was five timed married; I lost track of how many had ended in divorce or widowhood. I was also confused by the various children he had, and by whom; Ephraim had led a hectic life.

But all of that would pale in comparison when he told me that he had just returned from Jerusalem.

"I know you have seen Yeshu over the years," he said; "I assume you know what happened to him."

I had no idea which story Ephraim had heard, so I pressed him for more information. He had the story mostly right less a detail here and there. Most importantly, he knew of the crucifixion.

"But he is not dead, Avi."

I could not have been more startled. "What do you mean, not dead?"

"Some of his friends went to his tomb, and he was gone."

"Gone! What are you talking about?" I cried. What do you mean he was gone?"

"Not only gone from the tomb, but some of those followers claim that he has appeared to them. They say that there is no doubt that he is alive."

"Ephraim, Ephraim, please tell me you are exaggerating. You know how people get…….."

"Give me a little credit, Avi... Yes, I know the way people can get; with the life I've led, how could how could I not know the way people get. And I tell you that many are claiming they have seen Yeshu, raised from the dead."

Sinai could not have held the sheer number of thoughts racing through my mind. Risen from the dead? Jewish folklore was rife with stories of those who had died and lived again, either to do wonderful things or nefarious ones.

And testimony from his followers? Who, the same ones who had deserted their Master in his greatest time of need? Was all this talk of resurrection just the result of the collective guilt they must feel?

The questions continued forming in my mind even as I kept talking to Ephraim, and for a long while after he departed. One thing was sure; I could answer none of them in Nazareth. My sojourn had lasted far less than I had anticipated, and might not have accomplished entirely what it was designed to do. But if I was confident of anything in the universe that spring evening, it was that I must immediately return to Jerusalem.

Sophia's surprise and disappointment were both evident and gave me pause. Briefly, I explained my reasons.

"It sounds fantastic, Avi, but so much of Yeshu's life bordered on the fantastic. I'm disappointed, but I understand. I wish you well, but above all, I wish you care, care for your well being. Please promise me you'll watch out for yourself."

There was a tear forming in her eye as she talked. We embraced warmly, as two people who love each other do.

I left Nazareth within two hours of my conversation with Ephraim; there would be no circuitous route this time; I rode as fast as my horse would carry me. It was early morning when I arrived in the city, daybreak when I arrived home.

I was in shock over what Ephraim had told me. But the greater shock awaited me as I walked into the house.

~~ 48 ~~

Marcus saw me walk in and his jaw dropped.

"Avi, what are you doing here?"

"I had to come back, as soon as I heard......"

"You heard?" he asked with astonishment. "How could you have heard?"

"Ephraim, a childhood friend, had just returned from here. When he told me about the resurrection I had to come back immediately."

A look of understanding and a particular look of relief crossed my lover's face. "Oh, the resurrection! As far as that goes, everyone's pretty convinced somebody stole Yeshu's body. Father thinks it was the Sanhedrin, a continuation of their deception about Yeshu. I think it was his followers. But I'm leaving myself pretty open; he may have indeed risen."

"Oh, Marcus, that's so fantastic......"

"Not half as fantastic as what I have to tell you, my love. Something has happened with father. If you hadn't come, Simon was going to ride to Nazareth to try and find you."

"Is something wrong?" I asked fearfully.

"No, nothing like that. In fact, it's wondrous news. Father has been recalled to Rome. He has been promoted and will join the Palace Guard, the direct protectors of Caesar. It's a tremendous honor."

Now it was my jaw that dropped. "Rome!" I exclaimed. "You're going to Rome?" I couldn't even consider the possibility that Marcus would stay in Jerusalem.

"I have to, Avi. I'm all that he has….."

"And before you ask, you're coming too. I don't think either father or I ever thought you wouldn't. Of course, it's your choice…."

"Oh, Marcus!" I cried, "How could I ever be separated from you. But it's all so ……"

"Sudden, my love? I know that. And there isn't much time. It's been ordered that father is on board when a ship leaves Caesarea in six days. There's so much to do."

"Six days! That's no time at all. Can't he get more time to prepare?"

He laughed at my innocence. "This isn't a pleasure cruise, Avi. If they ordered father to leave tonight, he would have to be ready. It's not a matter of discussion in the Roman army."

I too laughed at my naiveté. "That was pretty dumb of me, I know. But Marcus, this is all happening too fast; I wanted to find out what happened to Yeshu."

"We'll find out Avi, and we'll find out before we leave, even if we don't sleep for the next six days. But take a moment. We're asking you to make a huge transition here. Father thinks it's best that you take a day or two to decide."

I answered my companion as honestly as I had ever answered anyone. "I don't need a minute. When you and your father set sail for Rome, I will be with you."

Marcus leaped into my arms. At that exact moment,

Nilsa entered the room. If I needed any further reason to follow my lover wherever he went, it was provided by the reaction we three had simultaneously. We all broke out in laughter.

"I will be cooking for Avi, then?" Nilsa asked with a smile.

"Yes, Nilsa, yes," Marcus said with a wide grin. "He's coming with us, as are most of the others. Only Simon remains undecided."

I could have easily predicted that. Especially with the possibility, however slim, that Yeshu was still alive. It made all the sense in the world.

Within an hour, Marcus described all of the preparations that had been made. Flavius had sold the house to another centurion, and a variety of farewells had been planned. Flavius would have three days to get 'settled' once we arrived in Rome, but after that, he would become a member (and a high ranking one at that) of the Imperial Roman Guard.

The subject of that honor arrived home. I didn't know exactly what to say, so I stood up and began applauding the man who had made so many good things possible in my life. He smiled appreciatively and embraced me. His first words warmed my soul.

"You are joining us, then?" and I nodded.

"That gives me great pleasure, Avi, it truly does."

We sat down with wine to discuss the practicalities. "I have to tell you, Avi that with this new position comes further scrutiny. We'll have to maintain the fiction that you are my servant."

A sense of melancholy crossed my spirit. Would there ever be a time and place where those like Marcus and I could live in public as we did in private?

"I will do what needs to be done," I responded.

We planned the next few days. I couldn't leave Palestine, most likely for forever, without telling Sophia.

I would return to Nazareth for a day. The rest of the time I would help the household with the transition. And of course, investigate the rumors about Yeshu.

"Will you see Levi?" Flavius asked earnestly

Shaking my head, I said, "No. I will not. I owe him much, and. I do not deny it. But I cannot forgive him for whatever role he played in the murder."

"If it was a murder," Marcus chipped in. "Any further news, father?"

"I need to apologize to Avi first, son. I'm sorry that I have not spoken of that yet."

"As always, no apology is needed, sir."

"Well, there isn't much news anyway. Everybody is treating it as a body snatch, except those courageous enough to identify themselves as Yeshu's followers."

"Anybody I know?" I asked although I was reasonably confident of the answer.

Flavius understood. "No, I'm afraid none of his closest apostles have shown their faces. There's a rumor that one of them committed suicide, but so far it's only a rumor. I thought you'd be able to find out more."

"I'll try, Flavius, believe me, I'll try. But unless I can contact Miriam, or James, or for that matter Simon Peter, I don't know if I can contribute much. And I'm rather sure I don't want to see Peter."

Marcus spoke. "Tell Avi what we discussed, father."

My lover's father grew very serious. "Whatever has happened to Yeshu's body, it doesn't change anything for Marcus or me. You should know that, Avi. If he rose from the dead, he was the Son of God. If he didn't rise from the dead, he was the Son of God."

If I had forgotten the strength of the centurion's faith, I quickly was reminded of it. But there was another issue I could see developing.

"Can you maintain that faith in the face of Roman culture? In your new position, will you not be required to participate in Roman ceremonies?"

Marcus' wit, as always, came to the forefront.

"Don't worry, Avi. We won't be sacrificing any virgins in Rome. For one thing, once you're there, you'll realize that there are no virgins in Rome. Not over the age of thirteen, at least."

After a hearty laughter that was much appreciated by all, we began discussing the details of our move. The night ended with the ever efficient Flavius drawing up a list of things we needed to accomplish in the next five days.

As I lay in bed that night, exhausted, a mixture of apprehension and anticipation filled my thoughts. Flavius and Marcus had often spoken of the splendor of the seat of the Roman Empire. I often dreamt of visiting, and now I would be a resident. As I was pulled off to sleep, I was sure my dreams would be of Rome.

Instead, they were of Yeshu.

~~ 49 ~~

Awakening, I was miffed when Marcus told me Flavius had gone to visit Levi.

"Calm down, Avi; he's bidding goodbye to an old friend, and someone should tell him that you are leaving Jerusalem. Besides, maybe he's heard something about Yeshu."

Flavius returned a short time later, and we asked him what Levi had had to say.

"He wished you well and hopes you enjoy Rome. As for Yeshu, Levi still maintains it was a body snatch; not surprisingly, he blames Yeshu's followers. I have to admit I agree with him to some degree; I can't see the Sanhedrin having anything to do with it."

To my mind, it almost wasn't worth discussing. My complete disdain for both the Sanhedrin and Yeshu's apostles was equal. Besides, I had decided to make for Nazareth that day. With constant travel and the time I would spend with Sophia, I computed that I could be back in Jerusalem within three days. I rode off for my native village, I thought, for the last time.

It was late at night when I arrived, but Sophia

seemed not to mind. I told her of my plans.

"Will you be returning?" she asked with hesitation. I looked at her doubtfully. She seemed to accept the fact that this would be the last time we would see each other. There were tears, but grateful appreciation also, on both sides.

She too had heard rumors of Yeshu, not only from me but from the Nazarenes who had spent the Passover in Jerusalem. The rumors were spreading throughout the town.

"It would be wonderful, wouldn't it Avi, for Miriam and James, maybe for all of us."

"I didn't realize that you were such a fan," I replied.

"We never discussed it, you and I, but I would hear of his preaching. And though I didn't know him well, I adored Miriam. The whole family seemed so nice. And I found some of his ideas to be rather stimulating. A world based on the equality of all, based on what is common between us instead of what separates us, how wonderful that would be. How could oppression and war exist in a world where everyone saw themselves as in the family of the God of All Things. It would be a kingdom itself."

"That it would be," I said, "but can't people live like that without needing the miracle of a man rising from the dead?"

"Well, it certainly gets people's attention, doesn't it?"

We spoke not only of Yeshu but of course father. By the time of our parting, tears had returned to each of our eyes. I would miss Sophia. I would miss her a lot.

Riding back, I estimated that I would have two days to seek the truth of what had happened with Yeshu. I wished I had time to stop in Sephoria, to seek out his brothers; but I was unsure they were still even there; Yeshu had never mentioned to me where their lives had taken them. I also debated stopping in Galilee to search for Simon Peter, but I couldn't; I was uncertain that if I did find him, I might not immediately throttle him. It was best for me to return immediately to Jerusalem.

I did take time to ride by the tomb where we had laid Yeshu to rest. It had become a bizarre tourist attraction; seemingly half of Jerusalem, whether they be Jew, gentile or pagan, wanted to peer into the empty tomb. Astride my steed, I saw twenty or so people milling around the crypt. Suddenly I heard "You! You on the horse! You were there that night. I recognize you."

It was a Roman soldier whom I faintly remembered from Yeshu's crucifixion. I had no desire to respond, and so I sped off into the distance. I didn't need any more trouble; Marcus didn't need any more trouble; Flavius didn't need any more trouble.

I found a hubbub of activity when I arrived home. Servants were packing, and the centurion who had purchased the house already was moving in some of his belongings.

I walked into the study to find Flavius, Marcus, and Simon in quiet conversation. I was about to leave, but Marcus motioned me over.

"Simon has decided to remain in Jerusalem, Avi." I nodded my head.

"You're certain, then, Simon?" Flavius asked.

"Very certain, sir. I have come to believe that the man Yeshu has truly risen. I will join a group of his followers as soon as my duties here are completed."

Flavius was concerned. "There could be trouble in that, Simon."

"All the more reason for me to be there. They might need me. He might need me."

The Cyrene had spoken out of no sense of self-importance. Instead, I could see the honesty of his reply.

Simon continued. "Please understand that my decision has nothing to do with your house. You have made my life as a servant full of joy, and I owe you much. But I believe Yeshu is the Son of the Living God. I do not pretend to understand all that he has said; I am a dull and ignorant man. If not for Avi, I would still be ignorant of letters and words. But my fate rests with Yeshu; of that I am sure."

Rising, master embraced servant. "You are the wisest of us all, Simon," Flavius said. "I thank you for your years of service. And I pray to the God of All Things that he watches over you and keeps you safe. And please be assured that if you ever change your mind, or if you need a sanctuary, or for that matter, if you need anything at all, you will always be welcomed in my home."

So Simon would not be joining us. I would miss the Cyrene, and the image of his taking up Yeshu's cross on that horrible night would be etched in my memory for all my days. I would discover weeks later that Flavius had provided generously for his former servant's well-being, an act that held no surprise for me. We would all miss the noble Simon, and often in the future, I would join Flavius and Marcus in praying for his safety.

Before we knew, the eve of our departure was upon us. To my chagrin, I had learned nothing of substance of Yeshu. Rumors were rampant, but the truth was elusive.

I went to bed early that evening, but sleep would not come to me. I rose, poured some wine, and stepped out into the backyard, to sit and think.

I was not the only one who couldn't sleep.

"May I join you, Avi?", Flavius asked.

I poured him some wine. "It's a beautiful night, isn't it?"

"Indeed it is. You will find the nights in Rome to be equally beautiful" he replied.

I chided myself for forgetting that in my apprehension about moving to a strange land, Marcus and Flavius would be returning to the place of their births. I said as much to Flavius.

"It will be wonderful for us; there is so much about Rome I miss. But I will miss Palestine also. I have enjoyed much of my time here; not all, but most. I lost my beloved here, the saddest day of my life. But Marcus grew up here and met his companion, a companion that not only changed his life but my own. If not for you, Avi, I likely would have ignored Yeshu, and a large part of my life would be empty. Now it is filled. I owe you a debt that can never be repaid."

"It is you," I replied earnestly, as earnestly as I had ever said anything in my life, "that has made all of the good things in my adult life possible. My faith rejects me; you accepted me. It's all my fault, but I could never talk to my father the way I talk to you. If there's any debt, it is a shared one."

He smiled. "Quite an interesting family we have here, then. It's a bit like Yeshu, isn't it? I understand very little of why it is the way it is, but I revel in the way it is."

"Pretty good way to describe it," I replied with a smile.

We talked until dawn, unaware of the passing of the hours. I can't even remember what exactly we talked about. I believe that was an indication of the family we had become.

~~ 50 ~~

But I knew it was more than physical. My journey was filled with doubts. I would know a total of seven people in Rome, and none were Jews. While Flavius had assured me that my people were allowed a certain freedom in the City of Light, I wondered how I would keep the Sabbath. With whom would I celebrate the Holy Days?

I worried too about my professional life. Where would I work? Again, Flavius assured me that scribes were in high demand in Rome, especially multi-lingual ones. That assurance lessened my concern but did not eliminate it.

More than I cared to admit, I was also worried about my personal life. When it came to men of my nature, Rome was to Jerusalem as Jerusalem was to Nazareth. Certainly, there were more men like Marcus and me in Rome; likely, they were more open about their preference. My trip to Sephoria so many years ago had convinced me of that. And they were Romans, not Jews. Marcus' next companion would carry none of the baggage his current one did.

All in all, a tremendous amount of uncertainty was my constant traveling companion for those five days. I found myself remembering Nazareth as an idyllic Eden. But I had not been cast out of the Garden; I had walked out voluntarily.

When we finally saw land, it was not unlike a religious experience. However, we had precious time to celebrate. Flavius' preparations had of course been meticulous, and within hours of landing ashore, we were walking into our new home.

It was very similar to our former house, a wooden and stone structure filled with a variety of rooms. There were only two differences: the rooms were larger, as the house itself was larger, and a spacious, ornate room abutted the kitchen. Flavius explained that in his new position, he would be expected to entertain often. Mixed with his natural sociability, I knew there would be many gatherings in that room.

The study had its own fireplace, and I knew at once it would be my favorite room in the house. Flavius also inherited two new servants; a valet of sorts who would tend to the centurion's personal needs, and another cook. Marcus and I both anticipated that Nilsa and the new cook would get along as well as the Romans and Jews did in Jerusalem. They would tolerate each other, neither comfortable with the situation.

The morning after, we toured Rome with the entire household. Flavius was right; Jerusalem's magnificence, which had so enthralled me as a child, was nothing compared to Rome's. We saw the Roman Senate, a tribute to their interest in representative government (even if that representation was limited only to specific groups). We visited the Coliseum, a tribute to their interest in athletic competition. We also toured the Institute, from where most Roman philosophical writings flowed, and where young, wealthy Romans received their higher education. Last, but certainly not least, we saw the outside of the Palace of Caesar, the place where Flavius would work. Solomon himself had never resided in such splendor.

At Flavius' insistence, we took a side trip to the synagogue. It was not small, but it wasn't the Temple either. In structure, it most resembled the synagogue in Nazareth, though of course, it was more substantial. It was a simple yet dignified structure. I assumed that some of the members of the congregation were of means. And I trusted it held none of the intrigues of the Temple.

Within weeks, Marcus and I found employment. He would scribe at the Institute, where he would be at the apex of Roman thought. And I again would be working within a religious environment.

I met Rabbi David at the synagogue and presented my credentials. As impressed as he was with my background, ("A Temple Scribe!"), he was equally curious about my biography. It was interestingly evident that news of Yeshu had reached Rome.

"Yes, I knew him, but not particularly well," I lied.

"We have had many strange reports; he worked miracles, he preached peace with the Romans, and yet he was crucified for his personal habits. Supposedly he was a Sodomite. Now comes word he has risen from the dead. Didn't know him well, you say......"

Again I lied; though I had the distinct impression Rabbi David wasn't swayed. And I wondered how word of Yeshu had spread to Rome so quickly. I would discover the answer to that question months later.

"Well, either way, I would like to offer you a position. An elderly man, Uriah, is our scribe, and frankly, none of his assistants appear to be able to take his place." The compensation offered was on the short side of what I expected, but my options were limited.

Rabbi David spoke further. "You know, Avrum, we

are not like the Temple. We deal with a variety of views here, from the very liberal to the very orthodox. This Yeshu fellow, he has excited the liberals, while the conservatives find him to be heretical. I'm sure both factions, and the ones in between, will be asking you questions."

I was less than excited about that possibility but thankful that I would be working. Nilsa prepared a celebratory dinner for Marcus and I. Repeating the conversation I had with Rabbi David, I was surprised when Marcus recounted that Yeshu had generated some interest at the Institute also.

"What are they saying?" I asked.

"Essentially that Pilate missed an opportunity. Here was a Jewish leader who didn't preach insurrection, and Pilate executes him. Just about no one believes the sodomy charge."

Incredible, I thought. People from hundreds of miles away could see the obvious truth, while those in the midst of the situation were confused. Within the confines of Jerusalem, many presumed Yeshu guilty.

"Seems like the Institute's view of Pilate echoes the military's," Flavius added. "They don't seem to hold him in any esteem, and they feel he may have caused more problems by crucifying Yeshu than if he had stayed out of the matter entirely. This is understandably especially true if Yeshu has risen."

"Interesting, isn't it?" I said. "The Sanhedrin was so convinced it was ridding itself of the problem by having him crucified. I wonder if Levi and Yusuf and the rest are having second thoughts."

"I imagine they may be, Avi, but treachery is often so rewarded," Flavius responded. "We'll have to keep a close eye on whatever news there is from Jerusalem."

He then raised his glass. "To an agreement then, gentlemen. We will all listen for news of Yeshu, sharing whatever we hear with each other. He doesn't need our protection now, either way. But we need to be kept informed."

Marcus added: "To Yeshu then," and we drank a toast. One thing would not be much different in Rome than it had been in Jerusalem, it seemed. Yeshu would continue to dominate our evening conversations.

And ultimately, he would dominate so much more.

~~ 51 ~~

Not unlike the first years, after I had migrated to Jerusalem, the early ones in Rome passed, to some degree, without incident. I grew acclimated to the City of Light, its cultures, and its customs. The concerns I had had about my relationship with Marcus proved to be unfounded. If anything, the passage of time deepened our relationship and our love. We spent our days working, and our nights appreciating the wonders of the big city. Being a Jew, however, I could not sit in the same areas as Marcus and Flavius. Since I was their "servant," I could still attend the events but had to sit (stand) in another area. As such I became acquainted with other servants and slaves; those friendships generated an informational fountain about Yeshu. The downtrodden of Rome were well aware of the Palestinian preacher who spoke of the equality of all, and whose life was beginning to take on mystical proportions.

Had Yeshu risen from the dead? Five years later I had no more solid information than I had had five days after his death. The theories were still the same; Yeshu had been removed from his crypt by the Sanhedrin, and buried in some secret place; the Romans had done the same; his followers had snatched the body, and disguised someone to act as the risen Yeshu; he had never died in the first place.

Flavius and Marcus were convinced he had risen. Marcus continued to say, "So what happened, then, Avi?" when I continued to express my doubts. "How do you explain the missing body and his appearances?" I had several answers that would explain both events, but neither father nor son was persuaded.

During those first years, the life of Yeshu (by this time I was tempted to call it a legend) began to interest all of the Rome, not just the marginal. Small covens of adherents to his teachings (or at least their interpretation of those teachings) began to spring up in Rome, as I heard they had in Palestine. Yeshu had told his followers to spread the good news of the kingdom; and that they did, very effectively to my reckoning. Simon Peter (of all people) had apparently appointed himself the leader of the movement. I wondered how he answered the question, "Where were you during the crucifixion?"

Some of the stories about Yeshu's life bordered on the bizarre. He not only rose from his tomb, but he did so carrying a twelve-foot high cross. He was physically taken into the heavens, like Elijah. Miriam had a similar assumption. Yeshu's childhood was spent raising other children from the dead; he must have been doing that in between the athletic games we had with each other. And of course, there was the wedding, where he turned water into wine. I was at that wedding, (actually, the bride was my cousin), and no such thing happened.

But I stood mute; who was I to question a legend? Maybe it was a wine I was drinking that day. But it sure tasted like water.

My friend's ministry had, through his followers,

reached further than I could ever imagine. Doubtless, his plea for the inclusiveness of all into the kingdom aided this growth dramatically. Jews, gentiles of all types, and pagans found comfort in the notion of a loving Father who cared for his children. Even if the Jews had to surrender their "chosen" status, it seemed not to trouble them. Women, who were (and sadly, still are), subjugated to men in just about every dominant religion, rejoiced at Yeshu's call for the equality of the sexes, and his prohibition against divorces, divorces which left women mostly homeless and destitute. Those who had led less than exemplary lives were captivated by the idea that the God of All Things forgave them for their transgressions. Those who had spent their lives as slaves were thrilled that they too could enter the kingdom, either (depending on one's interpretation) with their masters, or instead of them. Yeshu had generated a catholic appeal.

But there was also considerable confusion. Did someone have to become a Jew to follow Yeshu? The fear of circumcision, I thought wryly, kept many away. Was Yeshu's life foretold in Scripture, or were believers twisting and bending that life and the Torah to make it all fit? Most importantly, was Yeshu a Jewish prophet, a prophet who was only incidentally Jewish, or a prophet who was decidedly anti-Jewish?

It appeared the Greeks had embraced Yeshu the legend as much as any other group. I had some insight into this phenomenon from Marcus, who had, at the Institute, heard the great Roman orator Seneca describe Yeshu as a "Greco-Jewish" teacher. I understood Seneca's reasoning; there was more than a minor Greek "tinge" to Yeshu's teachings about monotheism, the afterlife, and the equality of all.

The Greeks had even gone one step further. Yeshu was not merely a Jewish prophet; he was the Messiah, the anointed one chosen by the God of All Things to free Israel from its oppressors. That he had done nothing to remove the yoke of the Occupation (and hadn't even said much about it) didn't seem to bother the Greeks. Instead, they declared him the "Christos", the Messiah. Followers of Yeshu thus became followers of the "Christos", or "Christians". By the time that interpretation had reached Rome, Yeshu bar Yusuf of Nazareth had been transformed into "Jesus Christ."

The Jewish hierarchy, who had plotted and planned his execution, was incensed by that interpretation, and the more popular it became, the more incensed they became. The Sanhedrin began condemning all talk as blasphemy, and those who ascribed to those beliefs as heretics. This time the Sanhedrin bypassed Rome entirely; they would deal with this Christian heresy themselves. Anyone expressing a belief in the "Christ" in public was stoned to death. I heard a report that a teacher named Steven was stoned to death right on the Temple steps, the very steps I had climbed daily on my way to work. Marcus had heard that Pilate remained silent as the Sanhedrin carried out its persecutions. Flavius thought that Pilate was acting on orders from Rome. Caesar, it was said, felt it was best not to involve the Empire in the internal squabbles of its conquered state. It appeared that Caesar placed the blame for all the unrest in Palestine squarely on Pilate's shoulders. Privately, Flavius thought the Roman governor was headed for suicide.

I thanked whoever or whatever was responsible for removing me from Jerusalem. All I knew was that I was safer in Rome than I would have ever been in Palestine. I also allowed myself the luxury of laughing at Levi and his cohorts; they had been so convinced that they had eliminated the "problem" of Yeshu by their nefarious efforts. Instead, their acts had spawned an entire movement that, even with its internal conflicts and contradictions, must be shaking the Temple at its very core. That I found very satisfying.

Through it all, the men at the synagogue continually prodded me about the boy they knew I had grown up with. Did he really raise people from the dead? What were his parents like? Did he ever get into any trouble?

I maintained my silence, deflecting all inquiries. Some thought me arrogant, but that didn't bother me. My knowledge of Yeshu was personal; I would share it with only those I respected.

Meanwhile, Uriah was retiring, and I was promoted to chief scribe at the synagogue. I was now in charge of all literary activity. Rabbi David may have made the appointment with some hesitancy, but he made it none the less.

Another three years would pass. Slowly, just as the Nazarene Avrum had been transformed into the Jerusalem Avrum, the Jerusalem Avrum was being transformed into the Roman Avrum. I was becoming more comfortable than I could have ever imagined, a comfortability encased by the love of my companion and my adoptive family. We were all growing individually; we were all growing as a unit.

Flavius and Marcus continued in their devotion to the movement. They spoke of Yeshu often and began to nightly intone the prayer they had heard him speak. Marcus especially announced to me that he had become a Christian.

In our ninth year in Rome, he would need his faith.

~~ 52 ~~

Marcus would lose his father, and I my third parent, on a cold and rainy day that had started like any other. Flavius had left for work early, as he often did, and then spent the morning attending to his duties. He had scheduled a noon meeting with his aide, and when the aide arrived, he found his commander lying on the ground, gasping for breath. Within moments, the noble centurion would be dead.

The Palace physicians immediately suspected poison, I was later told, because Palace physicians always immediately suspected poison. However, there was no evidence of foul play, and hence Flavius had died a natural death.

Marcus, of course, was devastated. Never had my lover so completely and utterly lost his composure as he did that day. It's said the passing of a parent is easier on older children, but that was certainly not the case with Marcus, as perhaps it is not with any only child, especially one who would now be parent-less. I was told that he knelt at his father's body, rocking and moaning until he was gently removed.

In the first of what would be several subtle, and not so subtle, reminders of my position in Roman society, I did not hear of Flavius' death until that evening. Marcus had asked a Roman guard to report the death to his house and to locate me at the synagogue. The guard went to the house, but no doubt felt the trip to notify me was unnecessary. In our private world, I was an integral part of Flavius' family. In the public sphere, I was a piece of furniture.

I raced to the Palace as soon as Nilsa told me what had happened, but was denied entrance because of my rank. For hours I stood outside in the cold rain, grounded by custom from comforting my soul mate at his hour of greatest need.

Marcus finally exited from the Palace surrounded by an escort there to see him home. He motioned to me, and I followed him at a distance. It was not until we were safely cocooned inside our house that we could mutually mourn the death of the great man.

My grief would have to be delayed; helping Marcus deal with his was the most important thing. When he wailed "I am now totally alone," I took no umbrage. Instead, I knew all too well the feeling of a parentless only child. It was a difficult evening.

The day that followed was my first introduction to the Roman method of disposing of the dead. Jews were buried in the ground the day they died, the only exception being on the Sabbath, and even then the burial was required to be the next day. The protocol for a Roman of rank, such as a centurion, was vastly different. Flavius' body would lie in state for two days. In his case, because of his assignment, it would be at the Palace. Those who had served under him, and those under whom he had served, would pay their respects. Military men of all ranks would do likewise, as well as a variety of government officials. It was rumored that Claudius himself would attend.

As the only family member of the deceased, Marcus would be forced to greet all the mourners alone. All of the while Flavius' corpse lay on a pile of flowers, surrounded by symbols of the Roman military.

It was an impossibly trying time for Marcus and one that I found utterly bizarre. Yet I was reminded that Flavius himself had found the Jewish burial ritual to be equally bizarre.

I could not attend any of these functions or the removal of the body outside to the Palace grounds, where it would be placed on a pyre of straw and incinerated. Marcus was forced by custom and prejudice to endure the entire ritual by himself. Outside of the Palace grounds, I mourned for the centurion and his son.

I also prayed to the God of All Things, and for the first time, I prayed to Yeshu. If he was in his kingdom, watching over these earthly events, I prayed that he would remember the man who had shown, in Yeshu's own words, "a faith unseen in all of Israel." I asked Yeshu to protect Marcus, as Flavius had protected him. And to comfort Marcus. And, yes, to comfort Avrum.

I thought that after the cremation, Marcus and I would finally have time to mourn together. That would not be the case, however. Roman tradition held that centurion's houses belonged to centurions, not necessarily to their heirs. Marcus would not be forced to sell the home, but he would be gently nudged. Within a month he did so, or more aptly stated, it was done for him. That put the two of us in a strange situation.

Between the sale of the house, and the inheritance from his father, accompanied by his earnings, Marcus was now on solid financial ground. For identical reasons of course, so was I. But we had no place to live, and certainly no place to house servants. In any event, we doubted that any servants would want to be in the employ of two men such as ourselves.

We decided to find other places of employment for the servants. All except Nilsa accepted. She confessed that she had, for a while, longed to return to her native Syria. She would take this occasion to do so. The parting was tearful, but made easier by the fact that Marcus had inherited his father's senses of responsibility and generosity; not only did he pay the cost of Nilsa's voyage, but she also left Rome with a considerable purse.

For weeks, Marcus and I rented rooms (separate of course) in an inn, with our belongings in storage. Strangely, it was Rabbi David of all people who would come to our rescue. An elderly Greco-Jewish woman, recently widowed, was returning to Greece and wanted to sell her home.

The house was nowhere near the size of our house in Rome; indeed, it was smaller than our house had been in Jerusalem. But the location was perfect. Situated on the outskirts of the city, it was still within easy distance by horseback of our respective workplaces and the center of Rome. We both fell in love with the house immediately, and the transaction was quickly completed.

In many ways, it would be an entirely different experience for both of us. There would be no servants. Marcus and I would struggle with domestic responsibilities. I had at least some experience, having had to provide for myself when I had first arrived in Jerusalem. But the tasks of cooking and cleaning were utterly foreign to my lover, who had spent his entire life surrounded by servants. His culinary talents would improve over the years, but I would tease him that they didn't do so by much.

We were comfortable in our new home within weeks. I believe that was partially true because for the first time we had something that belonged to the two of us, and only us (I had paid half the purchase price). We could look at the structure, humble as it was, and proudly say it was our home. We had been lovers for twenty years; the house was a symbol of our continuing commitment to each other.

With the "practicalities", as Flavius would always call them, handled, Marcus and I could now grieve for the fallen centurion. Marcus suffered an acute depression that would last for weeks. My attempts to console him were undoubtedly hindered by my personal grief. He spent hour upon hour in solitude, either in the little garden we had constructed at the back of our house, or in our small study. There were tears upon tears from both of us, both individually and collectively.

Again I was reminded that, as the Torah claims, time heals all wounds. Eventually, Marcus and I returned to a relatively normal existence. But Flavius' spirit would never leave me, as I was sure it never left Marcus. I would never forget Flavius; I did not want to forget him.

I knew Marcus was returning to normalcy when his sense of humor returned. One night he remarked to me:

"You know, Avi, I know that father is with Yeshu now, as is mother. Your parents are with them also. They are watching over their sons."

I appreciated my lover's sentiments, and even more his next comment.

"Let's hope they are shielding their eyes some of the time."

~~ 53 ~~

While all that was happening in my personal life, the Christian movement, now dubbed Christianity, continued to grow in geometric proportions. What had been a small cell of believers became a clan, and soon there were pockets of Christians within many cities and towns. Levi, if still alive, must be fuming. So much for the Sanhedrin's master plan of removing Yeshu from the collective conscience. Flavius would have been delighted.

Rome itself was growing a group of adherents, which Marcus joined. I would attend some of their weekly meetings, where the faithful would say the prayer that had now become well-known, and discuss what ought to be the Christian reaction to everything from world events to day-to-day living. Marcus kept his knowledge of Yeshu to himself, as did I. While Rome officially claimed to have no opinion of the growing religion, there were rumors that some in the government were said to be concerned.

The meetings themselves would have been an excellent source of pride for Yeshu. Syrians mingled with Greeks, Romans, and Cypriots, and just about every other nationality with each other. A man of means would be seen breaking bread with the lowest peon; women could speak freely of their opinions.

The movement also began to spill over into the world of letters, the world Marcus and I, of course, were the most comfortable with. Some, though not many, of the Christians were literate or at least had access to scribes. They began to translate the oral tradition of the movement into writings about Yeshu's life and ministry.

Like the oral traditions, however, some of the writings bordered on the fantastic, with stories that smacked more of pagan superstitions than the foundations of a new system of belief. At the same time, many were thoughtful and analytical pieces, written obviously from the heart, attempting to explain and interpret Yeshu's dreams for humanity.

The fantastic nature of the stories was not the most troubling aspect of the writings, however. There seemed to be utter confusion about what was meant when one claimed to be a Christian. Some wrote of Yeshu representing one thing, while others claimed he represented the exact opposite. Some had no doubt that if Yeshu were alive, he would do one thing; others, with equal certainty, insisted he would do the other; while others, again writing with complete conviction, claimed he would do something entirely different. There seemed to be little agreement on the significant issues of faith, and none on the minor ones.

All religions are a mixture of faith and ritual, and if Christians were confused about faith, they were entirely at sea when it came to rituals. What was the proper baptism? The ritual cleansing that Jews received at the Temple? Or the reenactment of the drenching the wild Yonni practiced? (It should be noted that Yonni, whom I remained convinced was either partially or totally mad, had become a folk hero of the movement.) Should the Christians reenact the night Yeshu had eaten his last supper with the apostles? Or was that sacrilegious?

There was a writer, a Jew who had been born in Tarsus, who was attempting to calm the confusion. Tarsus was a small village, not much larger than Nazareth, and in the same province of Judea. The writer, a man named Saul, initially had some connection to the Sanhedrin. He claimed to have undergone a conversion of sorts in the midst of persecuting Christians in his vicinity. The details of that conversion seemed a bit dramatic, but whatever happened changed Saul from persecutor to defender of the new faith. In the tradition of the movement, Saul changed his name to Paul and immediately began writing letters to other groups of Christians.

Paul was aware of the rampant confusion within the new faith; not only aware of it but especially bothered by it. How could Christians teach the world how to live if they themselves could not agree on how to live? Paul wrote of others knowing who the Christians were by writing "They will know us by how we love each other." Marcus quipped that in reality, you could tell a Christian by the confused look on his face.

But overall, Marcus and I found Paul's writings to be thoughtful and informative, if not a bit strange. The strangeness came from his seeming to dwell on matters like marriage, personal relationships, and yes, even circumcision. Yeshu had said very little, if anything, about these things, and yet they seemed to obsess Paul.

He had met with Simon Peter also, so while Paul admitted to never having met Yeshu, his letters claimed certain credibility. Peter, as I have mentioned, had been anointed (or had anointed himself) one of the chief leaders of the movement. From my view, his making such a claim was the height of chicanery. But Marcus said I was being decidedly un-Christian.

Paul also traveled extensively, which gave credence to the notion that he was a wealthy man. Everywhere he visited, Paul wrote; sometimes about the land he had journeyed to, sometimes in response to something he had heard about another area. There can be no doubt that Christianity's expansion into the collective consciousness, especially among the literate, was due in no small part to Paul. His literary style was excellent, with an ability to write in terms familiar to Jew, gentile and pagan alike. Again, my lover had a quick quip:

"Aristotle had his Plato, Yeshu has his Paul."

There were other noteworthy aspects of Paul's writings. Nowhere did he indicate the specific reason for Yeshu's crucifixion. That may have been a manipulation, but it was a useful one. The sodomy charge, of course, was false and outlandish, but its mere mention would dissuade many potential adherents. Perhaps Paul felt that it was a matter best left to future writers, to detail the facts of Yeshu's murder.

Moreover, he showed a remarkable ability to remain vague about the responsibility for the execution. Reading Paul, one could easily see the Romans blaming the Jews, and the Jews blaming the Romans. As a result, both nations could convert to Christianity.

Finally, Marcus and I both agreed that Paul's description of Yeshu as the Redeemer was brilliant. Yeshu had been a relatively obscure Palestinian preacher, but to Paul, he was the savior of all humankind, whose death washed away the sins of the world. Such an image fit a variety of religious legends (the Jewish Sacrificial Lamb, for instance), and indeed expanded Yeshu's appeal. Marcus thought the idea of Yeshu as Redeemer was likely; I was a bit more sanguine. But there was no doubt that it was a useful and popular description.

It was easy to see how Paul would be the chief proselytizer of the movement, a task he seemed not only up to but fit for. He would soon become so much a part of the Christian movement that Marcus and I joked that perhaps the adherents to the new faith should be called "Paulists" instead of Christians.

~~ 54 ~~

Yeshu would continue to be a focal point of my life, partly because of events that were happening at the synagogue. Rabbi David was stepping down, to be replaced by Rabbi Micah. While David had watched the Christian movement with a certain air of distance, Micah saw it as an integral part of Judaism. "We need to understand what this movement means to our faith," Micah said in his opening remarks to the congregation. "We have to find out as much as possible, so we can decide exactly how to react to it."

Many felt Micah's interest was spurred by his chief supporter, a wealthy member of the congregation named Yusuf bar Yeshu. The irony, as it turned out, just began with the name. This Yusuf had made his fortune as a mercantile trader, and everyone respected his cunning aptitude for business. He had been Micah's chief sponsor during the long and arduous process of selecting a new rabbi. More than one of our members remarked that Yusuf had purchased himself a rabbi. And Yusuf, who had done commerce effectively with the Romans, had even gone so far as to prefer being known as the Roman equivalent of his name. Many indeed called him "Joseph."

His campaign on behalf of Micah was not based on a desire for business advantage, however. Joseph had virtually retired from his trade, leaving the very profitable enterprise to his sons. It was his daughter's activities that motivated Joseph now. She had become an ardent Christian. Because of her, Joseph had become fascinated with the Palestinian preacher whose teachings had inspired his daughter's commitment. He decided he would use all of his wealth to determine what this Christianity business was all about.

Joseph was known to me, and I to him, only casually. Every synagogue has its caste system; a lowly scribe seldom associated with the wealthy members, and it was possible that Joseph was the most prosperous. But like many men with his set of talents, Joseph had never taken the time to learn how to read or write during his professional days. He had just of late become literate. Joseph attacked literacy with the same zeal he had shown in his business dealings. Within a year, he was writing articles, very well written I had to admit, addressed to the entire congregation. He had asked me to transcribe these letters, and because of that, our acquaintance was growing. Despite this work, I had always thought he was uncomfortable in my presence and viewed me with some suspicion.

But he also knew of my biography and reasoned that I had more knowledge of Yeshu than I had let on. Almost
underhandedly, he began mulling around my desk, asking what I was working on, and the like. Now I was the one feeling uncomfortable.

All of this was happening as Marcus, and I celebrated the twenty-fifth year of our union. For myself, I felt the same as I had that first night at Flavius' house when I had met him. That feeling had not waned; rather, it had developed a complexity and a growth that defined my entire existence. We had been through much with each other; through each step, my love for him had expanded.

I had never looked in another direction. I knew the same was true with him. We had a fidelity that I knew was unique for men of our nature, and even for traditional couples.

It was also our fifteenth year on Roman soil. We were no longer city dwellers, as our little cottage on the outskirts of town became our focal point. Nights that had been spent tramping to theaters and the Coliseum had been replaced by nights spent taking long walks in the countryside. Rather than seeing the multitudes of people on a typical night in Rome, most of our walks were spent in solitude. They served to deepen the nature of our relationship, as incredibly as we were still discovering things about each other.

Marcus' involvement with Christianity continued and deepened. He was now attending gatherings more and more often and even broached the subject of having one in our home.

It was the last thing I wanted. I did not need my experiences with Yeshu to become public knowledge, especially among the zealots who seemed to find every aspect of Yeshu's life (real or imagined) to be breathtaking. There was nothing wrong with them. In fact, most were very nice people. But they were obsessed, creating secret symbols with each other, using certain words in specific ways, and in general acting in manners I found odd. I was worried that the first time we showed these people where we lived, it would open the gates to them always being around.

I was able to convince Marcus that it was a bad idea by pointing out two things. First, transportation to our home would be difficult for many of them unless they owned horses. These were people who barely owned the tunics on their back, never mind horses.

But most significantly, there was no specific attitude on the part of Christians toward men like Marcus and I. What if it was determined that those of our nature were unsuitable to belong in Yeshu's kingdom? The movement was growing in large part because everyone was accepted into it. It didn't matter who or what you had been, you could become a Christian. What if, I suggested to my lover, that attitude began to change? Certainly, more details of our personal lives would be evident to visitors to our home. I preferred to keep those details hidden, and while I was sure there had been some talk of our relationship, talk wasn't knowledge. Marcus agreed with my reasoning.

There were also some unsettling things happenings with Christianity on the political front. Each year that passed seemed to intensify Rome's irritation with the movement. During the first few years, as I have mentioned, Rome saw Christianity as essentially innocuous. Why be troubled, many Romans reasoned, by a movement whose leader had preached cooperation with Caesar?

But others were less sanguine and saw a potential threat to the security of the Empire. More and more, as Christianity became more visible, there came official proclamations from the government. Christians would not be granted any special privileges. Their customs and rituals must conform to the Roman law. Excessively attended meetings were discouraged, especially meetings at night, and most of these meetings were at night. While not offering any official opinion of the new faith, Rome was making it clear it was becoming concerned.

That must have made the Sanhedrin happy. Israel's hierarchy continued its vicious attacks on the movement.

News of more and more persecutions was filtering through our synagogue. Most of our members were appalled, as only the strictest orthodox viewed Christianity as any threat. And indeed many like Joseph felt that the Sanhedrin needed to be restructured if they insisted on continuing in that direction. Joseph said as much in a letter written to our members, which I found myself happy to transcribe. Jews persecuting Christians, many of whom who were Jews by birth, was certainly not the way of the God of All Things. The Sanhedrin was showing the same animosity toward Christians as Romans showed toward Jews. That was not the way of the Lord, Joseph continued.

He was opposed by the conservatives, who continued to maintain that Yeshu was not a Jewish prophet, but a decidedly anti-Jewish one. The argument took up many of our services. I continued to keep my silence. Very simply, I did not wish to become involved. At the same time, I agreed with Joseph that persecutions did nothing to advance the cause of Israel. When I transcribed his letter to the congregation, I emphasized that point, an editing to which Joseph had no objection.

"Avrum," he said, "your talent with language far exceeds my own. Feel free to add or subtract things you find appropriate in any of my writings."

I did so in his other letters, and he never objected. Our relationship was strangely growing closer, partly, I discovered because Joseph wanted it to. He had his purposes, and shortly I would be made aware of them.

~~ 55 ~~

I had the feeling that some social invitation was coming from Joseph, and it did. The request (for the evening meal) itself was not surprising; that it included Marcus was.

"Romans are welcomed in my home always, Avrum. I could not have had the business success I've had without them."

I suspected he knew of the relationship Marcus and I shared. Apparently, it didn't bother him, and if it did, not enough to prevent his desire to socialize with me. Or maybe he thought it would make me more comfortable.

Joseph's house was easily the most beautiful home I had ever been in. It was huge; twelve of my childhood homes in Nazareth would have fit inside of it. Yet the size was not its most remarkable feature. Joseph had a taste for decorating that was truly unique. Or at least that was my first impression. Marcus readily agreed. We would shortly discover that the taste belonged to Joseph's daughter, who had inherited her mother's talent for decorating and arranging. Joseph's wife had been dead for five years, but she had trained her daughter well.

Joseph spoke to Marcus. "Enjoy my home, young man. I'm sure the taxes I pay to the Empire on it likely pay your salary." The comment was not said sarcastically, but rather in friendship.

After a sumptuous dinner, we adjourned to a large and ornate study. Joseph had acquired a large variety of alcoholic beverages through his business dealings, and Marcus and I sampled them all. And then we sampled them some more.

The liquor no doubt affected my judgment that evening. Joseph admitted that his invitation had an ulterior motive. He wanted, he claimed, to write the definitive story of Jesus of Nazareth, who had inspired the Christian movement. He felt that all the writings so far (including Paul's) lacked a precise accuracy. He said he wanted to provide a clear and concise telling of the events of Yeshu's life. To that end, Joseph wanted to do a de facto interview with me about the early life in Nazareth Yeshu and I had shared, and whatever other times our paths had intersected.

I overcame my initial hesitation and agreed. Was it because of the spirits I had consumed that evening? Was it because, when Marcus and I talked about the possibility, my lover urged me on? Or was it that I finally wanted someone to hear my story, a story that would clear up so many of the misconceptions that had been circulating about Yeshu. I had had my fill of the silliness of virgin births, of visitations by Wise Men, of a childhood filled with miracles. If people wanted to worship Yeshu, let them worship him for what he was, not for what they wanted him to be.

Marcus and I awoke the following morning with headaches. We both agreed that it had been a delightful evening and that it was likely I would enjoy Joseph's company when we started his project. Marcus teased me that if Joseph had not been significantly older than both of us, and of a different nature, he would be jealous.

During the next few days, I discovered more reasons to feel that I had made the right decision. Joseph told me that he had no intention of writing an "expose" of any sort. There would be no naming of names, no exposure of sources. At no point would he write that he had spoken to so and so, who had said this or that. His tome would be written in the third person, by what could be described as a disinterested observer.

There was also going to be quite a time lag between my interview and the actual writing of the manuscript. Joseph told me that shortly he was leaving to join his daughter in Jerusalem; he expected to be there for several months. Further, he would not be returning directly to Rome but would venture to Syria and Greece, to observe the progress of the Christian movement in those areas. It would likely be at least a year after our meetings that he would set pen to papyrus. In that year, if I had a change of heart about his using me as a source, I could tell him about it when he returned. Either way, he said he would honor my wishes.

Finally, Joseph assured me that since he would need scribes once the manuscript was completed, I would be more than welcome to participate, and the offer extended to Marcus also. So I would see the final product before it was released for public consumption. If I had an issue with any part of it that was based on my recollections, it could be edited before it was released.

All those assurances made my decision easier. And so Joseph and I began our work. The routine would be the same; each night, I would have the evening meal with him, and then we would adjourn to the study where the actual interview would take place. Whether it was the comfortability of the study, the extensive collection of spirits, or Joseph's innate ability to ask the right questions at the right time, I found myself speaking openly and comfortably. Often I would catch myself talking about just myself, and I would stop. But Joseph insisted I continue so that the sessions became as much the life of Avrum as the life of Yeshu.

Joseph was a complete and thorough interviewer. It was not enough to know that Yeshu and I had been to Sephoria; he wanted to know what we did there, down to the very last detail. He began to speculate that by working in Sephoria, Yeshu had been exposed to Greek philosophy and that perhaps he was not the simple small-town preacher generally assumed. When I mentioned Seneca had described Yeshu as a "Greco-Jewish" philosopher, Joseph nodded his head.

"Seneca is a wise man, Avrum. I've had the pleasure of his company twice; actually, he sat in that very chair you are sitting in. It would be wonderful if that man of ideas would succeed Claudius. Unfortunately, it appears Nero will."

(I had heard stories about this Nero from Marcus and others; stories about his strange sexual appetite, which apparently included members of his own family and his generally bizarre behavior. Neither Marcus not I looked forward to what seemed to be his inevitable reign).

The interviews were over. Joseph confessed to me that Yeshu's childhood, rather than being in any way mystical, was instead rather drab. "Perhaps," he said, "I will begin my manuscript with his public ministry."

"Then most of what I have said is of no use," I said.

"Not at all" he replied. "In fact, I now have a greater appreciation for Yeshu, the man than I could have ever had. You've painted some intriguing mind images, Avrum; I can easily picture this young Nazarene carrying his father's toolbox."

"And your description of the crucifixion is heart-rending, not to mention highly informative. Shame you were not in Jerusalem to witness the resurrection; I would be fascinated by your thoughts."

I left my thoughts on the resurrection to myself, along with the reason I had fled Jerusalem that Passover. The resurrection remained for me another Christian fantasy; Joseph believed the reports, it seemed, as did Marcus, as did many others. But that didn't make them real.

Marcus and I were part of the farewell party for Joseph, as he left on his voyage to Jerusalem and other points. I sincerely wished him well. I imagined he thought he was on a great mission of discovery. I hoped he wouldn't be disappointed at what that discovery revealed.

~~ 56 ~~

Now that I am old and at the end of my days, I realize that there are few days that define a man's existence. In my case, there was the day of my birth. Then there was the day I met Yeshu, the days I came to realize my true nature, the days I arrived in Jerusalem and met Marcus; other days when I buried my family and friends, and of course the bizarre Passover I had spent watching Yeshu's execution. The remainders of my days become fillers, in a sense, merely bridging the gaps between those events.

I cannot even begin to express the feelings and emotions that encompass the next significant day of my life. I would lose Marcus, and all of the losses that had occurred before would pale in comparison.

Like many of those momentous days, it began innocently enough. Marcus told me he was feeling ill, and would not be reporting to the Institute that day. I scolded him that he had drunk too much wine the night before. I went to the synagogue, and on my return home purchased some fresh fruits and vegetables, along with some meat. I would prepare my lover a healthy supper for his ailing body.

When I walked into the house, provisions in hand, all thoughts of supper disappeared. Marcus lay writhing in his bed, twisting and turning, clutching the area above his waist on the right side. He was crying and spitting up an ugly, greenish liquid. I held him tightly, asking what was happening. Through his writhing, he said he had had minor pain in that region for several days, and since that morning, the pain had intensified into a sheer and piercing one.

In our village was an older man who was an expert at making potions. Frightened as I was to leave Marcus, I ran to the man's cottage. He immediately recognized the symptoms and swiftly accompanied me back to my house with a satchel full of herbs. One look at Marcus convinced him that I was not exaggerating the circumstances. Working adroitly, he prepared the potion, and slowly, almost forcibly, poured it down Marcus' throat.

The potion worked wonders. You could see the pain subsiding, just by looking at my lover's face. The shaking and trembling began to subside, and he fell into a deep sleep. The apothecary motioned me outside.

"I have seen many such cases, Avrum. I have to caution you that I can only ease the pain; no one knows what the source of the pain is. Sometimes the patient recovers from just the potion, but I will be frank; frequently they do not."

He said those words matter-of-factly, in a hushed tone. As I imagine anyone would, I asked: "What can I do?" He had no response as he looked at the ground below.

"Do what you can to keep him comfortable. I will leave you a generous supply of the potion. Do not hesitate to use it liberally. I should warn you that sometimes a delirium develops from the potion. But it eases the pain, and that's what's important. In any event, do not hesitate to send for me if I am needed."

As he walked away, I realized perhaps for the first time how isolated Marcus and I were. I could not send anyone for the man, because I didn't have anyone to send. Neither of us had any living relatives, nor anything more than a perfunctory relationship with our neighbors.

I went back into the house to tend to Marcus. He was breathing heavily; the breaths were raspy and labored. I could tell that it was anything but a restive sleep. I sat next to him, rocking and crying as I had seen so many do as they watched over their critically ill loved ones. I was powerless to aid the love of my life, as I watched his chest heave and contract. I was crying; I was praying, hoping and despairing at the same time. Minutes that passed felt like hours.

I rose and paced the room. I tried to imagine what Marcus was feeling, but I couldn't. I tried to imagine my life without him, and that wasn't possible either. And so I spoke to Yeshu. I talked to him as a friend, as a prophet, as a God, or as a Son of God. Whatever he was didn't concern me at that point. I pled with him to intervene for Marcus, as he had done so many years before. As I'm sure others have and will do, I offered a bargain, my life for Marcus'. There was no heroism in my pleading, only the realization that there would be little worth living for without my companion.

My prayers would be interrupted as Marcus awoke. His eyes wandered around the room. Was it the delusion state the potion-maker had warned me of? Or did Marcus want to see, for the last time, the world he had lived in? He rasped heavily, his chest heaved violently, and his eyes closed as a ghastly pallor came across his skin. I was still kneeling next to him, speaking words of comfort, when I realized that he was dead.

"Marcus!" I heaved a guttural cry, as I rocked his

dead body in my arms. "Marcus, oh Marcus," I moaned through my tears. How long I stayed like that, I have no idea. Time was suspended. Thoughts of suicide raced through my mind; I wanted to rejoin my lover instantly. Whatever was on the other of the vast chasm between the living and the dead, I didn't care.

From somewhere I found the strength to wrap his body in linen, kissing the head that had encased his beautiful, ever- inquisitive mind; and his eyes, the eyes that had exposed his beautiful soul. I wrapped him tightly, and as I covered his face for the final time, I turned away to vomit, my entire being shaking and trembling. I needed air; I could barely breathe. I walked into our small garden to select a place for burial.

A few feet from where Marcus only weeks ago had done some planting, I began to dig. In an eerie way, the fresh air acted as a balm for my soul. I'm convinced that one day philosophers will discover that such feelings have a mental origin. The air might have felt coolly uncomfortable to others, but to me it was invigorating. Perhaps it was just that my mind was emptying of everything except for the digging.

The spiritual break was short-lived, however. I realized that my next task would be to drag the body, by myself, to the trench I had dug. With great physical, and greater mental effort I did so, and as I rolled him into the pit, his final resting place, the tears returned as strongly as they had been at any time that day. Or truthfully, any other day.

There was one final onerous task to complete. I covered Marcus' remains slowly, with each bit of dirt accompanied by even more tears. Eventually, I finished and knelt beside my lover's grave.

It was dark when I had begun the burial. The dawn was breaking as I finished. A new day had begun, the first day in untold years that Marcus' smile would not greet me. There were no tears left, only sheer and utter exhaustion. My mind raced with the matters before me. The "practicalities" as his father always called them, which had to be accomplished. But they would wait.

Perhaps Marcus was with his father now, and his mother also, their wondrous family reunited. Maybe Yeshu was there too, welcoming him into the kingdom. I prayed that it was so.

But I had to admit to myself that I was selfish. Wherever Marcus was, he wasn't with me. My tears returned as I sought rest.

~~ 57 ~~

In the late afternoon, I garnered enough strength to ride into Rome proper. The practicalities had to be attended to, the sooner, the better.

The Institute was almost deserted at this late hour, which was a useful thing. Jews didn't walk through this Roman bastion of higher education without raising some eyebrows. It was the first time I had ever actually been inside what had been Marcus' workplace. I entered the almost vacant building where I noticed an elderly man standing in the courtyard. He looked very ordinary, and I hoped he could pass along the sad news to the people that mattered.

"Yes, may I be of some assistance?" he asked quizzically.

"I beg the Roman's pardon, but are you connected to the Institute?"

The man surprised me by chuckling. "Well, that's one way to put it, my Jewish friend. I am Seneca, and I lecture here."

I was taken aback. Here I was addressing the most respected intellectual in the Empire as if he was a janitor. I suppressed my urge to flee.

I nervously detailed the reason for my visit, describing, for purposes of propriety, Marcus as my "master."

Seneca nodded. "A pain in the waist, you say. I have heard this is a particularly difficult way to die. On the other hand, there is no easy way, is there, Hebrew?"

I feared to say anything at all.

"I knew your master, though not well. A very bright and questioning mind, though it seems to have been blinded by this Christianity business. Had he converted?"

"I do not know, sir" I lied. "He wouldn't have discussed it with me."

Again, that quizzical look crossed Seneca's face. He nodded.

"Your master will be missed. I will inform the necessary officials. You have my sympathies for your loss. The loss of a .... master.... is always painful."

The way he spoke that the last phrase troubled me, and I couldn't wait to leave the Institute. I did so, as quickly as my legs would allow.

I had to ride to the synagogue and inform them of my whereabouts. I intended to take some time for myself; there was much to be done. Rabbi Micah agreed, favoring me with his response.

"Take as much time as you need, Avrum; your position will be here when you return."

We talked for quite a while. The rabbi was accustomed to this type of situation, if not necessarily this specific situation. There was no doubt that he understood that the bond between Marcus and I was not precisely master and servant. He spoke of no details, but the phrase the "death of a loved one" was often repeated.

Toward the end of his comforting conversation, the Rabbi gave me something to consider that in my grief I had hardly thought of.

"I assume Marcus legally owned your home."

"Why, yes he did."

Again, ignoring any specifics, he reminded me that the taxes on my property, if it were to become my property, would easily treble, if not more. As I have said, Jews could own property within the Empire, but the cost of doing so was often prohibitive. He also described the legal standing of any document that gave ownership of the house to me.

"You're literally on difficult ground here, Avrum. I would consult with men in the congregation who know of such things. I'm sure they would be willing to assist you."

As I rode home, the importance of what the rabbi had said played in my mind. Neither Marcus nor I had ever considered such things; I doubted that many couples had.

There was no document ceding ownership of the property to me. I thought wryly that men who spend their lives around documents would be expected to have one, and that it would be readily available. The truth was that I had no idea what would happen once the tax collector discovered that the owner of the property lay buried in the backyard.

I hoped that I would have some time to untangle that particular puzzle. Other tasks were beginning to take priority. No one dies, especially suddenly, without leaving a part of himself behind. There were clothes and other possessions my lover had accumulated, and they would have to be disposed of. That process occupied several days, not because of the number of items (actually they were quite few), but by the attachment each had for me. I buried all of Marcus' clothes, a seemingly simple procedure that I labored over a full day. I gathered many of his possessions into several large bags; I would leave them with Rabbi Micah to aid those in need. I had no interest in the silver Marcus had accumulated; I would deliver it to the Institute with the hope that some young scholar would benefit from my lover's talents.

I would save some items, those which held a special meaning for me. I placed them all in a trunk, vowing that I would never be without them. It would be inappropriate to describe those items; what may seem very ordinary to some was extraordinary to me. Over the next several years I would often open that trunk (I opened it again just recently, actually), and revel in the memories the items contained.

I spent many nights in the garden, talking to Marcus. It may sound eerie and perhaps demented, but those who have suffered such a loss will understand. I spoke of the past we had together, of the present which scared me, and of the future which I would spend alone. It was rumored in some Christian writings that Yeshu had said, on that fateful night in Gethsemane, that the Son of Man had no place to rest his head. I ascribed myself no such honorific, but now realized exactly what he had meant.

I sensed Marcus' presence throughout each one of those days; it was neither madness nor an overactive imagination. He was with me, and that gave me a strength I would hardly think I possessed. Over the next several months, I would make many crucial decisions; I could not have possibly made them alone.

For reasons that perhaps I will never understand, the most significant of those decisions would be the easiest. I would leave Rome, to return to Palestine. And not to the torch-lined streets of Jerusalem, but to the darkened roads of Nazareth. I would return to my point of origin; the story had begun there; the story would end there.

The ensuing months would be spent in preparation for that departure. I had arranged (the Romans would say conspired) to leave the property to a Roman family whose daughter had recently married; the house would be a gift from her family to the groom. Though I did not know them well, they appeared to be friendly people, and in truth paid me very handsomely for the house.

I took care of other matters expeditiously. Rabbi Micah was very thoughtful, summarizing my contributions to the synagogue in a very complimentary letter. I wasn't sure that my new life in Nazareth would require that I work; but if it did, I now possessed several glowing references.

Time passed quickly. I was within a week of setting sail to Palestine. On one of the last nights, I would spend on Roman soil, as I was sitting in the garden, I could see a carriage headed in my direction. I had received few visitors in the past few months and had no idea who would be calling on me at this late date.

The carriage stopped, and out of one side stepped Joseph, who had returned from his travels. I might have been surprised by his appearance, but it was from the other side of the carriage that my true shock would come. From that side stepped a man whom I never, in the God of All Things' universe, thought I would ever lay eyes on again. There was no doubt, however; I was about to receive a visit from the man I had reviled for years.

"Simon Peter," I said matter of factly, as I rose to meet him.

~~ 58 ~~

"Hello, Avrum," the ex-apostle said.

I stood mute, torn between my obligation to remain civil and my complete desire to physically assault the man I considered the greatest coward I had ever known.

Sensing the tension, Joseph spoke. "I wanted to stop and see you, Avrum. Rabbi Micah told me about your plans and of your unfortunate loss." Staring at the ground beneath me, he added: "this is where…'

"Yes, it is."

Joseph moved to the spot of Marcus' grave, and Peter joined him. They began to recite the Caddish. Perhaps Joseph had suggested this as they traveled to my home as a means of easing the difficulty of the situation. It was undoubtedly useful; my mood softened as I joined my guests in reciting the Jewish prayer for the dead.

I expressed my thanks and invited them into my house. Opening a bottle of wine, I asked Joseph about his travels, and about the progress of his manuscript.

"The book is complete, Avrum. Peter has helped me with it."

I raised my eyebrows.

"You've probably never thought of it in this way, but between you and Peter, most of the years of Yeshu's life are accounted for. The only missing period is those years you had left for Jerusalem and Yeshu stayed in Nazareth. I went to your native village to speak to those people who were there at the time. But they really couldn't tell me much. Apparently not much was happening with Yeshu."

I thought a whole lot was happening during that period when Yeshu had decided to pursue his fate. But this was not the time to discuss it, and I was still seething from Peter's presence.

Joseph continued. "In any event, the manuscript is now completed, and that's one of the reasons I wanted to visit you. Before you leave for Palestine, would you join me for dinner at my house? There's much about the book I want to discuss with you."

I remembered that Joseph had mentioned needing scribes once he had completed his work. So along with my natural curiosity about the finished product, I sensed the opportunity for a commission. I readily agreed to meet with him.

Joseph's next act startled me. "I believe the two of you have much to discuss. I am in need of some of this fine country air. I think I will stroll around a while and let the two of you talk."

He did not say this as a request, but more of a declaration. Before I could react, he was gone, leaving me alone with the man I had no interest in being with.

After a short awkward pause, Peter spoke. "We have a lot to talk about, Avrum." His tone was conciliatory, almost with resignation, and undoubtedly serious. My reply would not be any of those.

"What can we talk about, Peter? Where were you? How could you desert Yeshu the way you did? Did your wife resent you hiding under her skirt?" I essentially spat out the words.

"You're entitled to your anger, Avrum. I will not deny it. Nor will I defend my actions, save to try to explain to you why I did what I did. I only ask you to hear me out. Afterward, I will leave, and if you never want to see me again I will understand."

I stared at the Galilean. His sincerity and earnestness were apparent. So was that sense of resignation. He wanted me to know what happened and he was prepared to leave if I wouldn't listen. But above all he genuinely wanted me to understand. And I wanted to know. I needed to know. I put aside my feelings.

"Go ahead, then."

"Let me start with the last supper Yeshu shared with us. We expected a pleasant evening, despite what had happened at the Temple, and it started out that way. The food was excellent, as was the wine, and everyone seemed to be enjoying themselves. Even Yeshu, although he looked strangely distant."

"But suddenly, Yeshu turned to Judah and asked to speak to him privately. The two of them had been at each other for weeks. I thought this was a perfect time for them to make peace."

With certain sarcasm, I said, "I assume that didn't happen."

"Not at all. You could see Judah's irritation growing as Yeshu talked to him. I thought that rather than reconcile, the two might go at it physically. Instead, Yeshu walked away and silently came to the table. He started tearing the Passover bread and passing pieces to each one of us. He then described the bread as his body and the wine that we were drinking as his blood. He purposefully spilled some wine directly onto the table and said 'This is what will become of the man you have followed for three years.'"

"I know you have no sympathy for me, Avrum, but

please understand how scared I was. After watching Yeshu go off the way he did at the Temple that afternoon and listening to him that evening, I was totally frightened; frightened for his future and frightened for my own. For months he had been talking about his death, and his display made it seem so imminent."

"And you know what made it more frightening? Judah kept interrupting. Every time Yeshu said something, Judah yelled at him. He was screaming things like: 'Stop it! Stop it! You're mad' and 'you want your body torn like bread, and your blood spilled; you want to be bigger in death than you ever would be in life.' Finally, Judah screamed: 'You're just a man, Yeshu, a sick, sick, misguided man.'"

"Yeshu finally looked at him. 'Yes, Judah, I am a man, and as a man, I'm horrified to think of what will happen to me. You think I want it to happen? Then it is you who are mad. I'm sweating my blood from my terror at what lies ahead'."

"' But I must do what Our Father commands. He and I are at one with each other. A new covenant must be forged between the God of All Things and man; between Him and every man'."

"'How dare you!' Judah raged. 'How dare you speak of a new covenant? You're not another Abraham, Yeshu; you're not!' I tell you, Avrum, the man was ranting."

"Yeshu looked at him with that wry smile of his. 'That's the one thing you're right about, Judah. Abraham never had to finalize the sacrifice. No, I am not another Abraham. The cup that I have been given must be drained completely. Abraham never had to complete his sacrifice. But I must'."

"Judah rose from the table with a fire in his eyes. He ran to the door, yelling at us. 'You're all fools! Don't you hear what he is saying? Can't you see what he is doing? Do none of you care about the future of Israel?'"

"Yeshu shouted right back at him. 'Go, Judah, go! Go to your precious Israel, with its blasphemers who defile Our Father's Temple, and mock Him with their rules and rituals. Go! Go now; they're waiting for you'."

"Judah stopped at the door. He was crying, crying as a man whose whole world was collapsing around him. 'Why? Why are you forcing me to do this? Why, Yeshu, why?' Then he fled from the room."

I had listened to the apostle's exposition quietly, but it was time to speak. "I'm not defending Judah, Peter, but he was right in what he said to Yeshu. A new covenant forged between the God of All Things and men, not just Jews? The covenant sets us apart, makes us the Chosen People. Without that covenant, there is no Israel."

Peter sat silently for a while, shaking his head as he finally spoke.

"You are a man of letters, Avrum, and I am a fisherman. I've told you before that Yeshu had said things that I did not understand. But please, let me finish."

Peter continued. "I turned to Yeshu after Judah left, and said, 'I warned you about him. You'd better be careful'. Yeshu just looked at me and said: 'If this Son of God possessed caution, he would have never left Nazareth. Our Father does not want caution, Peter, but pure obedience and submission to His will. Judah will do what he feels is right. He does so actually in good faith. Don't be judgmental of him. Many will fail the Son of Man believing they are doing the right thing'."

"He was looking right at me when he said that Avrum; directly at me. I started to object, but he just turned away, saying he was going to Gethsemane to pray."

~~ 59 ~~

Peter paused to pour himself some more wine. It was apparent that what he had just said was difficult for him. There was also no doubt his next exposition would be even more so.

"James and my brother Andrew were right behind Yeshu, and the rest of us followed. Both Yeshu's brother and my own had expressed their worry about what Judah might do. At Gethsemane, Yeshu separated himself from all of us; he often did that when he wanted to be alone. James began to follow him but stopped halfway; he was torn between leaving his brother by himself and not wanting to bother him."

"The hours passed, and I convinced the others, and maybe even myself, that the danger had passed. It was late, and if Judah were planning anything, it wouldn't be that night. I was sure of it, so we all rested, some of us falling asleep."

"But suddenly James came running to us. 'Quick, something has happened.' I woke the other apostles, and we ran to where Yeshu was. We were all shocked by what we saw. Yeshu was standing in a clearing between the trees, but he was not alone. A circle of Roman soldiers surrounded him, all carrying torches and spears. At the edge of the clearing stood Judah; I couldn't fathom what he had done. One of the soldiers began menacingly addressing us."

"'Who wants to accompany this criminal to the magistrate? Come on now, this degenerate is your leader, isn't he? Are you men not dedicated to him'?"

"He scoffed at all of us. 'No, I guess not. Your flock is made of timid sheep, Nazarene, Get him out of here.'"

"They tied a rope around Yeshu's waist and led him out of the garden. I grabbed James and asked him what had happened."

Suddenly, Peter stopped his narration and, almost eerily, looked outside in the direction of Marcus' grave.

"James told me about the young man in the linen cloth, lying on the ground near Yeshu. Then he told me how the man had leaped up, naked, when the soldiers came. Even a man such as me could see the ingenuity of Judah's plot. Anyone coming onto the scene would believe he was interrupting a .... liaison....... between Yeshu and the young man. But I also knew Judah and knew he couldn't have come up with this on his own. He had to be an agent of much more intelligent men, men of power. Then I remembered the faces on the Sanhedrin as Yeshu was overturning everything at the Temple. I didn't have any doubt that they were the source of the deception."

"You shouldn't have any doubt, Peter" I answered quickly. "I can say for certain your impression was correct. Brilliant, wasn't it? The one crime that would get him arrested and discredit him at the same time."

I sensed there was much more to Peter's narration. There was. His next words came very painfully to him, as his eyes left the gaze from my lover's grave.

"Please don't take offense, Avrum, with what I am

about to say. But once you hear it, I believe you will understand my sin. Not forgive it; I doubt that you ever can, because I know I never can. But I pray that you can understand."

"I am aware of your nature, Avrum. Yeshu and I never discussed it, and please be confident of that. But I did discuss it with another, who is like you. You see, Avrum......."

Peter did not need to say it. Without being conscious of my perceptions, I knew it; I had known it for years. It was why Peter's brother had seemed so familiar to me.

"Andrew is......"

Peter nodded to my uncompleted statement. "He has struggled with it since we were children. My father never accepted it, so when the time came for me to marry, Andrew came with me. And when I left home to join Yeshu, Andrew followed me. He found in Yeshu an acceptance, despite what he is; an acceptance he had never found anywhere else."

I stared at the apostle, reminded again of what Yeshu had preached; all the mysteries of life were simple, you just had to see what was right in front of you.

Peter continued. "I pray you are beginning to understand, Avrum. I had protected Andrew all my life from those who would mock him, or hurt him because of what he is. I felt myself his guardian. As we followed the soldiers out of Gethsemane, they were taunting Yeshu with the same words that Andrew had been called. Andrew walked right next to me, the fear written all over his face. When the soldiers said they were taking Yeshu to the Palace, we hid under the trees. Andrew looked at me, pleading; I told him I would protect him, no matter what the cost."

"And that cost would be huge. A woman came upon us; she had seen the soldiers take Yeshu away."

"'You!' she cried. You are one of his friends. You and that one', she said, pointing to Andrew."

"You're mistaken," I said to her. I lied. I had to lie. Even in front of the other apostles, I had to deny the man that I knew was my savior. But that didn't satisfy the woman. She accused me twice more. Each time I denied knowing Yeshu. She turned from us and said "The Romans will pay for such information'. We saw her walk to the Palace, and talk to the guards outside."

The imagery of that night flashed before my eyes. Marcus and I had seen that very woman, whom we thought was a prostitute. Peter was telling the truth.

He spoke again. "I couldn't risk the Romans questioning Andrew; I couldn't. So we ran away. And we stayed away."

Peter's eyes misted over as he looked at me. Tears were forming in my eyes also. I rose to embrace him sincerely. I was crying for his courage, crying for the agony Andrew had endured through his life (an agony I knew all too well), and crying for the cost Yeshu had paid for this prejudice, which had denied him his closest friend at his greatest hour of need.

An apology was due, and I proffered it.

"You don't need to apologize to me Avrum; you couldn't have known the whole story. I did see Miriam the next day, and she told me about you and your Roman friends. They were......."

"The father and son whom you had met with Yeshu. It was the son, Marcus, whom Yeshu cured."

Peter held his head in his hands. "So the Roman was with Yeshu during his darkest hour, while the Jew lay in hiding. I will never outlive my shame."

He paused, and then asked, "The centurion.......?"

"He has passed" I replied.

"And his son?" Again Peter's eyes wandered into the garden.

I nodded.

"I cry for them, Avrum, as I cried for Yeshu. And for you also, who have suffered so many losses, I cry. May Yeshu calm your sorrows as he has calmed mine."

~~ 60 ~~

There was one more crucial issue to discuss with Peter, and I was relieved when he brought it up.

"I know Yeshu forgives me; He told me so after his resurrection."

I stared at my glass of wine. "So you saw him and talked to him," I said softly.

"Yes I did, Avrum. After talking to Miriam, Andrew and I fled back to Galilee. I wanted to put even more miles between Jerusalem and us, but we had no money, and I couldn't approach our supporters, not after what I had done. So we returned home and joined a fishing expedition. Fortunately, our skills had not been forgotten these past years. For several days, Andrew and I rediscovered our talents."

"But one night as we came ashore, we could see a lone, solitary figure standing there. I stood trembling and shaking as he continued to come into focus. There was no doubt; it was the Master."

I wanted to say something, but I didn't want to interrupt the only first-person account of Yeshu's resurrection that I was ever likely to hear.

"Go on," I said.

"Andrew rose to embrace him. But I stood behind. How could I run to him? I was ashamed and terrified at the same time, both for the same reasons. For all I knew, Yeshu had returned from the grave to taunt me for my desertion."

"Yeshu stood there, Andrew standing right beside him. 'Simon' he said,' whom I have named Peter, come to me.'"

"When he said those words, Avrum, I had no choice. I had to embrace him. I did so, with more tears than I would have thought a man could cry. I fell to my knees, and said, 'Master, forgive me.'"

"Peter, Peter, with all that you and I have been through, after three years of being in my ministry, after all the conversations we've had, you still question that I would forgive you? I should take more offense at your doubt that I did at your friend Thomas' when I appeared to him.'"

"'Stand up, Simon Peter of Galilee, to feel the warmth that Our Father has for the man His son once said would possess the keys to the kingdom.'"

"What could I do, Avrum? I hugged him tightly, still sobbing. It was him, alive, and un-bruised. It was no mirage, no trick."

Peter read the doubt in my face. "Please Avrum, let there be no question in your mind about that. He was as close to me as you are right now, alive, indeed full of life. He even teased me as he always did. He said 'Were you asleep when I foretold my resurrection? No, wait, you couldn't have been. The snoring would have shaken Sinai'."

"Yeshu," I cried, "'You've returned. It's really you'! Then the reality of it all struck me. I began to explain what happened, explain my sin. He stopped me immediately."

"'If Our Father spent all his time thinking about His children's transgressions, real or imaginary, He would have time for nothing else. He has no memory of the past, only of the present, only of the now. And in that now you stand in the love of His Son. What was means nothing. What is to be means everything'."

"We talked, Avrum. Yeshu, Andrew, and I. We talked. I swear by everything I've ever held sacred that it was just like the first time I had seen him, on that very shore three years before."

I had to ask the question that had been formulating in my mind since he had begun his narration about the resurrection.

"I believe you saw what you think you saw, Peter. But tell me, how did Yeshu get to Galilee? Did he walk from Jerusalem?"

"He didn't have to walk, Avrum. He had the ability to move around with no effort. He can appear and disappear like a spirit."

"So when your conversation was over, he just disappeared?"

"Exactly, Avrum. Listen; even I can appreciate how fantastic it all sounds. I know many of those who are opposed to our movement have mocked it for some of what we claim. One of the Roman soldiers did so just last week. He said 'This Messiah of yours who's risen from the grave, I hear he flies around like a little birdie."

I smiled.

"I can understand that," I said. "This talk of Yeshu walking out of his tomb, and all that stuff; it borders on the comical. Besides, it's eerie."

"It can be comical, and it can be bizarre, and it can be fantastic, Avrum. All that matters is that it is true."

I shook my head. "So where is Yeshu now?"

"He gathered us all together, his apostles. Our souls were filled with a mystical sensation Yeshu called the

Holy Spirit. He wasn't just explaining the kingdom as he had while he was living. He was letting us feel the kingdom. I tell you, anyone who had any doubt that Yeshu was who he said he was, was now convinced. All doubt was eliminated. I cannot explain the sensation in words. I can only say it was the most life-changing event that could happen to any man."

"As we were filled with the Holy Spirit, Yeshu told us we had a job to do; to go forth and spread the good news of the kingdom. We began to realize that this was his plan from the beginning, from the day he recruited all of us. We were the ones charged with telling the world what had happened."

A sense of wryness was occurring to me. "I don't imagine Judah was there."

Peter shook his head. "No one knows what happened to Judah, and Yeshu would not discuss it. Instead, he used Judah as an example of a good man who believes he is doing the right thing. Remember, he said the same thing on that terrible evening before the trial. Then he chided us about it: 'you are charged with the care of your own soul, and with spreading the good news. Let He who is to judge the living and the dead judge the Iscariot'."

"Does anyone know what really happened to him?"

Peter just shrugged.

"At the end our gathering, Yeshu began to rise, and his whole body became transparent. He was returning home, to the kingdom, to his Father. I know that as well as I have ever known anything. His last words to us were: 'Know that I am with you, even until the end of time.' And then he was gone."

"It's all true, Avrum. He returned from the dead to show us not to fear death. Instead, we should look forward to the day we are reborn into the kingdom, and be reunited with him. It's all possible, all you need is faith."

I wanted to believe Peter; I really did. How wondrous it would be if Yeshu had indeed risen from the dead, and now had returned to his kingdom, to be reunited with the God of All Things. Would I, at my death, be reunited with him? With my parents? With Marcus? I truly wanted to believe all of it.

But wanting to believe and believing are two different things. Peter read my thoughts.

"The time will come, Avrum, when you will believe the truth of Yeshu. Perhaps this is not the time. But it will come."

Joseph returned as Peter and I shared our last glass of wine. I sensed that he knew our meeting had gone well.

It would be the last time I ever saw Peter, and that conversation remains my most significant memory of him. Of Joseph, I would see once more, hardly realizing that that final meeting would so impact the rest of my life.

~~ 61 ~~

I arranged for the dinner at Joseph's house to be the last real activity I would do in Rome. Maybe I just feared being alone on the last night I would spend on Roman soil. With my mind occupied by the dinner, I would spend that night in neither morbid depression nor nervous anticipation.

The move itself, I had to admit, was less dramatic for me than my other two relocations had been. The truth was I was tired of Rome. Perhaps because of my advancing age, I longed for the solitude challenging to achieve in, or near, big cities. I wanted, as an Egyptian mystic had once described, the "serenity of silence."

I was, of course, leaving Marcus physically behind. But my experience as a scribe (not to mention my experiences with Yeshu) had led me to believe there were only two possibilities for my lover. Either his entire being had ceased the moment he breathed his last breath; in that case, as I spoke to him in his grave, I was somewhat silly talking to something that just no longer was. The other possibility that Marcus was in some "netherworld" or "great beyond" (perhaps even a "kingdom"), was indeed more appealing. In that case, my proximity to his remains was irrelevant; my words and thoughts could be heard by him as easily from Nazareth as they were could be in Rome.

I arrived at Joseph's house in the early evening. As always, the meal was sumptuous, accented with his usual collection of excellent drink. We adjourned to his study to further enjoy that collection.

Joseph began by discussing the details of his trip to Palestine and Greece. He had spared little expense on his journey, traveling first to Jerusalem, then to Sephoria, then to the river Jordan, and ultimately to Nazareth itself. Joseph had been to Jerusalem before but was a first-time traveler to the other locales. Jerusalem, he said, was pretty much the same, save for the advances of the Christian movement. Sephoria Joseph found boring; (he must not have gone to the baths!). And the river Jordan inspiring.

I was amused as he described Nazareth as "quaint" and its residents as being "extremely friendly" and "open." He seemed to think Nazareth was a bit more idyllic than I knew it to be. But if the big-city Joseph wanted to believe small-village Nazareth was something akin to Eden, I wasn't going to dissuade him and ruin his fantasy.

Apparently, he had spoken too many in both Sephoria and Nazareth, among them my old friend Ephraim, whom Joseph described as "quite a character." Predictably Joseph had concluded that there was little interesting about the early years of Yeshu's life. "Not much seemed to be different than any other childhood," he said, and (the specifics events of Yeshu's birth notwithstanding), I had to agree.

Joseph then described his trip to Greece where he was reunited with his daughter. As he had noted, Christianity was as popular in Greece as it was in Rome;

even, he said, as popular as it was in Palestine.

"There aren't small covens of Christians meeting in dark places, Avrum. Instead, there are large gatherings of men and women, sometimes held in large and ornate structures. Rather than hide and speak of one's conversion in hushed tones, Greeks celebrate their membership in the movement very publicly. They even have this charming ritual gathering where they re-enact the last supper Yeshu had with his disciples."

Joseph continued: "Yeshu appeals to Greeks, Avrum, with both his logical reasoning and his mysticism. And the Greeks have always believed the gods are intrinsically involved in human affairs, not some far off deities who are unconcerned. Yeshu's ideal of 'Our Father' has great appeal to them."

"But enough of my travels, my friend. Let's talk about why I wanted to see you before you left."

With that, Joseph went to one of his bookshelves and pulled out a papyrus-bound manuscript.

"I have completed the work that you and others have helped me with."

I took the opportunity to thank him for reuniting Simon Peter and myself.

"I'm delighted that it worked out so well, my friend. Extremely satisfied. I was a little worried as I walked around your neighborhood; I knew your opinion of Peter was not a fond one."

"I learned a lot that evening, Joseph; my feelings about the man have certainly changed."

'That's so gratifying to hear" Joseph replied. "You and he are the two men most responsible for my tome. I certainly pray for both of you, and wish you both the best."

"Now to some specifics. There are right now three copies of my manuscript. My daughter has the first, in Athens. She is negotiating with men of your talents to make copies, the first few of which will be given to various members of the movement there. I have a second copy and will be doing the same thing here in Rome, getting as many copies as I can into the hands of Christians on the continent. In both instances, once the free copies are distributed, I intend to make some money selling the other ones."

Pointing to the sheets by his side, he continued. "And this is the last copy. I wish to commission your services to make additional copies. There is a cloth inside the manuscript containing silver for those services. I would like to see as many copies in circulation throughout Palestine as possible. If you desire to sell them, feel free. I didn't write the book primarily to increase my wealth, but to spread the good news about Yeshu of Nazareth, the most remarkable man who ever lived. On the other hand, commerce is commerce, and I have no doubt people, converts and non-converts alike, will be interested in the life of that man."

I didn't need to look inside the pouch that rested inside the papyrus; I knew Joseph would be generous, perhaps exceedingly so, in his compensation.

The night was drawing to a close. I had a scant twenty hours or so to make the last preparations for my trip. My mind swam from those preparations as much as from the spirits I had consumed that evening.

I embraced Joseph and thanked him for all that he had done for me, and by entrusting me with his manuscript. He would likely never see the final edition that I would scribe, never see the final edition of his work that hopefully would be circulating throughout Palestine. But he trusted me to do that work justice, and I vowed to both he and The God of All Things to do so.

It had been a remarkable evening, but the real ramifications of my involvement with Joseph's gospel were only just beginning.

~~ 62 ~~

I had planned to read Joseph's manuscript on my voyage to Palestine. But once again my constitution would not allow it. If anything, the trip from Rome to Caesarea was more difficult than the trip the other way had been, and of course, I was now twenty years older. At no time during my seafaring was I up to opening the parchment.

The sight of land seemed miraculous to me. I spent a day in Caesarea and then hired a carriage to take me to Nazareth. It was perhaps the most luxurious thing I had ever allowed myself, but I had no intention of returning to my native village either on foot or riding on a team of horses that held my possessions. Joseph's tome was buried beneath those possessions, and other things were occupying my thoughts on the trip. Chiefly I was concerned with where I would live once I arrived in Nazareth. The synagogue still held some of my sheckles I had left years ago; at least I hoped it did. If not, I would be forced to spend my savings and my commission from Joseph more rapidly than I desired.

My carriage arrived at the town well in the early

evening. I had scarcely disembarked when I heard someone shouting my name from across the way. It was Ephraim, who while squinting, recognized his old friend from years ago. Quickly we remade acquaintance, summarizing the events that had happened since we had last seen each other. Like me, Ephraim was back in Nazareth and had been for about a year. We celebrated that two boyhood friends as ourselves would be able to spend our final years together. We also paused at the memory of the third member of our childhood trinity.

The most important part of our reunion, however, was when Ephraim gave me bits of information about my childhood home. Sophia had passed away five years earlier; I turned and gulped a deep breath as I remembered the woman who had meant so much to me. Ephraim explained that since she had no near relations, she had given the house to the synagogue, under the condition that if I were ever to return I was entitled to it without obligation. Again I was reminded of the remarkable woman my father had married.

Ephraim climbed aboard my carriage, and we rode to the house. I broke into tears as I walked between its walls for the first time in twenty years. Sophia had left everything, what little there was, where it always had been. It was as if she had supernaturally known I would be returning. We then rode to see the rabbi. Ephraim had warned me that he was a bit of an old cur, very set in traditional ways. Ephraim hinted that I should be careful around him; I knew exactly what he meant.

Ephraim's description was accurate. Rabbi Malachi was well along in years, and when Ephraim introduced us, his first words were:

"Ah yes, Avrum bar Jacob, the friend of the executed heretic. Well, he certainly got what was coming to him, didn't he? Well, sir, we will have no talk of the blasphemer in this synagogue, no sir we will not.

You are free to worship here, of course, but please keep your private thoughts private."

I had no curiosity about Malachi's religious orientations. In fact, I couldn't care less. The purpose of my visit was to reclaim my childhood home. I informed him as much, and he seemed more relieved than anything else. Quickly the business was concluded, and I would again be the owner of the house that I had grown up in.

As his final task, I asked the carriage driver to return me to that house. Ephraim volunteered to help me get situated, but the truth was that I wanted to be alone. Exhausted from my journey, and still getting over the shock of how many things had fallen into place, I would have been poor company anyway. Within an hour of arriving at my house, I was in bed, leaving the other considerations of my arrival to future days.

I have always remembered my dreams. Like many Greek philosophers, I believe all people dream, and some can remember them more acutely. I have never decided if this was a gift from the God of All Things or an onus. Yet anyone would have remembered the vivid images that visited my dreams that night.

The most remarkable was placed at Golgotha. I stood as Yeshu hung rasping on the cross. But one of the other onlookers I was standing with was Yeshu himself, a young Yeshu, and the Yeshu with whom I had grown up. I couldn't speak to the impossibility and remained mute as if my every effort to speak was stunted.

Suddenly the cross itself was uprooted and began to take flight above us. I ran among my friends, arriving at the spot where the young Yeshu stood. I grabbed him and pointed to the airborne cross. His only reaction was that wry smile of his, the smile I had seen so many times before.

Just as suddenly, Flavius emerged from the shadows

accompanied by an adolescent Marcus, the Marcus with whom I had first fallen in love. But before I could run to them, Flavius in that matter-of-fact voice that I had heard so many times, said: "Yeshu has done what he was sent to do; now Avi must do what he was sent to do."

There were other dreams that night, none with the impact of that one, even though all were very vivid. Yet I awoke the following morning strangely rested, despite the turmoil that had passed before my closed eyes the night before. It occurred to me that I hadn't eaten a substantial meal in days.

The same thought must have occurred to Ephraim. He appeared at my door with a basket full of bread, olives, and fruit. We sat, as elders do, in my backyard catching up on many of the years we had spent apart from each other. It was, I thought, simply wonderful.

I spent the rest of that day settling into my house, aware that this was likely the last unpacking I would ever do. That thought did not depress me; indeed, it invigorated me. As dusk fell, I visited the gravesite of my parents. The man who had purchased the groves from my father, and his heirs (he had long since passed), had kept their promise. The area around the graves was kept in almost pristine condition. The markers that indicated the individual graves had been well maintained, and even the most recent, Sophia's, had been respectively done. I made a note to thank the men who had so honored my three parents.

The remainder of that evening was spent at that very spot. I spoke to my mother, I spoke to my father, and I spoke to Sophia. I apologized to each of them for not being the man they perhaps had dreamed of while they were alive. I thanked them for being the wondrous, unique people they were, and for the beautiful way they had treated me. I may have been cursed with a nature that many reviled, but to them, I was a man, a person who deserved love. And love me each had done.

As I was leaving the site, I saw that one grave remained. The place my father had reserved for my remains was also well tended. My last thought as I walked away was that it would not be much longer before I joined them. Whether I would just be joining them in the ground, or perhaps in the kingdom, or maybe somewhere else, that I could not say. Each had led their lives in ways pleasing to the God of All Things, and, according to Yeshu, was now being rewarded. I was less sure of my own fate. That didn't trouble me, as much as the thought that they were now enjoying themselves gave me pleasure. They were worthy, and likely I was not.

~~ 63 ~~

Naively, I suppose, I had thought that my return to Nazareth would be quiet and uneventful. It had been more than forty years since I had walked my native village's streets, and few were still alive who would remember Avrum bar Jacob, and most of those had memories that were clouded by time. But everyone seemed to remember that I was a childhood friend of the boy now being called the Messiah. Children whose parents I hardly recognized were told by those parents that they had been intimate friends of mine and Yeshu's. Visitors to our hamlet in search of any miniscule information about the "Christ" were directed to my door; my home was becoming a bizarre tourist attraction. Not only did I not find these intrusions pleasurable, but I also began to detest them. I wanted to finish my own life, not re-live Yeshu's.

Ever the resourceful one, Ephraim had devised a plan to end all the intrusions. Rumors began filling Nazareth that the man Avrum was mad, that people who went to visit him were never to be seen again, or that he was a leper. The entire town partook in the deceptions, certainly more for their convenience than mine. While it didn't end the interruptions to my time, it did stem the tide quite a bit, and for that I was thankful.

I was also thankful that Rabbi Malachi offered me, however hesitatingly, the post of synagogue scribe. Not that the synagogue had that much work, but word began to spread through the town of my abilities, and that brought several attractive fees in my direction. Once again I was the scribe of Nazareth, handling business transactions and various other dealings. There was quite a bit of work, enough at least to fill my diminishing capacities; so much so that I began to mentor a replacement, Ephraim's grandson Yonni, a bright and energetic young man.

Whether it was my return to the world of letters, or my advancing age, or any of a variety of reasons, the idea of writing a memoir of my experiences begun to formulate in my mind. I decided that I would start that remembrance as soon as I was done with Joseph's manuscript; I had set aside a week to pour over and examine the gospel. I planned the night to begin but would be interrupted by a visitor, a most welcomed visitor.

"James!" I cried as I answered a knock at my door. I embraced Yeshu's brother, and poured my finest wine, in anticipation of a lengthy conversation. James looked terrific, as hale and hearty as I had ever seen him, as hale and hearty as I could ever imagine him being. He still spoke in the same soft tones he had as a child, yet with a depth that portrayed a deep maturity.

He began by telling me of his exploits since the last time I had seen him, during that fateful Passover. James had traveled extensively throughout Palestine and beyond, with news of his brother's ministry. He often was accompanied on those journeys either by Simon Peter or by Paul; thus he was at the forefront of the

Christian movement. As I listened to him tell of his travels, I mused that while Peter and Paul may be the brains of the movement, James was indeed its soul.

I was so enraptured by my friend's narrative that I had neglected to have immediately asked about Miriam; I interrupted him to rectify the error and my insensitivity.

Nodding his head, James said: "She is with Yeshu now, Avrum; they are once again united in the kingdom."

"So she has passed," I said respectfully.

"Oh no Avrum; she is still very much alive. Just like Yeshu, Our Father took her directly into the kingdom. She didn't die; she was assumed into the heavens."

Was this another of the bizarre stories that seemed to permeate the movement, I wondered. But I would not challenge the man; he was much too sincere for that. Instead, I felt my dead lover's spirit of wit descend on me.

"Well, for one thing, James, it seems that none of your family will ever have to worry about funeral expenses."

James smiled his (still, after these years) innocent smile, and continued. He seemed as eager to talk as I was to listen. I believe hours passed as we talked about each other's lives since last we had seen each other. Without dealing in specifics, I told him of my time in Rome, and of the writer Joseph, whose work I was about to begin transcribing.

"I've heard of the books being written about my brother, Avrum; and Paul has read me some of the letters he has written. But you know me to be a dull and ignorant man, not very knowledgeable about some of the things Yeshu spoke of. It's best I leave that portion of the movement in the hands of more capable men than myself."

I wondered if there were, in fact, any more capable men than James, but didn't pursue the issue. Instead, I returned to the crucifixion drama and asked if he had heard what finally happened to Judah.

James had a distant view in his eyes as he answered. "No one knows, Avrum; there were all kinds of stories, but no one is certain what happened to the Iscariot." Then, my friend's jaw set in a certain, almost vengeful way. "If I should ever meet him, I would kill him."

The venom of his statement, so unlike anything I had ever heard James say, shocked me. James continued in that same vein. "When I think of what he did to Yeshu, to mother, and yes, Avrum, even to me, I could easily slaughter him with my own hands."

I paused, framing my next words carefully. "First of all, James, I'm sure your brother himself would disagree with you. Isn't the kingdom all about forgiveness? I know, it's difficult, but I can tell you from personal experience, Yeshu was right about that. I hated a man you know well for many years for what he had done. Yet when I discovered the reasons why he had acted in the way he did way, my appreciation for him grew in ways I can scarcely describe. It may not be the same, but......"

James nodded his head. "I understand, Avi; and I think I know of whom you speak. We never got into details, but Simon Peter has told me of your meeting in Rome with him. I can only pray that I someday will have the same forgiveness for Judah. But it would be very difficult...."

I did not want our evening to end on that sour note, and so I reminded James of our childhood spent together, a childhood when none of us could have possibly foreseen the events that awaited us. I mentioned that I had considered penning a memoir of sorts about that childhood, and James readily agreed that I should do so. "So many strange things have been written about my brother's history; maybe it is time for a more accurate retelling of that history. You have my blessing to say whatever you need to say about Yeshu and my entire family in your work."

I could not express my joy at James' reaction and assured him that nothing I would ever write would ever compromise in any way the most wonderful family a man could have ever known.

The night was drawing to a close. I told James that my traveling days were over, and I would spend my final days right where I was. He said he would try to visit me again. We embraced as fondly as we ever had, and I wished him well on his journeys.

As he walked away from my home, I thought of the unsure, nervous and shy young man he had been, and of the assured, calm and outgoing man he had become. Christianity indeed, I thought, is the religion of rebirth.

~~ 64 ~~

The time had arrived to examine Joseph's manuscript. Yonni had advanced far enough with his talents that he was able to handle the work coming in from Nazareth. Moreover, if I did go fully ahead transcribing Joseph's tome, I would need Yonni's services. Beyond that, while the notion of writing down my own experiences was beginning to obsess me, I owed Joseph his time.

I decided I would treat Joseph's manuscript as I had done other similar assignments. At the beginning of my career, I had been encouraged by Levi never to approach a book piecemeal. Instead, my mentor had said, the scribe should read the entire contents of the work first, to attain the "flavor" of the author's intent. After the first reading, depending on the material, a second complete reading may be called for, and perhaps even a third. Only after the scribe could ascertain the underlying theme of the work should the actual business of transcribing begin. It was a technique that had served me well throughout my career. I would continue it with Joseph.

A glass of wine in hand, and a long candle burning on my table, I opened the sheets of papyrus that held Joseph's gospel. Reading the first sentence of the first chapter, I was immediately discouraged and discomforted, however. Joseph had deceived me when he told me that his book would be an objective discussion of Yeshu's life. Instead, he had begun with:

"The Beginning of the Gospel of Jesus Christ, The Son of God."

Those first few words spoke volumes about the slant Joseph was about to take. "Jesus Christ" of course meant "Yeshu the Messiah, Son of God"; informing all that Yeshu had, and still held, that special and unique relationship with the God of All Things. Joseph could have begun with "the gospel of the great prophet Yeshu," or something similar. Instead, he made it clear from the outset that this gospel would accept completely what the Christians were proclaiming.

Or did it? I pondered that opening statement for quite a while. It occurred to me that, while in Greece, Joseph may have learned of a style popular among Greek writers, especially philosophers. They would make a statement at the beginning of a work, implying that it was true. Then they would spend the rest of the book demonstrating that it was instead false. Perhaps that was to be Joseph's technique. The teachings of Levi resounded through my mind; digest the whole of the manuscript first.

And so I proceeded. Joseph had suggested to me that since none of the recollections of my youth with Yeshu indicated anything remarkable, he might omit them from his gospel entirely. I had to admit to myself my disappointment that he had. There was nothing of Agatha, nothing of the somewhat strange events that surrounded Yeshu's birth, nothing of his childhood at all. Miffed as I was, I could almost understand Joseph's reasoning. Besides the somewhat scandalous events that surrounded Yeshu's beginnings, events that would add nothing to the mystique of the man (and might even detract from it), Yeshu's childhood had been, I admitted ruefully, just too mundane to write about. As had my own, I supposed.

So Joseph's gospel began with Yeshu's baptism by the strange man Yonni. His description of that baptism smacked more of Greek theater than the reporting of actual events, however. Doves descended from the heavens, the skies opened up, and the voice of the God of All Things was heard by all. This was far from the bizarre and barely clad Yonni thrusting people into the river Jordan that I had witnessed. Joseph's description was indeed imaginative, but also overly dramatic.

It must be based I mused, on Yeshu's account. Doubtless, Yeshu had told Peter the same details he had told me about his baptism. Peter would have repeated those details to Joseph. But there was a difference between Yeshu's and Joseph's versions. To Joseph, everyone there that day had seen and heard what Yeshu told me only he had experienced. I found that difference troubling.

And yet that was far from the most discomforting aspect of Joseph's retelling of the baptism. Any educated reader would have a significant problem with the story as a whole. If Yeshu was indeed the Son of the God of All Things, why would he need to be baptized by a mere mortal in a ritual that almost defied the ritual of the Mick bah? Would this be the only inconsistency in Joseph's text? I paused and then plunged more in-depth into the manuscript.

Joseph next wrote extensively of Yeshu's ministry. Some of it was, I had to admit, fascinating reading, as Yeshu began to explain his belief system, most notably about "Our Father" and the "kingdom." There was much substance to many of the things Yeshu said, or perhaps that Joseph, no doubt inspired by Peter, had Yeshu say. It made for some very thoughtful reading, especially the seemingly endless amount of parables Yeshu was fond of telling. Rather than confronting major philosophical issues directly, he instead channeled somewhat tricky positions into stories and fables, perhaps reasoning that the apostles, who were mostly illiterate and uneducated would more easily understand them that way. While some of the parables were clumsy, I could easily see where they would be instructive.

But again, there was an immediate danger to Yeshu's methods. Everyone interprets stories in their own way; this appears to be self-evident. And it certainly was evident from Joseph's text. Frequently, the apostles just seemed to miss the whole point. Yeshu seemed to be endlessly chiding them, Peter most frequently, about their lack of understanding. Yeshu could be like that, I remembered. But if the apostles, the chosen ones, could not correctly interpret their master's parables, how could those who hadn't known Yeshu personally be expected to do so? I saw that as another major issue.

Philosophical ramblings were not the totality of the ministry, as Joseph was quick to point out. There were a variety of miracles Yeshu had performed along the way. I had no opinion of them; perhaps they did happen. And certainly, my experience with Marcus' illness led me to believe that Yeshu was indeed blessed with the ability to heal. But the leap from "healer" to "Messiah" was a huge one.

Immediately I realized another issue as Joseph described Yeshu's miracles. Anyone who had read the Torah would identify the "feeding of the thousands" and "walking on water" as miracles performed centuries earlier, by the prophet Ellisher. Did Joseph assume that few, if any, of his readers, would be familiar with the

Second Book of Kings, where Ellisher performed those same miracles? Perhaps Joseph's assumption was sound. Many of his readers would likely be gentiles, unfamiliar with the Torah. Yet many would just as probably be Jews who would quickly see the similarities. It seemed a bit of a gamble on Joseph's part. More seriously, if the reader did not accept Yeshu's miracles, seeing them as only plagiarisms from Kings, could they accept the rest of Joseph's reporting? As before, this would require scrutiny later on.

I paused to consider all that I had read. I did not immediately continue. Instead, I walked, first into my backyard, and ultimately around Nazareth. I believe at several points, I talked aloud to myself. Fortunately, the hour was late, and I did so unseen.

I decided to digest what I had read before I went any further. I would leave the gospel alone for the rest of the evening.

~~ 65 ~~

Or so I thought. Sleep would not come to me as I tossed and turned, over the contents of Joseph's manuscript. I surrendered to the fates, rose from my bed, and relit the candle; I would complete my reading as the sun rose over the Palestinian horizon.

My career as a scribe had given me access to some of the world's greatest fiction, fiction I always considered an honor to transcribe. But nothing could have prepared me for the final chapters of Joseph's manuscript. They were all very dramatic, all very moving. And most were untrue.

Joseph began his last chapters with an account of Yeshu's arrest. For the most part, this would be the most honest of his retellings of the events of those days. Though I wasn't there, his description of what had happened in Gethsemane meshed with the eyewitness accounts Peter and James had given me. From then on, however, Joseph fell into a narrative of complete fantasy.

Rather than being taken directly to the magistrate, Yeshu was, according to Joseph, taken first to the

Sanhedrin. As to why he was taken there, Joseph did not explain. In any event, Yeshu winds up eventually in Roman custody. And from there Joseph's imagination begins to truly get the best of him.

According to the author, Yeshu, a poor itinerate Jewish preacher, was given a grand and ceremonious trial, presided over by Pontius Pilate himself. The absurdities of this portrayal were too numerous to count. Jews (and just about anyone else who wasn't a Roman citizen) received almost no protection under Roman law; arrest meant guilt, which meant punishment. True, there might be a hearing of sorts, and I knew Yeshu had had one. But presided over by Pilate? Pontius Pilate was a military man, unused to the nuances of Roman law; Marcus had suggested to me years earlier that Pilate was only semi-literate. Even if the accused were famous (which Yeshu certainly was not), Pilate would have no real standing in a Roman court besides that of an interested observer.

The absurdities didn't end there. Yeshu had been given a hearing before the magistrate, cursory at best. But according to Joseph, he had been tried before thousands of Jews, in some great courtyard. These "crowds", which had saluted Yeshu earlier as he entered the city, were now screaming for his blood. But why? Joseph again does not explain.

At some point in the proceeding, Pilate addresses the crowd, asking them what should be done with the accused. A Roman governor asking a crowd of Jews how to handle a Jewish prisoner? I wryly assumed Joseph had consumed too many of his fine spirits before he had penned those words.

Incredibly there was more. Yeshu was being tried as an enemy of the state, a subversive. A man who had preached non-violence; a preacher who had told his followers to pay their taxes and render to Caesar what was Caesar's; a prophet who had spoken of a kingdom open to Jew and Roman (and everyone else) alike.; a man who had instructed his tribe to love his enemies and to turn the other cheek when assaulted; this man was suddenly a threat to Roman security. How ironic that the preacher who had been chided by his people for not being anti-Roman now stood accused of being just that.

At no point did Joseph mention the real crime of which Yeshu had been accused. Nowhere. No mention of the young man in the garden, and the accusation of sodomy. Would Joseph describe it later? Was he trying to be tasteful in an off-kind of way?

Larger absurdities were about to come, however. According to Joseph, the Romans had a custom of releasing any prisoner the Jews wanted to be released, during the Passover. I could not imagine in what state Joseph had written these words; who would believe such a thing? Certainly, no one who lived in Palestine.

To compound this fiction, Joseph had Pilate offering the crowd the choice of Yeshu, or a man named Barabba. For reasons Joseph didn't give, the crowd chooses Barabba.

Who was this man Barabba, I wondered; Joseph gave little information, beyond that this Barabba had achieved some notoriety as a rabble-rousing Jew. I had never heard of this man, and I had had access to much information about these things from both the Temple and from the Palace (through Marcus).

I was forced to quickly conclude that there was a simple reason why I had never heard of Barabba; he didn't exist and never had. Why would Joseph fabricate such a person? What possible purpose could it serve to Joseph's manuscript? Beyond all that, there was something distinctly odd about the name "Barabba." I was tempted to stop my reading and investigate the matter further, but Levi's words rang through my mind;

read the whole first, to parse how the pieces made the whole.

But the difficulties continued. According to Joseph, Pilate asked Yeshu: "Are you the King of the Jews," to which Yeshu replies, rather mysteriously, "It's you that say I am." What an incredible and bizarre exchange! What could Joseph possibly be thinking?

I was relieved when the action of the gospel moved away from the "trial"; I had been sated with its inaccuracies. My mood evened as I recognized perhaps my only real contribution to the whole gospel; Joseph accurately described Simon the Cypriot hoisting up and carrying Yeshu's cross. Even this portrayal had its elements of fiction. Joseph made it appear that Simon had just been passing by and that the soldiers had forced Yeshu's cross upon him. That description troubled me deeply, even if I understood how difficult it would be to explain why Simon was on the road to Calvary. With sadness, I accepted the fiction, all the while wishing Joseph had spent more time describing the completely heroic acts of a completely heroic man.

Joseph's rendition of the scene at Golgotha was also relatively accurate, with of course the now-common exaggerations; the curtain of the Temple being torn in two; the "crowd" of onlookers to the execution, etc. The tearing of the curtain was nice symbolism, I thought, indicating that Yeshu had indeed "torn" the covenant of Abraham. As for the crowds, Joseph just seemed to enjoy placing throngs of people everywhere.

I was again given pause, this time appreciatively, to the retelling of Flavius' pronouncement that: "Indeed, this was the Son of God." Even as Joseph offered no information about the man, beyond his being a centurion, the passage had the same effect reading it as it had when I heard it. Still, because of the lack of background, Joseph had almost ignored entirely the noblest man I had ever known. As I read the passage, I wept at the memory of that man.

But all the accuracy and integrity Joseph had shown describing the crucifixion quickly vanished, however. Yusuf the Arithmithean, one of the most sinister of the plotters of the outrage, was transformed into a kindly old man. I bristled at the very notion; that sanctimonious Sanhedrin personified all that I detested about my faith; here he was being saluted for his "generosity"; my stomach churned at the very suggestion.

Joseph ended his gospel with the two Miriams arriving at the crypt, to anoint Yeshu's body. This had likely happened as I was fleeing to Nazareth. They are shocked however when Yeshu's body is not there. Instead, there is a man (an angel?) who says "He is not here." The women run off, scared out of their wits.

What a confusing and unsatisfying ending, I thought. Joseph's entire gospel had been spent describing Yeshu as the Messiah, the son of God. Why not detail his (supposed) resurrection?

I set the manuscript down on my table. I had done what my mentor had taught me to do. I had read Joseph's gospel in its entirety to appreciate the underlying theme of the work, its "flavor."

But I did not appreciate the flavor. I was confused, I was adrift, and I was more than a little angry. Well written as it was, the tome was fraught with inconsistencies, impossibilities, and incongruities. How could such a work convince anyone that Yeshu bar Yusuf had indeed been the Messiah, the Son of God, and the Redeemer of mankind? How would it convince anyone of anything?

I placed the sheets of papyrus aside. There they would sit, for quite a while.

~~ 66 ~~

It would be several weeks before I would take those sheets off the shelf. I could blame the amount of work I had coming my way. Not only had I employed Ephraim's grandson Yonni, but the rabbi himself had a grandson who was interested in my craft. I agreed to take him on as an acolyte. The circular nature of a rabbi's grandson wanting to be a scribe, working for a rabbi's grandson who had fostered similar ambitions when young was not lost on me.

But that blame would be misplaced. The truth was that I was so confused by Joseph's gospel that I could not even begin the transcription process. Ephraim had more than once criticized me that my chosen profession was a simple one, merely writing down another man's words. I would explain to him (an explanation he seldom paid any attention to) that the physical process of writing the words was the most natural part of the scribe's task. Indeed, I had often looked forward to the time when the manuscript was ready for copying. It was the getting it ready, the editing, that was always the significant labor. And the major challenge.

I had to be faithful to Joseph's intent. O the other hand, the one thing I was sure about was the scorn with which it would be greeted. Joseph was too fine a man, as was his subject, to be laughed at. And laugh Palestine would do as they read of a peasant preacher given an elaborate trial before the Roman governor himself. Parts of many of Joseph's other narrations would produce a similar effect. I worried that if I were to leave them in the gospel, it would be met with scorn and ridicule by all. I couldn't let that happen.

That was the primary obstacle blocking my path, but there were others of course. Any copyist knows them well. Joseph had written his gospel in traditional Greek, and the primary reason he had paid me the fee was my talent for translating. The Aramaic version would be much more accessible to even the less-educated Palestinians who, while they might understand the spoken Greek idiom, likely wouldn't be able to fathom the classic Greek style Joseph had used.

Moreover, the style of Greek Joseph had used did not always translate easily into other languages. Frequently, the copyist who is also a translator finds himself trying to solve this problem in a clumsy and cumbersome way. And that was far from the only technical issue.

The task in front of me was an arduous one, especially when I considered the nature of the work. I briefly considered abandoning it. But I couldn't. I had accepted Joseph's commission for the job. Honor, not to mention the Torah, demanded that I performed it.

Of course, I knew there was more to it. For whatever reason, I had come to believe that this would be the most important thing I had ever done in my life; all that had preceded it merely a preamble to transcribing this gospel. It was not only to Joseph that I owed this obligation, it was to Yeshu, to Miriam, to James, and to

Simon Peter. I had a responsibility to all of them, to correctly complete the task I had been given.

I was also self-aware (self-critical perhaps) that my desire to complete the work was intrinsically entwined with the memory of the man who had been my lover for decades. The spirit of Marcus permeated every thought I had about Joseph's work. My companion had come to believe while he was alive that Yeshu was who he said he was. Here was an opportunity to legitimize that claim, to make it widespread, to introduce to the many the man my soul mate deemed the Messiah. And not just the Messiah of the Jews, but the Messiah of all of mankind.

With all these thoughts in mind, I began again to completely and thoroughly read the manuscript. I quickly decided I would change nothing of the miracles or healings Joseph claimed Yeshu had performed. They were essentially insignificant anyway. Moses had parted the Red Sea and spoken directly to the God of All Things; Noah had saved civilization from extinction. Walking on water seemed trivial compared to the feats of those heroes of the Torah. And none of them had claimed a direct decadency from the Almighty.

I began taking copious notes as I read. Every time I found something objectionable in Joseph's work, I made a note of it. In fact, I had so many notes that the notes themselves began to outnumber the pages of the gospel. The shelves on which I kept the manuscript and notes started to sag under the weight of its contents.

Day and night I obsessed over the gospel. Day and night I tried to make sense of what Joseph was trying to say. It became more than an obsession. Sabbath obligations went unheeded as I poured over the tome. Social invitations (not that they had ever been numerous, to begin with) went ignored. I ate too little; I drank too much. Even personal hygiene went neglected. On more than one occasion, I was uncharitable to Yonni as he reported to me in the morning. I believe he developed a fear coming to my home.

I was saved from the obsession by an unlikely source. Answering a knock on my door one morning, it was not Yonni but Ephraim, who immediately physically grabbed me from my home and forced me to walk in the morning air, and to walk around the village. He forced me to eat solid food, to ignore my bottles of wine, and to pay attention to my grooming.

By the end of that day, it was as if all the exhaustion from my obsession had spilled into that one evening. I collapsed into my bed, and sleep, which had been infrequent and restless, became sound and restive. I slept the entire next day.

I woke the next morning as a newborn, refreshed and rested. When Yonni came to my door, I greeted him heartily and cheerfully. He would admit later that he feared that morning that I had gone totally mad. Preparing an extensive morning meal, I laid out a plan for the business before us, and for completing all of the work I had neglected.

With Yonni busy at work, I once again approached the gospel. I dropped the manuscript on the table, and the sheets opened to Joseph's description of the trial of Yeshu. I looked at those pages and felt a personal epiphany. Right in front of me was the answer to every question I had asked, and every question that had left me stupefied. It was as if the God of All Things (Our Father?) had blown the manuscript open to the exact location that would answer all of those questions.

The pages had flown open to the story of Barabba.

~~ 67 ~~

The character Barabba had confused me; it had confounded me; it had perplexed me. Why had Joseph invented such an obvious fiction; what purpose could it serve? By discovering the answer to that question, I discovered the portal through which I would understand the whole of Joseph's gospel.

I had spent untold hours reading the gospel in literal terms, peering at every word, every phrase. I had analyzed the truthfulness of every statement, pulled apart sentences, written volumes of notes, referenced and cross-referenced all that Joseph had written.

And I had wasted all that time.

Various conversations I had had throughout my life began to swirl around within my mind, an eddy of quotes heard over my lifetime. Joseph had told me that he had wanted to write the definitive history of Yeshu of Nazareth; Yeshu himself had said to me that words were not the truth of Scripture; the truth of Scripture was that it was true. I had been doing precisely what Yeshu had chided the Sanhedrin (and myself) of doing; looking only at the words.

The cacophony of quotations continued to permeate my mind. "Words are like bread," Yeshu had said; by itself, it is only bread. It is only when we ingest the bread, allowing it to circulate within our system, that the bread becomes the sustenance of life. So too were words; by themselves, they are merely words. But placed with a man's (or a woman's, I was reminded of another conversation) soul, they become the sustenance for that soul.

I needed, to understand the whole of Joseph's work, to go past his words. I had to get past the impossibility of the man Barabba; past the spectacle of Yeshu's baptism by Yonni; past the huge "crowds" that had witnessed my friend's miracles, healings, and demise; past the narrative of his hearing before the magistrate as some grand legal proceeding. I had to sift through the accuracies of each event. Yeshu had indeed been baptized by Yonni, worked miracles and healings, had been arrested, tried and executed. How much did it matter that those events did not happen as Joseph described them? It didn't, because Joseph had paid the ultimate compliment to his subject.

Yeshu had spent his entire ministry describing complex theological and moral issues by way of the parable. He seldom spoke directly, except when he explained the God of All Things as "Our Father," and even that description required the listener to think, to analyze. He told stories, he made up scenarios that led the listener toward the path of the truth of our lives.

In a way I could only now understand, Joseph had followed Yeshu's lead. The entire of Joseph's gospel was a parable, a parable about the life of Yeshu of Nazareth. Did it matter that there weren't "thousands" fed by Yeshu multiplying loaves and fishes? I had spent hours attempting to understand where those "thousands" had come from, and how they had gotten there.

No, it didn't matter. What mattered was the message that Yeshu provided sustenance for the soul, and that the nourishment was unending and insatiable, always to be replenished when needed. There was no end to the loaves and fishes, Joseph had written; of course, we knew that there had to be some end to them. But if the bread represented the essence of Yeshu, of his wisdom and guidance, then indeed there was an endless supply.

So the entire of Joseph's gospel was a palpable, a parable about the master of parables. And what of Barabba? Who was he? What was he?

The name Barabba didn't exist in Palestine, nor its Roman counterpart, Barabbas. But the phrase "bar-abba" most definitely did. "Bar-abba", the "Son of the Father", was the name Yeshu had called himself continuously. What could Joseph have meant by the parable of Barabba?

There was little question in my mind that the "throngs" of onlookers that had (imaginatively) attended Yeshu's trial represented Israel itself. Pilate was offering Israel the choice between a Son of the Father who embodied all those things traditional Jews prayed for; a political, military leader who no doubt would eliminate the Occupation and protect the exclusivity of Israel's covenant with the God of All Things.

Or they could choose a Son of the Father who was decidedly non-political, a pacifistic leader who preached the inclusion of all of humanity into the kingdom of the God of All Things, a kingdom attainable through the covenant that Yeshu represented and embodied. Israel made it's choice, conspiring with Rome to eliminate the man who would have changed its face forever; it had chosen the past instead of the future. And in the process had made the rise of Christianity possible, indeed inevitable.

A religion which preached the equality of all

presided over by a God who cared for every one of his creatures in a fatherly way, would appeal to all, even more so if its herald was a charismatic leader like Yeshu. The message was appealing; the messenger was appealing. The rapid growth of Christianity that I had witnessed in my lifetime was evidence of the enormous error Israel had made. Jews were flocking to the movement, as were their pagan brothers and sisters, all inspired by the life and teachings of the man Yeshu, a life of which Joseph had written so eloquently.

The scope of Joseph's gospel was now apparent, as was its range and depth. This time, it was a conversation that I had had with my grandfather that raced to the front of my mind.

We were discussing Noah and the miracle of the flood. I had questioned grandfather as to how it was possible Noah knew the whole world was flooded, besides the somewhat clumsy image of the dove. Grandfather looked at me intently, then just laughed, saying, "Well, Avi, it must have rained a lot."

I had to think when I considered the parable of Noah; readers would have to think when they read the parable of Yeshu, as authored by Joseph. It was brilliant, and in the end, saluted the Creator who had made thought possible.

I was now ready to prepare and transcribe Joseph's manuscript. I would commission Yonni (the rabbi's grandson was not quite prepared for such intricate work, I reasoned) to prepare multiple copies, to scribe as fast as he could. I wanted to put as many copies in the hands of those who were in Jerusalem for the next Passover as possible; I knew Yonni would be faithful to his charge.

But I knew there was one change to be made. One alteration to the text that was demanded. It would take me many days to accurately make that alteration.

~~ 68 ~~

Joseph had written a brilliant, compassionate parable about the life of a man I had loved as a boy. A man that Joseph believed was the Son of the God of All Things, the Messiah, and the Redeemer of all mankind. Once readers grasped the style of the work, I thought, they too would understand the essence of Yeshu of Nazareth.

But there were internal inconsistencies in the manuscript. These inconsistencies I knew would make readers question the validity of the story. In Joseph's name, I had to deal with those contradictions.

I returned to Joseph's gospel after several days. I had already begun the process of transcribing it and had Yonni working on making a second copy. Together we had worked long hours, leaving the regular business of Nazareth to the Rabbi's grandson.

As each hour passed, I knew I would have to make alterations to the text. The first would have to do with Joseph's failure to mention the resurrection; a resurrection that I knew would be the focal point, as it already was, of the Christian movement.

And so I added an additional chapter, with Yeshu

appearing to his disciples after his rising. I wrote it with some drama and some imagery. Although I would never claim to be a writer, I was reasonably satisfied that my version of those events followed the lead that Joseph had set, both in style and in substance.

That would be the easy alteration to the text. There was a far more difficult one to be made, and I struggled with how to do it for many nights. Joseph's description of the charge that had led to Yeshu's execution was fraught with problems; not only of the ordinary type but even when the style of the parable was taken into account.

To Joseph, Pilate had Yeshu crucified for calling himself a king, a "King of the Jews." There were several problems with that portrayal. First, Yeshu had never called himself a king. True, he had spoken of a kingdom, but one ruled by the God of All Things, "Our Father."

It was moreover very difficult to believe that a preacher who may have been the least political preacher in all of Palestine had granted himself a title that was inherently political. Yeshu would have no more called himself "king' than he would have called himself "Caesar."

And what if he had indeed called himself a king? Levi's rantings resounded in my mind. If Yeshu had indeed anointed himself "King of the Jews", Rome wouldn't be upset, they'd be excessively pleased. Yeshu was more than they could ever dream of as a King of the Jews. He told his followers to love their oppressors while honoring their wishes; above all, to 'turn the other cheek" if struck down by those oppressors. Rome could not have been happier than if Yeshu was the leader of Israel.

Nothing about the charge had the plausibility that it required. I was not unsympathetic to Joseph's plight. The crime that Yeshu had been framed for was not a comfortable topic. Sodomy remained a distasteful crime, and Sodomites were by definition distasteful to many. I remembered the reaction in Jerusalem as the rumor that Yeshu was a Sodomite spread on the day after his death. It had made Yeshu an object of ridicule and disgust. I knew Joseph wanted no hint that such a charge could be true.

I was far from being unaware that the matter had personal relevance for me. I had witnessed my friend being executed for a crime of which he had no guilt, but I did. Yeshu was not of my nature, and any indication that he was would, regrettably, compromise him in ways I dared not to imagine. I could not allow that to happen.

Neither could I go into great detail about the true cause of the crucifixion, for two reasons. The character Barabba had been my own personal portal into the realization that the gospel was a parable, and I wanted it to be a similar portal for other readers. The entire "trial" scene in the gospel may have lacked truth, but it was sated with the essence of Yeshu, a spirit I was loathed to change. And I would not.

But the readers of Joseph's gospel deserved the truth of what had happened that fateful Passover. I struggled mightily with how to do just that.

The answer (again I was reminded of Yeshu's saying that the answer was always right in front of us) was simple. I would insert the story of the young man exactly when and where it had happened, omitting nothing of his nakedness or of his fleeing away from the Romans.

I imagined the readers of the gospel would likely be stunned by this added verse. They would rightly ask "Who was this young man," and "What was he doing there?" and "Why was he naked?" And I wanted them to ask those exact questions. Genuinely, the insertion would solidify the nature of Joseph's work as a parable.

No one in Palestine would believe the trial scenes as

Joseph had described them; this had been obvious from the beginning. But the reader would understand that there had been a trial, and at least a hearing, and there had been a reason for that trial; even the Romans wouldn't arrest someone (even a Jew) and crucify him for no understandable reason. The nature of the parable would then be reinforced, along with the obvious conclusion that the charge was false. The reader would immediately recognize the trickery that had caused my friend's execution. And who bore the brunt of the responsibility for that trickery.

And so I made the addition to the gospel. I made it as Yonni was transcribing that scene in the manuscript. He asked no questions, but I could sense the confusion he was experiencing. I was satisfied with that confusion; the insertion of the verse had had the exact effect on the gospel's first reader that I dreamed every reader would have. I silently saluted myself for my inspiration.

The work was done. I estimated that between Yonni and myself, we would have several copies ready by the time he went to Jerusalem for Passover. When he finished the first of those copies, I treated my acolyte to a fine evening meal. I invited Ephraim to join us, and I knew both were appreciative.

As they left me for the evening, I went to my yard to celebrate our achievement with a tasty bottle of wine. My life's journey had led me to this exact moment, I concluded. Flavius had told me in my dream to do what I was sent to do; I felt at that very moment that I had done just that. I had helped Joseph proselytize the life of the remarkable Yeshu of Nazareth, someone I had loved as a boy, admired as a man and remembered with deep emotion after his death.

But it wasn't just Yeshu I remembered that night. It was all of those who had peopled his life and mine, and how they had intersected, beginning with my grandfather, my mother, my father, Yusuf, Miriam, and James, and extending through Marcus and Flavius, two men who had defined my whole existence. I remembered all the others whose lives had intertwined with the lives of two childhood friends, in an out-of-the-way village in a troubled land. Indeed, how could I possibly forget any of them?

They had formed the landscape of my life, and it was to them that I drank a toast, individually and collectively.

And then perhaps for the first time in that life, I drank a toast to Avrum bar Jacob.

~~ A ~~

My name is Yonni bar, Malachi. I was the apprentice of Avrum bar Jacob, whose manuscript you have just read. I am sad to inform the reader that my mentor has passed.

I arrived at my teacher's home one morning three weeks ago to see him prostrate in the middle of his room; I could not feel the life force within him. A pungent odor permeated the room, a scent I know as the smell of death. I ran to retrieve my grandfather, who was a childhood friend of my master. Grandfather knelt next to his friend's body, shaking his head, and covering his tear-soaked eyes with his hands. I knew Avrum had died.

The funeral procession for my mentor was fairly unremarkable. Having no living relations, the responsibility for his burial fell to grandfather and myself. We were joined by our rabbi, who I knew had always viewed Avrum with a certain suspicion. For the most part, I think that was because of Avrum's lifelong friendship with Yeshu, the native of our village who has inspired an entire movement. But only for the most part.

We laid my master in the ground alongside his mother, his father, and his father's second wife. There were few mourners and no Shiva; how strange that he who had sat Shiva for so many would have no one sit for him. Perhaps that is the nature of things.

It was decided among the elders of the synagogue that I would be responsible for the final disposition of Avrum's earthly possessions. He had left notice with the rabbi that he wished his house and most of his silver be left to the synagogue, to be used to procure manuscripts, and to encourage and facilitate literacy among the residents of Nazareth. I fulfilled my master's wishes and thought I had disposed of all the items in his home.

That was until I discovered a trunk. He had disguised the chest with a wooden top so that it appeared to be merely a table; in the two years in which he was my instructor, I thought it was just that.

Discovering the truth of that trunk has been a source of revelation for me; inside of it, along with some other items, was the manuscript you have just read.

There was much of that manuscript that I had already known; certainly of my master's friendship with Yeshu, whom some have called the Messiah. I have been copying the man Joseph's manuscript faithfully for months, as Avrum wanted it to reach the broadest possible audience. Indeed, one of my last conversations with my master was his instructing me to take the copies to Jerusalem for the coming Passover, and distribute them freely. Avrum would not make the trek; he had refused to ever step inside the city many years ago, he had told me.

But there was much in the writing that I did not know. My grandfather had told me, right at the beginning, that Avrum was not like other men, but that I should not let that fact dissuade me from being his disciple (grandfather could not have known how ironic that advice was). So I knew all about Avrum's true nature, though the matter was never discussed between he and me.

But I knew nothing of my mentor's struggle with that nature, nor of the role Yeshu had played in those struggles. I knew nothing of the man Marcus, and his father Flavius, nor of any of those unique and unique characters that had peopled Avrum's life. I knew nothing of the actual events of that Passover week that had led to his (and grandfather's) friend's execution. Like many Nazarenes, I had heard the rumors but knew little outside of them.

Like my mentor Avrum, I have been surprised by the breadth of the movement Yeshu inspired. On my Passover trip last year, Christianity was the dominant topic at the Temple. Many were in favor of the Sanhedrin's reaction against the movement; Yeshu indeed had brought into question the foundation of Israel, the sacred covenant of Abraham

Yet many were opposed to the persecutions. At worse, the said, Yeshu was a misguided martyr, perhaps too taken with his own importance. The beauty of his message rang true; the God of All Things as a merciful parent, who invited all into his kingdom. I admit I joined the latter group. As a Jew, I may have lost my "chosen" status, according to Yeshu; but I gained the brotherhood of all humanity, as we strove to live as the Almighty desired us to live. And I won a religion rooted in love, the love the Almighty has for His children.

For the first time, I have felt like one of those children. My master Avrum never knew (or perhaps never let on that he knew) that he and I shared the same nature. I too have the feelings he described; I also struggle with those feelings, as he had.

I have learned from the gospel of Joseph and the manuscript of Avrum that I am also one of Our Father's children, that he cares for me as much as he cares for all of us. I have also learned that my nature should not, and cannot prevent me from living as one of those children. My brothers and sisters may mock me, but I still must love them. Avrum did, and expressed that love throughout his entire life, by his words and his actions.

I will not speak of this revelation with any of my family or friends. I have never discussed my nature with them, nor do I have any desire to; it is mine, it belongs to me.

But I will celebrate that nature in the way my master Avrum celebrated his, by making the life of Yeshu as public as possible, through the distributing of Joseph's manuscript. I will not only bring them with me to Jerusalem; I will have several copies available, so that many can read, and ponder, the remarkable story of Yeshu bar Yusuf.

I will make my own alteration to the manuscript, however, which is not an alteration, but more of a dedication. As my master wrote in his last chapter, ultimately it was the spirit of his dead lover Marcus which propelled and inspired the work that Avrum put into Joseph's manuscript. I also know that Marcus accepted Yeshu as the true Son of the Living God of All Things. For those reasons, I will title the document "The Gospel of Yeshu the Messiah, the Son of God, According to Marcus."

Perhaps the movement Yeshu founded will treat men (and women) such as Avrum, Marcus, Andrew and myself differently than others have treated us. I can only dream and pray to Our Father that this will be so.

ABOUT THE AUTHOR

R.A. Giuggio
lives in Western Massachusetts.

Please feel free to correspond with him and the community at
https://mgiuggio.wixsite.com/ragiuggio

Made in United States
Orlando, FL
19 December 2023